ALSO BY JUDITH A. BARRETT

Grid Down Survival Series

Maggie Sloan Thriller Series

Riley Malloy Thriller Series

Donut Lady Cozy Mystery Series

Danger in the Wind

Grid Down Survival

Book 2

Judith A. Barrett

DANGER IN THE WIND

GRID DOWN SURVIVAL SERIES, BOOK 2

Published in the United States of America by Wobbly Creek, LLC

2020 Georgia

wobblycreek.com

DANGER IN THE WIND is a work of fiction. Names, characters, businesses, places, events, locales, and incidents either are the products of the author's imagination or used in a fictitious manner. Any resemblance to actual persons, living or dead, or actual events is purely coincidental.

Cover by Wobbly Creek, LLC

ISBN 978-1-733-12417-1

DEDICATION

Danger in the Wind is dedicated to the color turquoise and to the talented artists whose tools are hammers and nails.

PREVIOUSLY...

MAJOR

Shadow, my German shepherd, and I lived a quiet, lonely life on my farm after I retired from the Florida Highway Patrol until my son and his wife died in a crash, and my granddaughter, Aimee Louise, who is now eighteen, joined us. I became the guardian of Rosalie, Aimee Louise's friend from school, after Rosalie's mother died.

When the nation's power grid collapsed, I invited the county sheriff and his family to move from their house in town to the farm, and we adjusted to being without electrical power from the grid. Our farm family expanded once again when Mr. Young, a nearby neighbor and retired farmer, and Vanessa, the town lawyer, came to live with us.

As the sheriff and I suspected, the economy crumbled, and gangs of thugs soon terrorized the countryside. Our nearest neighbors were murdered, and we took in their two children. The attacks on my farm, though, seemed more targeted than the other attacks from roaming gangs. When we realized we had the information that would stop the planned takeover of the US government, Sheriff and I took action.

It might sound like Sheriff and I are pretty smart, but we rely on Aimee Louise and her gift that I didn't understand at first.

Aimee Louise is autistic and smarter than all of us. She doesn't see facial expressions; instead, she sees what she calls *clouds* that reveal a person's true feelings, but most importantly, she sees danger in clouds.

ROSALIE

I'm seventeen, and Aimee Louise is eighteen; we've been best friends for only a year, but we're like sisters. Aimee Louise wanted me to tell you more; she's not really much on talking.

Pops left out the most important part: he married Vanessa, and it was a grand farm wedding.

Aimee Louise and I attended an amateur radio class before the grid went down. No surprise, she's an electronics whiz. Mr. Young gave us a radio antenna and transceiver, so we listened to the hams every morning and evening.

Deputy Stuart likes Aimee Louise, but I'm not supposed to talk about that.

CHAPTER ONE

Major Dave Elliott, retired Florida Highway Patrol, and his black and tan German shepherd, Shadow, patrolled along the fence line of his north Florida farm.

As the wind gusts from the northwest intensified and the late afternoon temperature dropped, Major shifted his rifle sling, zipped up his brown canvas jacket, and removed his gloves from his pockets. He was tall and lean, and the years of being in the sun weathered his hands and face except around his eyes. *Trooper eyes*, he called the paleness left from his sunglasses. He scanned the dirt road, and Shadow raced to the north pasture in search of rabbits.

When Major was halfway to the driveway gate, he narrowed his eyes. *Two men on the road.* He strode to the cover of the stand of white oak trees between the house and the fence, and Shadow joined him. As the tall figures drew closer, Shadow wagged his tail.

"Good boy. You're right. It's Sheriff Starr and a deputy."

Shadow dashed to the fence line and yipped.

After the three men met at the gate, Major said, "Where's your car, Sheriff? I thought you were on patrol tonight. Want to come inside for coffee?"

"I left it at the deputies' house because I didn't want to announce our arrival. We need to have a private discussion," Sheriff Jack said. "Deputy Stuart has a problem."

Major closed the gate. "Let's go to the barn. No one will interrupt us there."

Sheriff and Stuart strode toward the barn while Major scanned the road. Major and Shadow trotted to catch up with them.

Sheriff lost his middle-aged spread last year when he and his family lived at the farm, and he ran with Aimee Louise and Rosalie. He had stayed lean despite his wife Molly's cooking, but the new deep lines on his face revealed the stress of ensuring the county's safety with the new instability of the power grid. He'd moved his family back to Major's farm three months ago.

Stuart was the youngest of the sheriff's deputies, and only four years older than Aimee Louise. After the sheriff began running with the girls, Stuart did too.

"My folks live in southwest Georgia," Stuart said. "I got word through the sheriffs' communication network that Dad fell and Mom needs help. Their farm's about two hundred miles from here."

When they reached the barn, the sheriff leaned against a stall door, Stuart paced, and Major sat on a hay bale and scratched Shadow's ear.

"I could hike it in ten days, but I'd rather get there sooner," Stuart said. "Before the grid and the economy collapsed last year, it took me less than four hours to drive to the farm."

"Gas rationing has limited our use of the department cruisers, but we've maintained over half a tank of gas in each," Sheriff said. "We have four personal vehicles and could fill one tank by siphoning from two of them, but the cruisers are targets, and the cars would be fine unless we travel on dirt or muddy roads. Deputy Jim has a motorcycle, but that's even more of a target. Any ideas, Major?"

"We've set aside the farm fuel for equipment and generators, but we have a tank and a half of gas we could use for Mr. Young's old truck. My truck has a full tank and is diesel, four-wheel drive, more reliable, and more comfortable for travel, but Mr. Young's work truck is less conspicuous. The trip is too dangerous for one person. I'll go with you." Major rose and crossed his arms.

"I agree it's safer to send two. I'll go." Sheriff headed to the door. "Let's go, Stuart. We've got things to do."

Major's face reddened. "You have four little kids and the responsibility for the county, Sheriff. You need to say here."

"I go with my deputy." The sheriff slammed his hand on the stall door.

Aimee Louise, Major's eighteen-year-old granddaughter with autism, stood at the barn door. Her long black hair reminded Major of her mother's, and he saw her grandmother in her clear blue eyes. She wore her favorite T-shirt with a German shepherd on the front.

"I will go with Stuart," she said.

"What do you mean? Were you eavesdropping?" Major scowled as Stuart strode to stand next to Aimee Louise. *Not sure I approve of Stuart hanging around Aimee Louise so much.*

Seventeen-year-old Rosalie followed Aimee Louise into the barn. Major was Rosalie's legal guardian, but he considered her a second granddaughter. Rosalie was seven inches shorter than Aimee Louise, but Major said it was impossible to overlook her because she had her mother's feisty nature, copper-red hair, and emerald green eyes.

"No, we weren't," Rosalie said. "We came outside to look for you and heard voices that got louder."

"Rosalie's right," Stuart said. "You two cranked up the volume. No one else has Aimee Louise's talent to see what she calls clouds and what we call people's intentions."

Aimee Louise gazed above Major's head. "Protective."

Major thought, *Aimee Louise's ability to recognize people's feelings by the clouds she sees still surprises me.*

"You're right; I'm protective," he said.

Sheriff narrowed his eyes. "I could have told you that. No disrespect intended, Aimee Louise."

"Worried," Aimee Louise said. "Stay with your family."

Sheriff stared at her. "You're right."

"Well, I'm calm," Stuart said.

Rosalie chuckled. "He's joking, Aimee Louise."

Aimee Louise gazed at Stuart. "Calm."

Stuart and Rosalie laughed. "Sometimes your jokes are hard to understand," Rosalie said, "but that was awesome."

"Thank you." Aimee Louise bowed.

"I wonder if we should take Mr. Young's truck? My truck provides more value for the farm." Major returned to his hay bale. Aimee Louise sat next to him, and Rosalie stood on his other side.

"The reason we came outside was to tell you the ham radio news, Pops." Rosalie tapped the spiral notebook that she used to record her notes. "There's an illness going around, and babies, children, older people, and even young adults have died. Some hams called it a flu bug, but others said it was nothing they'd ever seen before. Town officials have panicked and closed their roads to keep any outsiders from passing through. The hams said it's worse than the cholera outbreak last summer."

"Do we plan to go around the small towns on our way?" Stuart asked. "The hams reported the illness erupted in large cities then the sickness followed the interstates, but now it's creeping out to more rural areas."

"We have informal roadblocks in place to keep out the criminal element. I need to get on my radio with our surrounding county sheriffs first thing in the morning to discuss a regional plan," Sheriff said.

"Can we leave first thing in the morning?" Stuart rubbed the back of his neck as he paced.

"If we can plan and pack tonight, we can. We may need four-wheel drive; we'll take my truck. I'll want basic tools, and we should take food along. What else?"

"I'm jotting down notes for the list," Rosalie said. "Major, Stuart, Aimee Louise, and me. Is Shadow going too, or is he staying?"

Major said, "Rosalie, you can't go. Stay here and operate the radio."

"Mr. Young can operate the radio, and Annie can take notes. Aimee Louise needs me."

Mr. Young was a retired widower in his eighties and a neighbor until the grid went down. He hauled his trailer to the refuge at Major's farm then offered his farm to the town's pastor and his family.

"Stuart understands Aimee Louise too. Can you give me a compelling reason you should go?" Major asked.

Rosalie straightened her back and glared at Major. "I'm the best shot with a rifle on the farm. Josh calls me Dead Eye Red."

"My older son has a way with words," Sheriff said. "I don't think he realized you knew that though."

"I have the excellent hearing of a redhead, but the truth is Aimee Louise told me." Rosalie snickered.

"You're right about your shooting skills, but that's another reason we need you at the farm," Sheriff said.

"What do you think, Aimee Louise?" Major asked.

Aimee Louise stared at the far corner of the barn. "Rosalie knows."

"I do too," Stuart said.

Major narrowed his eyes. "Is anybody going to tell me?"

Stuart glanced at the girls. "Rosalie and Aimee Louise are safer when they are together."

Rosalie nodded and recorded more items on her list.

"Yes," said Aimee Louise.

"I think you're outnumbered, Major. I'll talk to Molly and Mr. Young. Molly can talk to the kids. I'll send Vanessa out, and you can explain to your wife." Sheriff chuckled as he strode out of the barn.

Major mumbled, "Thanks a lot."

"I've got a barebones list," Rosalie said. "We'll work on it while you talk to Aunt Vanessa."

Major and Shadow met Vanessa as she stomped out of the house. Glittery silver framed her face and streaked through her shoulder-length brown hair. Major smiled. *I still get a catch in my throat at the fire in her blue eyes.*

"What's this about you leaving? When were you going to tell me? Where are we going, and when do we leave?"

Major cleared his throat. "Let's walk to the garden."

"Absolutely not. You are not sweet-talking me in front of the broccoli." She faced him and put her hands on her slender hips.

Major placed his hands on hers. "Stuart needs to help his parents on their farm in Georgia. It's not a trip a person can do alone."

"You're telling me you're going and I'm not. Why do you have to go?"

"Stuart will need help with the farm. Sheriff can't go because the ham radio news reported an outbreak of a deadly flu virus. He'll organize roadblocks to stop people from spreading the flu through the area. You're needed here."

Vanessa narrowed her eyes. "There's more."

Major sighed. "Because of Aimee Louise's clouds, she'll provide extra protection, and she and Rosalie are a set."

"Unbreakable, I suppose. I'm not convinced about any of this." Vanessa stormed to the house and slammed the back door.

"Maybe she'll see the logic later." Major and Shadow returned to the barn for the planning session.

After he loaded the truck with supplies for the next day, the sun had set. The chirps of crickets and katydids and the buzz of cicadas accompanied Major and Shadow as they completed their evening patrol under the illumination of the moon. When he went inside, his pillow and a blanket were on the sofa.

"She's still mad, Shadow."

He pulled off his boots.

"Honey?" Vanessa whispered in the dark. "Sorry. Would you like to come to bed?"

Major picked up his pillow and followed her to their bedroom. After he closed the door, she ambushed him with her pillow.

When Major laughed, she shushed him and giggled. "Want to wake up the whole house, old man?"

* * *

Major woke before dawn and grabbed his clothes then slipped out of the bedroom. After he fed Shadow, he strolled to the pens to check on the animals. Cirrus clouds promised clear weather as they drifted across the pale, blue-gray eastern sky with its hint of daylight to come. A barred owl hooted, and its mate returned the call from the nearby woods. As Major and Shadow approached the porch, the back door creaked. Vanessa set two cups of coffee on the table near the rockers.

"I didn't want you to leave because I was afraid something might happen to you. I'm still afraid, but I won't allow my fears to come between us," she said.

They rocked and sipped their coffee.

"We should be on the front porch if we want to watch the sunrise," Major said.

"Too much trouble to move except for coffee." Vanessa rose and returned with the coffee pot. After she refilled their cups, she asked, "How did the girls talk you into letting both of them go?"

Major shook his head. "I walked into the dark alley of logic unarmed."

"What about Sheriff and Stuart? Weren't they there?"

"Stuart jumped ship and joined the pirates. Sheriff hid." Major grinned.

Vanessa laughed. "I believe it. Stuart's in awe of Aimee Louise. Have you noticed? Molly's making egg sandwiches for breakfast, and Sheriff already left with his in hand. Rosalie's going over her notes with Annie, and Aimee Louise is briefing Mr. Young on the radio and the hams she has talked to. Mr. Young's beaming face shows how proud he is with how far Aimee Louise has come. We have a talented extended family here."

Rosalie opened the back door. "Stuart's here. Aunt Molly said we could eat then leave. Are you ready?"

When Vanessa rose, Major hugged her and kissed her forehead. She smiled and raised her face for a kiss. Major kissed her lightly.

Rosalie said, "Aw, that's sweet. Let's go."

Vanessa laughed. "Be safe, honey."

"You too." Major's kiss lingered on her mouth.

"We're eating," Rosalie called from the house.

Major released Vanessa. "Promise me you won't worry unless we send you a message to worry."

Vanessa swatted his arm as he rushed inside. The girls and Stuart had eaten and headed to the truck. Major grabbed his sandwich, jacket, and backpack.

When he reached the truck, Aimee Louise was in the passenger's seat and Stuart and Rosalie were in the back seat of the four-door crew cab. All three of them wore tan baseball caps. Shadow sat between Stuart and Rosalie.

Major finished his last bite of sandwich then turned to the back. "Rosalie, I'm still not convinced. I have a feeling you're needed here."

Aimee Louise glanced back at Rosalie. "What about Annie?"

"Annie and I talked last night. She worries we won't come back. She gave me her mom's stuffed brown dog to bring along. She said I'd need it."

"That's her prized possession." Stuart raised his eyebrows.

"I think her idea was that if I had her stuffed dog, I'd have to stay safe to return it."

"Or you might need it," Aimee Louise said.

"Annie is so talented at construction sometimes I forget she's only eleven years old." Major backed the truck away from the house. "Where did you get the caps?"

"I brought them," Stuart said. "Aimee Louise said we needed to have similar profiles."

Before Major turned onto the paved road that led to Plainview, Stuart said, "Stop a second. I don't think we want anyone to see the four of us leaving town. People can't help but speculate. You, Aimee Louise, and Shadow going somewhere is less interesting. Rosalie and I can ride in the back. The topper's tinted windows are opaque enough that no one will see us."

"You're right," Major said. "Slide that back window open so we can communicate."

After Stuart and Rosalie hopped out of the truck and into the bed of the pickup, Shadow sprawled across the back seat.

"Good cover, Shadow," Major chuckled and turned toward town.

"Nobody's at the roadblock on this side of town; it must be too early." Major said. "That will probably change after the sheriff's meeting is over."

As he approached the roadblock on the far side of town, Major slowed. "Pete's here." He lowered his window.

"Morning, Major; hey there, Aimee Louise. You're out early. Ya going to Mickleton?"

"No, we're just going up the road. Will you be here all morning?"

Shadow stuck his head out Major's window, and Pete scratched the dog's ears. "No. Butch will be here soon. I got to get to the diner and set up the tables for this week's swap. Our swap's growing again. We're getting fewer deliveries in town, especially groceries and hardware. The truckers tell me when a truck breaks down, they can't get parts, and fewer truckers will drive because they're afraid they'll break down away from home and won't be able to get back. I hear that's what's wrong with the power: they can't get parts when the equipment fails. You tell the vet hello for me, Shadow."

"How did you know?" Major asked.

Pete chuckled. "Nobody down that way for miles except for the vet. Easy guess, right? See ya later."

Major raised his window as he drove away. "Thanks, Shadow. Good timing on your part."

When Major approached the vet's place, she was at the side of the road near her mailbox. She stepped away from the road and shielded her eyes with her arm then waved as the white truck drew closer. *Everybody in the county drives a white truck.* When he neared her driveway, he slowed, and Aimee Louise lowered the passenger window.

"Coming to see me?" She leaned on the truck and peered at the back seat. "Shadow feeling okay? Everybody all right at the farm?"

"Doing fine. Did you hear about the flu going around?"

She frowned. "I don't think it's a run-of-the-mill flu. I hear the mortality rate is close to fifty percent. The medical community worries this might be another pandemic virus like that last one before the grid went down, but it will be worse because we don't have the personnel, facilities, or medicine."

Major narrowed his eyes. "Any idea how it's spread?"

"Could be a sanitation issue. Not sure hand washing is a priority when people are hungry."

After he drove away, he asked, "You get all that?"

"Good reason to stay away from big cities and the interstate," Stuart said.

"We can check in with hams as we travel," Rosalie said.

Aimee Louise turned on the mobile radio and pulled her list of repeaters out of her backpack.

Stuart peered through the window. "What are you reading, Aimee Louise?"

Rosalie piped up from the back. "She's going over our list of repeaters in north Florida and south Georgia that could pick up and retransmit our transmissions to increase our distance. We know which repeater to use close to the farm. We need to find another repeater closer to your farm in Georgia. She'll check to see which ones are active."

"The list is old." Aimee Louise consulted the list and turned the frequency dial. "Nothing there."

"But it's all we've got. Just need to keep going down the list and checking," Rosalie said.

No traffic passed them as they sped away from Plainview. Aimee Louise glanced out her window. "Fields are empty, Pops. No cows or goats and no equipment."

Major scanned the road ahead. "I'll pull over so you two can ride in the cab."

As he slowed to the side of the road, Stuart said, "Wait. A vehicle is coming over the rise ahead. Looks like it's traveling fast."

Major accelerated and turned at a dirt side road lined with oak and pine trees. He slowed and pulled into a thicket then lowered his window before he shut off the engine.

"I think I should stay back here," Stuart said. "I can monitor what's going on behind us. Rosalie can sit with Shadow."

"It might be simpler if I stay back here. Two girls might be too much of a target," Rosalie said. "Although, I can crawl through the window to the back from the front."

Major stared as the vehicle sped by. "Looked like a surplus army truck, and it's empty, from the sound of it. Don't think anybody around here has a truck like that. Rosalie, you can move up here if you like. I didn't think about you being able to get through the window."

"Time for a break?" Rosalie asked.

"Excellent suggestion. Let's stretch our legs. I think Shadow wouldn't mind a break too."

When Major stepped out of the truck, the underbrush crunched under his boots. "It's been dry at the farm too." He glanced at the sky as he headed to the rear of the truck. "We could use some rain."

Rosalie poured water into Shadow's bowl, and Shadow drank his fill then trotted after Aimee Louise.

"We won't be far," Rosalie said as she followed Aimee Louise and Shadow down the dirt road.

Major strolled along the dirt road. *Only tire tracks are ours.* The stench of a dead animal wafted from the nearby field, and buzzards circled above. Major strode across the stubble into the field to investigate and found the source: the carcass of an emaciated cow surrounded by more buzzards. Major scanned the field then returned to the truck.

Stuart climbed out of the back. "I did some rearranging."

Major peered at the pickup bed. "Did you pull everything closer to the back?"

"In a way," Stuart said. "I can see out the side and back windows now, and I left a path from here to the cab. I cleared a spot next to the cab for Aimee Louise and Rosalie to sit or stretch out without being seen, and if I shift the largest duffle bag in a position in front of the window, the back will appear full front to back."

Aimee Louise, Rosalie, and Shadow reappeared and climbed into their seats, and Major turned the truck around and headed north.

After an hour, Major said, "We're close to a small town, and looks like a roadblock ahead. Rosalie, hop into the back. Aimee Louise, what do you see?"

When they were closer, Aimee Louise said, "One, protective; the one on the right is scared."

Major slowed as he approached the roadblock; when he lowered his window, Aimee Louise lowered hers.

CHAPTER TWO

"I'd rather you kept your window up." Major spoke in a quiet calm voice, and Aimee Louise raised her window. He placed his Florida State Police badge with his rank on the left corner of the dash then kept his hands visible on the top of the steering wheel.

The first man approached the driver's side of the truck. "Need you to go back where you came from."

The second man tapped on Aimee Louise's door. "You need to go back."

Aimee Louise whispered, "Good boy," as the second man tried to open her locked door, and Shadow wagged his tail.

The second man said, "Get out of the truck."

"Oh look," Aimee Louise said, "my dog likes you."

Shadow placed his chin on Aimee Louise's shoulder.

"Hi, puppy." The man scratched the rash on his hands and wiggled his fingers at the window then turned his head and choked back a cough. Shadow emitted a low growl.

Major squinted at the first man. "Don't I know you?"

The man glanced at the dash and Major's badge. "Major? You taught my boy how to shoot. Remember Scooter? He's a doctor near Atlanta."

"Isn't that something." Major chuckled. "We were worried he wouldn't graduate from high school."

The man grinned. "My wife won't let me remind him of that." His face changed to somber. "Be careful. We've heard there's something bad going around. My son says people have a little cough and a rash then three days later they hemorrhage and drop dead. It's moved so fast, there hasn't been enough time to understand how it's spread. Limit your contact with people is what my son advises."

"Thanks, Phil, we will. We'll be returning home later in the week. Is there a good bypass we could use?"

"Yes, there is. Did you see the road four miles back next to the Baptist church cemetery? Take that road, and you'll miss all the towns between here and the Georgia state line if you're going that far. Road's not paved, but it's passable except in heavy rain. Stay to the right. When you get close to the state line, there's a road that veers to the left, but it's rough."

"Thanks, we'll do that. Will we lose much time?"

"Ordinarily, I'd say maybe twenty or thirty minutes, but with the roadblocks, it's probably faster these days. We let an old army truck headed south go through earlier this morning. They said they were going to Orlando to pick up medical supplies. Fred here told them not to come back this way but to use the interstate. Guess the interstate makes them nervous because the passenger got twitchy. Thought he would shoot ole Fred for a minute there. People are scared."

Major shook his head. "Scared people are dangerous."

The two men stepped back, and Major turned the truck around. As he headed back to the detour, Aimee Louise said, "The man was sick."

"Like Phil said, we'll have to limit our contact with people."

After two hours of traveling past empty fields and abandoned equipment, Major slowed down. "There's a barrier across the road ahead, but I don't see any people."

"Do these side windows open, Major?" Stuart asked. "Looks like they slide."

"They do, but I can't think I've ever opened them though."

Stuart disappeared, and the sound of scraping and grunting came from the back of the pickup, first from one side then from the other. Stuart reappeared at the window. "Got 'em cracked a bit. Rosalie's positioned on your side with her rifle ready, and I'll be on the passenger side. We'll holler if we see any movement."

When they reached the barrier, Major stopped the truck. "I don't see anybody. Aimee Louise, scoot over here behind the wheel. I'll check the road."

He stepped out of the truck and used the door as a shield for a few minutes. Aimee Louise slid into position behind the steering wheel as Major opened the back door.

"Come on, Shadow. Let's take a break."

Major made his way to the barrier, and Shadow followed him. When he reached the barrier, he stared at the bridge that had collapsed on the other side of the rushing stream. He scanned the riverbank along the road and hiked through the brush to the left. Shadow stayed at the shoulder while Major pushed through the wild blackberry bushes with briars that caught onto his jeans. *Should have pulled out the machete.* After thirty feet, he came to a fire road that curved away from the river. He trudged the rutted fire road and came out behind the truck. He whistled for Shadow, and Aimee Louise flashed the truck lights.

Major strode to the back of the truck. "No place to cross the river. Found a fire road, but it brought me back here. We're better off turning around. Why don't you two move to the cab? We're not likely to come across anyone, and I expect we'll be traveling some bumpy roads."

Aimee Louise slid over to the passenger side then Major jumped into the driver's seat as Stuart and Rosalie climbed into the back of the cab with Shadow.

"Hang on. The ditch will be bumpy."

After a half hour, Major turned right at the fork in the road.

Aimee Louise lowered her window. "Pops, the road is red, and the sand looks different from the sand at the farm. The air smells salty."

"We're closer to the Gulf coast where there're more shells in the sand. The red dirt is red clay. We don't have any clay around the farm."

Major slowed as the truck creaked and rocked on the rough road with deep ruts.

"It's been quite a while since a road crew scraped this road."

"There's a creek ahead," Aimee Louise said.

"Hang on." Major sped up to cross the sandy creek bed with a trickle of water. The rear tires sank into the sand, but the truck's momentum propelled them onto the other side.

Rosalie pointed to the right. "There's a dirt road beyond the trees."

I'll check it out on foot," Stuart said.

Major pulled closer then stopped. "The machete is under my seat. It makes going through blackberries easier." He handed the machete to Stuart.

Stuart jumped out of the truck then hurried to the back and grabbed a long-sleeved shirt and leather gloves.

* * *

Stuart hacked through the tangles of vines and the blackberry thickets. His foot got caught in a vine, and he fell into a blackberry bush. "Dang tanglefoot vines." When he rose, the blackberry thorns snagged his shirt and jeans and scratched his arms and face.

Before he broke through the brush to the road, he crouched to rest and listen. A mockingbird trilled through its repertoire, and birds chirped. *Birds say it's clear.*

He rose, pushed back the brush, and eased to the road. He walked two hundred yards each way before he turned back through the brush.

When he neared the truck, Rosalie poked Aimee Louise, and Aimee Louise ducked her head. Stuart glanced at Major, who glowered at Rosalie. Stuart frowned to hide a smile. *I'll bet Aimee Louise would say, protective.*

"What did you find?" Major asked.

"The dirt road runs north and south. It's a forest area. No signs of homesteads, but I saw planted pines and *no trespassing* signs, so it's not uninhabited. I didn't see any way to get the truck to the road, though. It would take heavier equipment than the machete to get through the trees and brush in less than a day."

Aimee Louise handed Stuart his thermos of water.

"What's the condition of the road?" Major asked.

"Thanks, Aimee Louise. The road's not as bad as this." Stuart stuck his gloves into his back pocket and gulped down the water.

"Let's keep going. Maybe we'll come to a crossroad." Major opened the back door for Shadow, who leaped to the middle of the bench seat.

Rosalie reached for the passenger's door then frowned at Stuart's almost imperceptible shake of his head. He raised his eyebrows and inclined his head toward the back door, and Rosalie shrugged and climbed into the back seat.

Stuart glanced at Major who smirked then turned his head. Stuart returned his long-sleeved shirt to the back of the truck and exhaled. *Guess I won't be left on the side of the road after all.*

As Major reached for the ignition, Stuart said, "Wait. Do you hear that?"

Loud rumbling on the road came from behind them. "Sounds like a big truck is headed south," Stuart said.

Major started the engine and backed into the thicket Stuart had cleared. "Let's throw some of that brush in front of the truck. Maybe they won't notice us."

After the pickup was far enough away from the road, Major and Stuart jumped out and threw branches in front of it and onto the hood.

The truck rumbled past them then Major held up his hand. "I hear another one, but it's coming from the south. I didn't expect this much traffic on the back roads."

Stuart pointed to the stand of trees close to the road. "That looks like the best position to see who it is."

Stuart pushed through the brush. When he neared the road, he paused. *No birds. Truck must have scared them off.*

He searched for a surveillance position where he could see but remain hidden. He settled in position in the stand of planted long-leaf pines with blackberry bushes and tall seed weeds. He crouched low as the rumble of a truck grew louder.

Stuart's eyes widened at the heavy-duty truck as it sped north. The canvas sides of the body of the truck billowed in the wind, but tiebacks anchored the flaps across the back. Children sat on crowded benches inside the truck and wore identical short-sleeved light tan T-shirts, jeans, and surgical masks. Two men leaned against the support frame and cradled rifles. Their dark brown shirts had an unidentifiable patch on the pocket and the distinctive outline of bulletproof vests underneath, and they wore full-face masks that resembled self-contained breathing apparatus. *Who are they?*

Stuart slipped back to the path and hurried to the truck.

"Trucks are filled with what looks like kids to me. Maybe in a school uniform, and they are wearing face masks. At least two armed men. They're in a rush."

"Let's break for lunch. I'll take my sandwich and sit near the road for a while." Major handed out sandwiches while Rosalie set out water for everyone. He adjusted his holstered belt and headed to the road with Aimee Louise and Rosalie following him.

"No." He growled. "I'm doing this alone."

"I need to see the people," Aimee Louise said.

Rosalie slung her rifle over her shoulder and stepped closer to Aimee Louise. "I'm back up."

"Rosalie, take cover in the brush and back up Stuart. Let's go, Aimee Louise," Major said.

Another truck rumbled from the south. Aimee Louise dashed through the brush to the north then faced south as she crawled to hide behind a culvert near the road. Major scanned the trees and brush and dropped into a crouch perpendicular to the road ten yards from Aimee Louise.

The truck sped past him, but he swiveled for an unimpeded view of the rear of the truck. *Just like Stuart described.* He glanced at Aimee Louise who had crawled closer to the road.

After the truck passed their position, Aimee Louise stayed low as she made her way to Major's position.

"The front seat passenger had a danger cloud and pointed a gun at the driver," she said. "The driver's cloud was worried and protective. The men with the rifles in the back had danger clouds. The rest were young and scared or sad except for a few that were protective."

Major's eyes widened. His view of the cab had been a blur.

"I wondered why you went for the culvert. That's two trucks with kids in surgical masks under guard. We didn't have time to see who was in the first one. You hear anything like that on the ham radio?"

"No. Ask Rosalie."

When they reached the truck, Major said, "Let's load up. Maybe we can travel without contact with the trucks. Just keep your eyes open for any side roads."

After they were on their way, Rosalie stuck her head through the window between the cab and the pickup bed. "Did you notice the shift in the wind? We may get rained on tonight."

"Rosalie, the hams say anything about children in trucks on the radio this morning?" Major asked.

Rosalie frowned. "Not really. Except one ham mentioned four boys in his town had gone to visit relatives then another man said he'd heard five boys hadn't returned from hunting. The hams joked that boys have invented excuses to skip chores for generations. That was about it."

"Doesn't seem like much of a pattern." Major peered out his window. "Is it worth checking the ham radio?"

Rosalie leaned back then a few minutes later, Stuart stuck his head through the opening. "The hams don't know Aimee Louise this far away from the farm. Rosalie and I don't think it's wise for her to be on the radio. We can listen, but either you or I should do the talking, Major."

"That okay with you, Aimee Louise?" Major asked.

Aimee Louise adjusted the mobile radio. "Local first."

"Rosalie has her notebook and is ready to take notes," Stuart said.

At the sound of a squelch break on the radio, Aimee Louise adjusted a dial to pick up the weak signal and adjusted another dial to stop scanning other frequencies that would override it.

"I got two…" The male voice drifted out.

"I'm pulling over so we can catch a better signal. Maybe. Hang on back there." Major braked hard and pulled to the shoulder.

"Got anything?" Rosalie asked from the back of the truck.

"Dump the…on the side…" The transmission broke up.

Aimee Louise waited. "Out of range."

She changed the radio back to scan. "They used simplex, which is short range, and they faded out because we're getting farther away. Nothing on the nearby repeaters."

Aimee Louise lowered her window, shaded her eyes with her arm, and peered at the sky. The white, fluffy clouds had become dark along the bottom edge and had grown in size and height. The earlier soft wind had strengthened and shifted. Aimee Louise shivered in the chillier northwest wind gusts and reached for her sweatshirt as she raised her window.

"The wind has shifted. It's stronger," she said.

"You two come up here," Major said. "Rosalie can keep track of the weather."

Rosalie and Stuart slid into the back seat and set their backpacks on the floorboard while Major eased back onto the road.

"Did you see the dark wall cloud behind us? We've got a storm chasing us," Rosalie said.

Major peered through his side mirror. "That's a big storm. The wall cloud is rotating and has a tail."

"That's not good. A rotating wall cloud frequently spawns a tornado." Rosalie rubbed at her neck. "I think I have a tick." She leaned her head to the right, and Stuart examined her neck.

"Yep, you do. Do you have tweezers in your backpack?"

Stuart removed the tick. "We'll check for ticks when we get to the farm this evening."

The rain fell in fat drops then sheets of rain blew across the hood. Major squinted to see the road and shifted to four-wheel drive when the truck slipped in the mud. The crosswinds rocked the truck.

"Wind's shifted again. The storm's coming at us from the southwest," Rosalie said.

"Maybe we can leave it behind." Major clutched the steering wheel to keep the truck on the road. A gust of wind shoved the truck to the right, and Rosalie squealed and grabbed onto Shadow as the truck slid into a ditch. Major rocked the truck then gunned it out of the ditch.

"That was amazing, Pops, but I'm not sure we can outrun it," Rosalie shouted over the pounding rain and roaring wind.

"Part skill, mostly luck," he mumbled as he focused ahead. Major fought the wind and kept pushing the truck forward.

"We need a place to ride it out. We can't afford to get stuck in a ditch," Major said. "Watch for a driveway. Maybe we can find a building to shield us from the wind."

After five tense minutes, Aimee Louise said, "Driveway, Pops."

"Don't see it." Major slowed the truck.

"I did," Stuart said. "It's behind us. I'll run down the driveway to see what's there."

"We can run faster," Aimee Louise said.

"Not enough room to turn around." Major stopped and peered around the vehicle. "I'll back the truck. I'll need a guide."

Rosalie said, "Aimee Louise and I will run."

"I'll guide." Stuart threw on his rain jacket and jumped out.

As Aimee Louise and Rosalie pulled their ponchos out of their backpacks, Major glanced at his side mirrors. "Stay in the truck. I can't even see Stuart."

Stuart tapped on Major's window then signaled toward the back with his palms parallel, and Major put the truck in reverse and eased back as he watched Stuart. He squinted to keep Stuart in focus. *Driving blind.*

"Watch that side," Major said. "Let me know if I'm headed into a ditch."

Aimee Louise and Rosalie pressed their faces against their windows. When Stuart put his wrists together with his fists tight, Major stopped, and Stuart waved to the right. Major turned until Stuart motioned forward. After Major straightened the wheels, Stuart held two thumbs up and jumped into the truck. Rainwater ran off his gear and soaked his seat.

"The driveway's gravel, and I thought I saw a structure ahead. The road is fairly straight," Stuart said.

"You're drenched." Rosalie moved Stuart's backpack on top of hers at her feet.

"Better one of us than three of us." Stuart pushed back his hood and dripped on the seat. Shadow moved closer to Rosalie.

The rain pounded the roof and windshield, and the wind buffeted the heavy truck. Major tightened his grip on the steering wheel with both hands as the truck crunched down the graveled driveway. The grating of the gravel faded in the cacophony of howling wind and pounding hail the size of peas that bounced off the roof and hood.

"There." Aimee Louise pointed. "A barn on the right."

Major turned and pulled up to the barn. "Looks sturdy enough."

Aimee Louise reached for her door handle.

"Just a second. Let me check it out." Stuart jumped out of the truck and disappeared in the deluge. The intensity of the hail increased.

Stuart returned and opened his back door. "Found an unlocked side door. It's a horse barn and sturdy. Grab your stuff and run inside. Hurry. The hail's getting worse."

Aimee Louise snatched up Major's backpack, the handheld radios, and her backpack while Rosalie grabbed the backpacks and the cooler at her feet. Shadow jumped out with the girls then the three of them dashed to the side door.

"Major, there's a barn door. Want to see if we can get it open and drive the truck in?" Stuart asked as he headed to the rear of the pickup.

The hailstones grew to quarter-sized, and Major said, "Let's check it from the inside."

Major and Stuart grabbed the rifles and ammunition then rushed to the side door. The hailstones pelted them, and the wind intensified.

Stuart leaned against the door to close it, and Major slid the wooden bar across the door to keep it closed.

"We found a tack room, Pops." Rosalie's eyes were wide, and her hands shook.

Aimee Louise stepped out with her hands over her ears. The wind was deafening, and the rafters creaked as the building swayed.

"In the tack room." Major shouted over the monstrous crescendo of the violent storm as debris slammed into the side of the barn. He wrapped his arm around Aimee Louise, and Stuart grabbed Rosalie's hand as they dashed into the tack room and dropped to the floor. Major pushed his feet against the door to hold it shut, and Shadow leaned against him.

When the noise increased, Rosalie leaned against Stuart. Aimee Louise ducked her head, and Major wrapped his arms around her. She hid her face in his chest as the building groaned. He covered her head with his hands then the air pressure plummeted, and Major felt his ears pop as Aimee Louise clapped her hands over her ears.

The building heaved, and Major cringed as a sudden dead calm and intense pressure assaulted his eardrums. An explosion and a splintering crash ripped through the silence then all was black.

CHAPTER THREE

Shadow whined, and Major opened his eyes. He was on his back, and he stared at the clear sky through the tree branch that came through the roof and rested on a rafter. He tried to rise, but a board from the tack room wall pinned him down. Shadow wiggled out from under the heavy board that pinned Major and barked.

"Aimee Louise. Rosalie. Stuart." Major struggled against the lumber but couldn't get the leverage to push it away.

Aimee Louise hugged Shadow then knelt next to Major. She had an abrasion on her forehead, a bruise on her cheek, and a cut on her lip.

"Stuart, help me." Aimee Louise called out then rose to her feet and bent her legs to heave the board off Major. After Major scooted to the side, she dropped it and helped him to sit up. Major clutched his shoulder.

"I don't know where Stuart and Rosalie are," Aimee Louise rose to clear the debris that blocked the door.

"Stuart, where are you? Rosalie?" Aimee Louise's shouts bordered on panic as she pushed and tossed boards. Shadow faced the missing tack room wall and barked.

"Here," Rosalie said.

"We're in between the tack room and the stall next to it under some shelves and plywood," Stuart said as the sound of boards banged against other boards. "I've almost got our way cleared. It'll be easier to get out through the stall side."

"You okay, Pops?" Aimee Louise asked.

Major pushed away the neck of his shirt and inspected his shoulder. "I think it's just bruised."

Aimee Louise took off her sweatshirt and fashioned a sling for Major's arm then removed the last of the splintered shelves and wood that blocked the door. Stuart pushed open the door. His ripped shirt flapped and revealed the gash on his arm.

Rosalie peered into the tack room. "We landed under a support for the stall and tack room. I'm fine. Looks like I'm the only one. Is Shadow okay?"

Shadow bounded to her. "Guess he is." Rosalie scratched his ears.

"Good to hear," Major said as Aimee Louise helped him to his feet.

"Be right back," Stuart said. "I'll check the truck."

Rosalie came into the tack room. "There's more space in here than anywhere else."

Major peered out the door. "The structure of the barn is solid; it held together fairly well. There's only that one hole in the roof where the limb breached it. All the splintered wood is from the stalls. Glad we were in the tack room."

Rosalie examined Aimee Louise. "You will have a black eye."

"Really?" Aimee Louise touched her left cheek. "Ouch. Tender."

Stuart returned. "A limb landed on the truck and smashed the topper, and another branch crashed into the driver's side of the truck at the back door. Doesn't look like any damage to the truck other than the door, but it's stuck until we clear a path to move it. The storm tossed the limb into the roof. There are no trees nearby."

Rosalie opened the first aid box and pulled out a triangular bandage. "Pops, if you'll sit somewhere, I'd like to replace Aimee Louise's sweatshirt with a sling."

"I'm fine." Major headed to the door, and Rosalie stepped in his path.

"Maybe so, but I can't reach the back of your neck to untie Aimee Louise's sweatshirt."

Aimee Louise cleared her throat, and Major dropped to one knee.

"Okay, Rosalie. Make it fast." Major fidgeted while Rosalie untied the sweatshirt then replaced it with the triangular cloth and tied the knot to the side of his neck.

"Keep your arm back into that pocket," Rosalie said as she tied the knot in the material at his elbow. "It'll keep the weight of your arm off your shoulder. Let me know if you feel your arm drooping or if your fingers tingle, and I'll adjust your sling."

"Thanks." Major rose to his feet.

"Ready to walk around the barn to check the structure then inspect the driveway to the road to see how much work there is for us?" Stuart asked.

Major headed to the door then paused. "Aimee Louise, you and Rosalie gather up what you can find of our things. We'll need an inventory. Stay close to the tack room. We know it's solid."

After they left the barn, Major strode to the truck. "You're right. Doesn't look like any damage that would affect drivability." He stepped back and circled the barn, and Stuart followed.

"Roof looks intact on this side," Major said.

When they reached the other side, Stuart said, "That limb looks like a spear."

Major inspected the roof. "Bigger than I thought. The owners will have to take it out in pieces."

"Driveway doesn't look too bad so far. Mostly branches and limbs we can clear by hand," Major said.

Stuart tossed branches to the side, and Major dragged the smaller branches with one hand to clear a path from the truck to the driveway then headed down the driveway

As they neared the road, Stuart said, "Trees down across the driveway. Do we have a chainsaw?"

"A small one. Let's check the field to see if it's too soft to go around." Major sloshed as he stepped over the downed fence into the field of clover. "Too wet. May be okay in a few days. Let's get the chain saw and the axe. If you cut the trees into manageable pieces, Aimee Louise can chop off the large branches to make it easy for the girls to drag the branches to the side."

On the way back, Stuart said, "Should we pull a few things out of the back of the truck for the night, or are we going to push on?"

"I'd rather clear the driveway and leave before first light. We can pull out sleeping bags, the camp stove, and food for tonight later."

When they returned to the barn, Major said, "Let's see what we can reach in the back of the truck."

After Stuart lowered the tailgate, Major said, "I don't think there's enough room for you to maneuver, but I'll bet there's plenty of room for Rosalie."

After Stuart left to get the girls, Major lifted out the gasoline cans that were next to the tailgate.

"Stuart said we need to clear the driveway first then we can leave in the morning. What do you want us to do?" Rosalie asked when they reached the back of the truck.

"We need the chainsaw and axe. Can you find them, Rosalie?"

"Sure." Rosalie jumped onto the tailgate and pulled out the chainsaw and the axe.

"What shall I do?" Aimee Louise asked.

"Go with Stuart, and clear the driveway."

Stuart carried the chainsaw and gasoline, and Aimee Louise carried the axe down the driveway to the first tree.

"What next, Pops?" Rosalie asked.

"We need the camp stove, food, water, and sleeping bags in the tack room."

Rosalie moved the items to the tailgate then they carried them inside. After they set down the gear, Major said, "Let's help clear the driveway."

Stuart cut the massive trees into sections then Major and the girls rolled or dragged the pieces of wood and branches to the sides of the driveway.

"After we clear this last tree, can I have the truck keys?" Aimee Louise asked.

"We'd like to listen to the radio," Rosalie said. "It's getting close to the time that hams get on the radio for the day's check-in."

Major handed the keys to Aimee Louise. "Go whenever you're ready."

"We'll clear brush on our way back," she said then raced down the driveway with Rosalie.

* * *

"Which direction do we move the brush?" Rosalie asked.

"Tree line side, but not into the ditch," Aimee Louise said.

"Makes sense." Rosalie dragged two light branches away from the driveway.

After ten minutes, they had cleared the driveway of the remaining brush and dashed to the truck. Aimee Louise started the engine while Rosalie rushed inside the barn for her notebook.

When Rosalie jumped into the truck, she asked, "Got anything?"

Aimee Louise pointed to the radio.

"Tornado went through here. We're all okay. Our house lost some shingles, and we've got trees down but haven't heard of any injuries."

"Saw an old military truck going north on the back roads before the tornado hit."

"Hope they got to where they were going or found shelter. You hear about the sickness? Kids have colds, but nothing else around here."

"Everybody's well here. Few colds, like you said."

"About to lose electricity again. It's supposed to be because of the illness. I don't quite understand that. Out."

"If it weren't for the electricity going down all the time, I'd be skeptical about that illness thing. I'm out."

Aimee Louise stared at the display as it scanned the repeaters.

"I don't understand what that flu bug or whatever it is has to do with electricity. Do you?" Rosalie asked.

"Ask Pops."

The radio picked up a high-pitched voice. Aimee Louise pointed to the display that stopped at a frequency most often used for simplex.

"Anybody there? Hello?"

"Sounds like a kid," Rosalie said. "You going to answer?"

"Go get Pops."

Rosalie jumped out of the truck and raced to the driveway.

"There was a bad storm," the child said. A younger voice added from the background, "We been walking."

"It's okay," the older child said. "Somebody will hear us. See? The light goes on when I press this switch."

Stuart jerked open the door. "That's a kid. Have you said anything?"

"No," Aimee Louise said.

"Hello? We found this radio in the field."

"Are we losing them?" Stuart asked.

"No."

"Hello? Anybody there? We were in a truck, but the men made us get out."

Major came up behind Stuart. "Go ahead, Stuart. Girls, could you move our gear back into the truck?"

"On it," Rosalie said as she and Aimee Louise raced to the barn.

"See? Light's green. Hello?"

"I hear you," Stuart said. "Where are you?"

"Somebody's there. Did you hear that? Hello. We're in a field next to a road. There was a bad storm then I found a radio."

"Who's with you?"

"Me and this little kid. What's your name, kid?"

"What do you think?" Stuart asked Major.

"I think we head north. Aimee Louise can drive. You ride up front with her. Rosalie can ride behind Aimee Louise, and I'll back you up."

"Kid's name is Henry. My name is Brandon."

"Hello, Brandon and Henry. I'm Deputy Stuart. Do you see anything close? A building? A water tower?"

"No. The trees are all knocked down. Wait. Henry's pointing. Oh. A sign on the road up ahead. Should we go see what it says?"

"That'd be good."

"It's kind of far."

"I'll wait while you check."

Major said, "I'll help the girls load up. We can pick up our tools on the way out. There's only one more tree in the way, and it's small. Should be easy to drag it out of the way."

After they loaded the gear, Aimee Louise drove to the driveway and headed to the road. When they reached the tree, Stuart shifted it out of the way, and Rosalie helped him load the tools into the back of the pickup. After they climbed back into the truck, Aimee Louise turned north.

"Watch for a truck. Could be in a field," Major said.

"How far away do you think they are?" Stuart asked.

"Hard to say. Simplex works on line of sight, and typical range is less than thirty miles, but it depends on the radios and the topography," Major said.

"Hello? Hello, Deputy Stuart?"

"I'm here, Brandon."

"We're at the sign. It says *Dessater County*. Or maybe *Dess Ater*."

Stuart furrowed his brow and glanced at Major. Major shook his head and shrugged.

"Brandon, I'm not sure where that is. Can you spell it for me?"

"Capital d-e-c-a-t-u-r capital c-o-u-n-t-y. Dessater County."

"Perfect. I know where you are. I'll be there soon."

"Hello? Deputy Stuart? Wait, Henry, don't run away. Are you in a big truck? Henry wants to know."

"No. I'm not in a big truck. Henry's smart."

"I guess. Henry wants to hide. Stop at the Dessater sign, okay?"

"Will do. Watch for the white pickup truck with a smashed top. Out."

"Oh yeah. Roger Wilco Out. That's radio talk, Henry."

"Dessater?" Major asked.

"Decatur County. They're at the Florida-Georgia state line. Maybe five or six miles away."

Aimee Louise maintained a steady speed on the road going north. After five miles, the dirt road turned onto a paved road, but Aimee Louise maintained her slower speed.

"There." She pointed to the left farther up the road. She slowed as she approached the truck that was upside down and split in half around a tree.

"Stop here," Major said. "I'll check the truck. If I'm attacked, it's your call, Stuart, but I'd feel better if you sped away and kept the girls safe."

"Understood." Stuart frowned. "Keep Shadow inside the truck, Rosalie, in case we need to take off in a hurry."

Rosalie lowered her window and trained her rifle on the wreck. Stuart stepped out and used the body of the truck for cover.

Major slipped his rifle into his sling then stepped into the ditch and continued to the trees for cover in his approach to the rear of the crash site.

As he made his way to the truck, he glanced to his right at the body of a man face up in the ditch. *Dead.* Next to the man were the bodies of two children. Major forced his attention back to the truck. He slipped to the next tree. Still no movement. No sounds. He hurried from tree to tree until he was at the rear of the truck.

He pulled back the canvas tarp and retched at the sight in the back of the truck. The second man and the children in back were dead. He dropped the canvas curtain then froze at the sound of a whimper.

He jerked back the tarp and stared at the tiny body wedged between the bodies of two teenaged boys. Her wide dark-brown eyes peered over the surgical mask that covered most of her face and her ears.

He held his index finger up to his lips, and she cringed. He eased the curtain closed and waited. *Silence.*

He peered around the corner and scanned the length of the truck then scanned the area near the front of the truck. *Where is the passenger door?*

When he reached the cab, he discovered the engine compartment entangled with the passenger's body. The splintered trunk of the tree had crushed the driver's side of the cab and the hood, but the driver's body wasn't visible. Major climbed around the front of the truck and found a fallen tree across the hood on the driver's side. A man's body lay on its side in the weeds and close to the tree. A branch from the tree was across his legs. When Major shifted to get closer, he slipped on the debris but caught himself before he fell.

"Don't shoot," the man's voice was weak.

"I'm here to help." Major made his way to the man and knelt next to him. "Where are you hurt?"

"I can't see or move my legs."

"There's a branch across your legs." Major examined the branch. "I can't move the tree. Maybe we can dig you out, but I need help. I won't be long."

"What's your name?"

"Dave Elliott, but they call me Major. I'm retired state police."

"Nice to meet you, Major. I'm Rodney Cabello. I'm a judge in Miami. What about the children?"

"You too, Judge. I don't have good news about the children because we've found only three survivors so far."

Major made his way to the road and waved. Aimee Louise pulled the pickup parallel to the crash and parked. Stuart, Rosalie, and Shadow jumped out, and Aimee Louise remained in the driver's seat.

"We have a man trapped on the other side of the truck near the driver's side. I think we can dig him out of this soft sand. Stuart, grab our trench shovel and see what you think. He's a judge from Miami."

Mayor lifted his cap and ran his fingers through his hair. "Rosalie, there's only one survivor, a little girl, in the back of the truck. I'll lift her out then you can take her to the pickup."

Rosalie and Shadow followed Major to the back of the truck.

"Stay back, Rosalie. I'll bring her out to you," Major said. He lifted the flap, and Shadow rushed past him and jumped into the truck.

"Hello, doggie," the tiny girl said, and Shadow wagged then jumped out.

"Can you come out too?" Major asked. "Come out with the doggie?" He eased closer to her as she struggled.

"Just a second, this big boy will move a little for you. Excuse me, boy." Major rolled the boy's body that pinned the girl away from her, and she jumped up and darted to the back of the truck. Major stared at the rash on the dead man's hands and scanned the children. *No rashes.*

Rosalie lifted her out. "Our dog's name is Shadow, and my name is Rosalie. What's your name?"

"Dolly. Where's Gramps?"

"Not sure. Let's get you a drink of water, Dolly, and a snack. Would you like a snack?"

"I'm hungry. Can I take off my mask when I have my snack?"

Rosalie carried Dolly toward the truck. "You can take off your mask anytime you like."

Major checked the remaining children then paused before he dropped the flap. "Rest easy, young souls."

He trudged around the truck and joined Stuart, who had dug a trench on one side of the judge's legs.

Stuart straightened up. "Getting there. I found Judge's glasses."

"I have a broken frame, but at least I can see," the judge said. "What about the children? I'm afraid to ask. My Dolly. She was in the back. Did you see a girl?"

Major stared at the judge. "I found her between two older boys. I think they died trying to protect her. She told me her name was Dolly. Dark brown eyes and hair? About five?"

"That's her. That's my granddaughter. I didn't think she'd…" His voice broke and trailed off.

"See if you can straighten your legs, Judge," Stuart said. "If you can shift your left leg closer to the trench on your left side and drop your right knee to the ground, we may have enough room to slide you out."

The judge wiggled and scooted his left leg then straightened his right leg. "Let's get me out."

Stuart stooped, grabbed the judge under his arms, dug his heels into the sand, and leaned back. Stuart held tight to the judge and slid him clear of the tree.

"Thanks. Can you help me up?" the judge asked. "I need to know if I can walk."

"Sit up first," Major said. "Let's see what you can do on your own."

"You okay here, Major?" Stuart asked. "I want to get to Brandon and Henry."

The judge sat up then held out his hand. Stuart shrugged and gave him a hand up. When the judge rose, he winced. "My right knee is iffy. Can you get me a stick, Son?"

"We've got plenty of sticks." Stuart picked up a sturdy branch. "Try this."

The judge held onto the stick and put his weight on his right leg. "This will work. I'm ready."

"Lean on me, Judge. The terrain's rough until we get up to the road," Stuart said.

Major picked up the tools and hurried to his pickup then tossed the tools into the back.

"We'll be a little crowded after we pick up the boys," he said when he reached the cab. "We'll see what works. We've got the judge coming."

Dolly climbed over Rosalie to the window. "It's Gramps. You found him." She leaned out the window and squealed as she waved. "Hi, Gramps."

The judge gazed at Dolly, and his eyes welled as he limped to the truck. "I'm so happy to see you, sweet girl."

"I didn't know where you were. I couldn't move until Mr. Major helped me get unstuck. Rosalie said I could take off my mask. It was scratchy and hard to breathe. Rosalie is nice."

Stuart helped the judge into the truck while Major climbed in the other side. Shadow squeezed next to Major.

"We'll squeeze everybody in, but it won't be for long," Major said. "Any problem clouds, Aimee Louise?"

"No."

"Thanks. Good to know."

After everyone had a seat, Aimee Louise pulled back onto the road, and Stuart picked up the microphone. "Hello, Brandon. Deputy Stuart calling."

"Hello. This is Brandon. Over. We're hiding, but hurry. The grass is itchy. When will you be here?"

"Five minutes. We'll stop at the sign, and I'll wave so you'll know it's me."

"Roger wilco. Wait. Henry wants to say something."

"Wave two times so we know it's you," Henry said.

"I will wave two times. See you soon. Roger wilco out."

Major patted Stuart on the shoulder. "Well done, Stuart. I was afraid at first that we'd have to hunt for them. I'm looking forward to meeting ole Henry."

"Henry's a stinky boy," Dolly said. "We don't like stinky boys, do we, Rosalie?"

CHAPTER FOUR

"Some stinky boys are okay." Rosalie said. "Henry's one of the okay boys."

"Oh. I didn't know about okay stinky boys. Henry's okay?"

"Yes, and we won't even call him stinky."

Major snorted.

"Do you need a tissue, Mr. Major? Henry needed a tissue. His wiped his runny nose with his mask. I told him that was gross. The man got mad and made him and a boy who coughed get out of the truck," Dolly said. "Rosalie can give you a tissue. Rosalie has everything. She gave me a snack."

"You're right, Dolly. Rosalie is amazing." Major turned to the judge. "I have so many questions, but now isn't the time to ask."

"You're right. We can talk later, but I didn't realize what was going on when we stopped. I should have paid attention. I should have done something." Judge stared out the window and rubbed his face. "There were four trucks when we started. We followed one, and I had the impression the other two took a different route to a point where we were to rendezvous. Did you see them?"

"We heard one going south then saw two trucks with kids in them going north; the second one must have been yours. Where were you headed?" Major asked.

"I don't know. I overheard something about the interstate, but I don't know which one or which direction."

"Is that a sign up ahead, Aimee Louise?" Stuart asked.

"Yes." Aimee Louise slowed as she approached the sign then parked next to it. Stuart opened his door and stood on his running board. He waved once then paused before he waved a second time.

"Here we are." A boy popped up in the tall field grass ten feet from the road. A second, smaller boy appeared two feet away from the first one. Stuart waved them in, and the two boys dashed to the truck.

When the boys reached him, Stuart said, "I'm Deputy Stuart. Hello, Brandon. Hello, Henry. Do you think you could squeeze into the front seat with me?"

After the boys scrambled into the truck, Stuart closed the door. "I'll tell you everybody's name. Aimee Louise is our driver. Behind me is Major. He's a state trooper. He's in charge. Shadow is Major's dog."

Henry leaned over the seat and held out his hand, and Shadow sniffed then licked it. Brandon gulped, then he squeezed his eyes shut and held out his hand for a sniff.

Brandon opened his eyes. "That tickled."

"Next to Shadow is the Judge, and his granddaughter is next to him."

"That's Dolly," Henry said.

"I knew that," Brandon said.

"No you didn't," Henry said.

"Did too." Brandon's face reddened.

Rosalie broke in. "I'm Rosalie."

"Rosalie is very smart. She has everything. You want a snack? Rosalie has snacks," Dolly said.

"Aimee Louise, we can go now," Major said.

Rosalie reached into her backpack and gave each boy a bottle of water then handed out crackers. The boys settled back in the seat with their snack, and Aimee Louise sped up to highway speed.

"Hang onto your bottles, boys," Rosalie said. "We refill them."

"Where are we going, Major?" Judge asked.

"We're on our way to a farm in southwest Georgia. The folks there need some help. We're about two hours away, barring any more unplanned events."

After the boys finished their crackers and water, their heads drooped, and they leaned together. Dolly snuggled against her grandfather.

Major tapped Stuart on the shoulder. "Boys asleep?" he asked in a quiet voice.

Stuart nodded.

"Dolly and the judge are too."

After an hour, Stuart asked, "Need a break, Aimee Louise?"

"No. When we get closer, we can switch."

Stuart stretched. "Major, after I turn at the driveway, there's a perfect spot to pull into the woods then we can walk to the house."

"Do we send Rosalie or Aimee Louise with you?"

"Aimee Louise and a hand-held. If Mom or Dad are afraid, she'll know, and we can alert you."

"And Shadow," Aimee Louise said.

The judge stirred and yawned. "Glad these kids are getting some rest. That's the first chance I've had to nap. We'd been on the road two days when the tornado hit."

Aimee Louise slowed.

Major leaned forward. "Something wrong?"

"Deer crossed the road up ahead. Looked like a doe with two fawns," Stuart said.

Aimee Louise resumed her speed, and Major relaxed. The sky at the horizon to the west deepened from pinks and blues to a blaze of orange.

After another twenty minutes, Stuart said, "It's almost dark enough for headlights, but we're close. Pull over after the curve, and we'll switch."

"No," Aimee Louise said. "Headlights behind us."

"I'll direct you to the driveway," Stuart said.

Major turned. "The wrecked topper's blocking my view. How fast are they coming?"

"Not fast," Aimee Louise said. "Could I make the turn without braking?"

"We won't have to," Stuart said. "There are two curves in the road then the driveway. Slow down." Stuart leaned forward to peer at the road. "It's a left turn after the second curve. This is the first curve."

Aimee Louise accelerated through the curve.

"That was good," Stuart said. "The second curve's coming up."

Aimee Louise coasted through the curve.

"Perfect. Driveway's across from that mailbox. Here."

Aimee Louise tapped on the brake and turned at the driveway in one motion.

"Continue down the driveway past the curve then we can switch." Oak and pecan trees and wild brush grew on the left, and wildflowers decorated the shallow ditch between the trees and the driveway. A fenced field of tall grass was on the right.

After the curve, Aimee Louise parked and slid into the passenger seat as Stuart rushed around the truck and jumped into the driver's seat. He continued down the driveway then backed through an opening between two oak trees.

"The trees and brush are deceptive," Major said. "Great concealment."

Stuart chuckled. "It was a perfect hideout when I was a kid. Dad kept it groomed and my nieces play here every summer. Ready to go, Aimee Louise?"

Aimee Louise grabbed the handheld radio and followed Stuart as he stayed in the shadows on the way to the house.

"When we get close to the house, I'll hail my folks then approach the side door. If you see something, we need a signal. How's your barred owl call?"

"Whoo-whoo who-whoo?" Aimee called.

"That's excellent. Warn me if there's a problem."

When they reached the end of the trees near the farmhouse, Stuart said, "Stay out of sight."

Stuart strolled half-way to the house then put two fingers to his mouth and whistled. "Hey, Mom? Dad? It's Stuart." He whistled again.

The side door opened, and his mother rushed outside. Her tears streaked her cheeks as she hurried to him. She threw her arms around him, and he embraced her.

"Everything okay?" he whispered.

"Is now that you're here," she said. "Your dad told me that would be the first thing you'd say. Nobody here but your dad and me. We had some trouble earlier in the week, but the neighbors stepped in. We heard you might come, but we didn't expect you so soon."

"You mind staying here, Mom, while I check the house?"

She chuckled. "Dad said you'd want to clear the house. We don't mind your caution. Go right ahead. Your dad's in the living room. We don't have electricity this evening."

Stuart stepped into the dark house and turned on his flashlight. "Dad, it's me."

He strode from the kitchen to the living room where his dad sat in his chair. A worn footstool elevated his legs. A kerosene lantern on the fireplace mantle lit the room with a warm orange glow. His dad smiled and saluted as Stuart continued his search of the downstairs area then he took the stairs two at a time and checked the upstairs bedrooms and bathrooms.

When he returned to the living room, Stuart said, "I'll get Mom. We need to talk."

Stuart stepped to the kitchen door. "Come on in, Mom. I've got some people for you to meet, and they're hungry."

"Gracious, I better throw together a bite or two."

Stuart called out. "Aimee Louise, tell Major to bring the truck on down to the house then bring everybody inside."

When Stuart returned to the kitchen, his mother had lit a lantern in the kitchen, put a pot of water on the stove, and pulled out a larger pot. "How many people, Stuart?"

Stuart breathed in the familiar aroma of the fresh-baked bread that cooled on the counter. "Eight."

Stuart's dad limped into the kitchen. His cane supported him as he eased into his chair at the table. "I didn't want to miss out," he said.

Aimee Louise knocked on the door, and Stuart opened it. "Come on in. Folks, this is Aimee Louise. We have six more in the pickup, and they'll be here in just a minute."

"I'm Sandra," Stuart's mother said, "and this is Scott."

"Nice to meet you, Ms. Sandra and Mr. Scott," Aimee Louise said.

"You too, Aimee Louise. Eight of you?" Sandra said. "That's easy. Spaghetti, green beans, and fresh bread. Won't take over fifteen minutes." She opened the pantry and pulled out a quart jar of home-canned spaghetti sauce and two jars of green beans.

Aimee Louise held open the door as Major helped the judge inside then Rosalie, Shadow, and the children spilled into the house.

"Hello, I'm Rosalie. Is there a bathroom we can use?" she asked. Dolly clung to Rosalie's shirt and peeked at Stuart's folks.

"Second door on your left then there's another one past the living room into the hall on the right."

"The boys can use this one," Stuart said. "You and Dolly can have the bathroom in the hall."

Rosalie switched on her flashlight, and she and Dolly hurried down the hall. After the girls returned, Stuart introduced everyone, and Sandra wiped her eyes on her apron and waved her wooden spoon at the crowd in her kitchen. "Y'all find somewhere else to chat. You're slowing me down."

"Who wants a farm tour?" Stuart asked as he headed to the door. Brandon, Henry, and Dolly rushed to follow him outside.

"We can help you," Rosalie said as Aimee Louise moved extra chairs to the table.

"Thank you. Plates there; silverware here." Sandra pointed to the cabinet and a drawer.

After the men moved to the living room, Scott settled into his well-worn recliner. Major helped the judge ease into the overstuffed chair near Scott's recliner then Major sank into the three-cushioned sofa. He leaned back and closed his eyes. "It's going to be hard getting up from here."

"I'll bet when Sandra says food is on the table we'll move fast." Judge chuckled.

"How did this squad get together?" Scott asked.

"The original plan was for Stuart and me to come see you, but my two granddaughters made a pitch to come along," Major said.

"We picked up the judge, Dolly, and the boys after a tornado hit the truck they were in."

Stuart strolled into the living room. "Rosalie replaced me. They're chasing fireflies."

"Stuart, while we waited in the pickup, I got through to Mr. Young. The sheriff will get in touch with the local sheriff about the truck," Major said.

"I didn't hear about a tornado. Where was that?" Scott asked.

"South of here in Florida. Maybe a hundred miles. There were twelve children in the back of a surplus military truck that crashed," Major said. "The judge and the three kids were the only survivors."

Scott exhaled. "That's rough. Who were the children?"

"I have a theory they were all children of law enforcement officers," Judge said. "Dolly and her parents live with me in Miami. My son's an FBI agent, and his wife is a trainer. My schedule is the most flexible, so when the babysitter called early Friday morning and said she was sick, I called my clerk to shift my hearings to Monday. He told me other judges were cancelling Friday hearings too because of the bad flu epidemic in Miami."

Major peered at the judge. "Why were you their driver?"

"I wasn't part of their plan. When the front door glass broke, I hid Dolly and grabbed my gun. Two men stormed into the house, and I shot one of them; but after the third guy came through the back door and found Dolly, I surrendered my pistol. From what I overheard, their original orders were to snatch Dolly, shoot the babysitter, and blackmail my son. Their boss wanted my son to cooperate, but I don't know the details. I think the only reason they didn't kill me is they were short a driver."

"Did you catch any information about the boss?" Major asked.

"Not really. They said something about the boss and the Florida principal office and expressed their disgust with the boss who didn't think the sickness in Miami was important. They put masks on the kids." The judge shifted in his seat to face Major. "I'm not familiar with ham radios. You talked with someone where? At your farm? How did you do that?"

"The hams around here keep their repeater operational, and it boosted my signal. Little more to it, but that's the basic idea. Mr. Young monitors our farm radio and heard me sign on. He'll notify the closest county sheriff who will send someone to investigate the crash site."

Brandon, Henry, and Dolly rushed into the living room. "Ms. Sandra says to wash your hands and come to the table," Brandon said.

"We already washed," Henry added.

"I washed better," Dolly said.

Scott chuckled as he rose from his chair. "On my way."

* * *

While they ate, Judge asked, "How long have you been farming here?"

"My parents bought the property right after World War Two when he came home from Italy. All I ever cared to do was farm," Scott said. "What about you? Are you a Miami native?"

"Sure am. My grandparents left Puerto Rico in 1952 and settled in Miami."

"What does your dad do, Brandon?" Major asked.

"My dad builds houses. Mom says he's the best there is. I want to build houses too." Brandon beamed.

"What about your mom?" Rosalie asked.

"Mom's an FBI agent. Dad says she's the best."

"My dad is a policeman," Henry said. "Mom says he's the best too."

"That's great, Henry," Major said. "What does your mom do?"

"She takes care of me and Dad and works in an office. Dad says she's important."

"Dads and granddads are smart," Stuart said.

"That's right. They are," Sandra said.

At the end of the meal Stuart said, "Mom, the kids and I can take care of the dishes, but we'll need you out of the kitchen."

Major said, "Outstanding idea, Stuart. Sandra, would you show me around the farm?"

Scott laughed. "Well played, Son. Go on, Honey. We've got this. I'll supervise."

"I'll pitch in," Judge said.

"I know a conspiracy when I see one," Sandra said. "There's a pot of boiling water on the stove to wash and rinse the dishes. Let's go, Major."

Major offered his good arm, and Sandra grinned and slipped her arm through his.

As they strolled to the barn, Shadow trailed along. "Can you give me a rundown of your priorities for repairs?" Major asked.

"Sure can, but I'll tell you my number one priority was getting Scott out of his depression. Those children put the first smile I've seen on his face since he fell. I can't tell you how much that meant to me."

"I understand," Major said. "I struggled with depression then Aimee Louise and Rosalie came into my life."

Sandra stopped at the goat pen. "I can take care of the house and garden, but I can't repair the fences around the front and back fields, and the tractor needs its regular maintenance. The goats got out, and I fixed their fence and pen the best I could. I think if y'all put in one solid day's worth of work we'd be back on track. We had two hours of electricity every day for quite a while then it dropped to every other day. Lately, it's sporadic. Makes it hard to know when I can catch up on laundry or fill my water barrels."

The hum of an engine interrupted their stroll.

"Is that a generator?" Major asked.

"Stuart must have started the generator for baths and showers."

"After the kids go to bed, let's discuss our plans with Scott and Stuart then get an early start in the morning. I suspect the judge will do what he can. I know the girls will pitch in."

When Major and Sandra stepped inside, the kitchen was clean, and Stuart was drying pans.

"Judge is supervising the boys' baths, and Rosalie took Dolly upstairs for her bath. Do you have clothes packed away somewhere?" Stuart asked. "We need underwear and shirts at least for the three munchkins."

Sandra chuckled. "You couldn't have asked for anything else that could have made me happier. I have kids' clothes catalogued and stored by size. Let's go attic shopping."

"Need a little help here," Judge called out from the bathroom, and Major strode down the hall and peeked into the bathroom.

"Major, I need tweezers. The boys have ticks."

"Top left drawer, and the alcohol and cotton balls are under the sink," Sandra said as she and Stuart slipped past Major on their way to the attic.

"Can I help?" Major asked as he entered the bathroom. "Lots of bites too, I see. I'll bet I can find something for the itch."

As the judge plucked off ticks, Major applied antiseptic to the sites.

Stuart tapped on the door. "I've got pajamas for the boys. Mom guessed sizes."

Major opened the door, and Stuart handed him the clothes. After the judge and Major cleared the boys of ticks and treated their bug bites, the boys dressed.

The judge gathered the towels and dirty clothes for the next day's laundry, and the boys followed Major into the living room.

Scott asked, "What happened? Somebody took all your grime away, boys. I'll bet you smell better too."

The boys grinned and poked each other.

"Did anybody tell you about the Newton farm rule for baths?" Stuart asked.

The boys' eyes widened as they shook their heads.

"Bath then snacks before bed. It's the rule."

"It's true," Sandra said. "Come with me to the kitchen. I have crackers. We'll make cookies tomorrow."

Dolly skipped down the stairs.

"You look great," Major said. "Ms. Sandra has a treat for us in the kitchen." Dolly followed him to the kitchen.

"I had a bath," Dolly said.

"You're in luck," Brandon said with his mouth full. "Farm rule. Bath, snack, bed."

Dolly swished her nightgown then plopped in her seat at the table. "Bath, snack, bed."

"Where do we sleep?" Henry yawned.

"We have a boys' bedroom and a girls' bedroom upstairs," Sandra said.

After the children settled in bed, the adults gathered in the living room while Rosalie and Aimee Louise showered.

Scott cleared his throat. "Major, the judge and I had a lengthy discussion. He and the children will stay here. There's no way Rodney could get to Miami by himself with three children. I'll heal soon, and so will he. We can work together to keep the farm up and the children safe. And I cleared it with Sandra."

Major smiled.

"We've got the room and the resources. A teacher down the road developed monthly lessons for distinct age groups. We'll be fine," Sandra said.

Rosalie bounded down the stairs and sat on the floor next to Aimee Louise, who had taken her shower downstairs. The girls' shirts were damp from their wet hair.

"Water was nice," Rosalie whispered. "I was happy to see no more ticks."

"One more thing, Major. I'm reluctant to contact the parents," Judge Rodney said. "If word of the crash with no survivors gets back to Miami, doesn't that take away the leverage for blackmail? Except I hate the unnecessary pain the parents are suffering."

"Tough decision." Major rose and paced. "We aren't leaving until the day after tomorrow at the earliest. Let's think about it and talk tomorrow."

"Y'all will come up with something," Sandra said.

"I'm sure you're right," Major said. "Scott, Sandra and I talked about priorities for tomorrow. We came up with repairing the fences and the goat pen and maintenance for the tractor. Anything else?"

"That's a good list of our critical tasks," Scott said. "Wouldn't hurt to plow the north field for planting, but I'm afraid that's a full day's work. What do you suggest, Son?"

"Aimee Louise, Rosalie, and I can repair the fences in the morning if we get an early start and have enough boards and wire on hand," Stuart said. "We'll use the tractor to haul the supplies then I'll do the maintenance on the tractor and till the field."

"Scott, don't you think the three of us could repair the goat pen and fencing?" Major asked.

"Sure could. It'll wear us out, but I'm looking forward to getting out of the house and getting my hands dirty again."

Aimee Louise and Rosalie headed upstairs.

CHAPTER FIVE

"Judge, we have a guest bedroom on the main floor next to the guest bathroom," Sandra said. "That's yours. Stuart, I assume you set up cots in your bedroom for the boys and a cot for Dolly in what we've always called the girls bedroom. Is that right?"

"I did. Major, there's a third bedroom upstairs that's yours. There's a guest bath between your room and the girls. My bedroom has a bathroom with a shower."

"Anybody want anything before showers or bed? I can make coffee or hot tea," Sandra said.

"I'm fine, Sandra. I can't tell you how much I enjoyed your cooking," the judge said.

"Don't anybody worry about water pressure. We built this house for a farming family that got dirty," Scott said.

After all the showers, Major and Shadow accompanied Stuart outside to turn off the generator then strolled the grounds.

"What do you think, Stuart? Will your folks be okay if we put in a day's work?"

"I expected to be here longer, but I'm confident Dad and the judge can manage after we're gone, and Mom will keep the kids busy. The kids sure put a spark in Dad's eyes, didn't they?"

Before Major headed up the stairs he said, "You coming, Shadow?"

Shadow trotted to the front door and flopped down on the rug.

Major chuckled. "No surprise. See you in the morning."

* * *

Major woke and dressed while it was still dark. When he entered the kitchen, Sandra smiled. "Pot's on. Ready for some coffee?"

"You're up early, Sandra. Coffee sounds great."

She poured a cup and handed it to Major. "I got in the habit of getting up before everybody else when my children were little. It was the only time of day I had a little peace. I'd read or stand at the window and watch the birds."

Major sat at the table and inhaled the coffee aroma from his cup. "I do that at the farm. I take my coffee out to the porch and watch the sun rise. We've got four young children at the farm besides Aimee Louise and Rosalie. It's nice to gather my thoughts in the morning before the day explodes with their energy."

"Scott has had trouble sleeping since his fall until last night. I suspect those days are behind us." Sandra smiled. "I've got cinnamon rolls ready to pop into the oven, and we have eggs. Simple and quick."

She cocked her head and gazed at Major. "Is Aimee Louise autistic? I noticed Rosalie does most of the talking for the two of them, but she seems to follow Aimee Louise's lead."

"She is. The two of them are quite a team. I have trouble keeping ahead of them."

"Stuart seems tuned to Aimee Louise too, and I've noticed there's something extraordinary about Aimee Louise beyond the autism. I just can't put my finger on it."

"Aimee Louise has a talent." Major sipped his coffee. "Like others with autism, she doesn't recognize facial expressions. You may have noticed she doesn't look at your eyes but over your head instead. She sees what she calls *clouds* that indicate a person's feelings or intentions. She tells us when she sees a person with a danger cloud with a code she suggested: *Uncle Dan*. Dan for danger. Her mother called her clouds a gift, and I agree. I still don't understand it, but I accept it. She has saved our farm family more than once."

"I sensed there was something." Sandra refilled her cup. "After breakfast, the kids and I will plan our day and maybe walk down to the teacher's house to talk to her. If we get a few hours of electricity today, they can help me with the laundry."

Aimee Louise and Rosalie tiptoed down the stairs. "We didn't know if anyone was up," Rosalie said. "We're going outside to watch the sunrise." Shadow hopped up from his spot near the door and trotted out with them.

"I'll join you," Major said.

Sandra waved the coffee pot, and he stopped for a refill. When he went outside, he found Aimee Louise and Rosalie on the east side of the house near the garden. The girls sat on an upside-down wagon in silence.

Major smiled. *The Aimee Louise sunrise rule is no talking.* He stood behind them and sipped his coffee. *Good rule.*

Rosalie squirmed until Aimee Louise said, "Good morning, sun."

Rosalie jumped up. "That last minute is the longest one of the entire day. About the time I think I'll bust, the sun comes up."

The girls ran inside as Major lingered and gazed at the sunrise. Shadow leaned against his leg, and Major scratched his ear.

"Sandra told me I'd find you out here." The judge sipped his coffee. "After she slid those cinnamon rolls into the oven, the kids came bounding down the stairs."

"I've been thinking," Major said. "We could get word to your son, Brandon's mother, and Henry's father through the ham network and have them contact my local sheriff. If they want to pick up their children, we have a built-in screening process with us as their intermediate contact. If they're coming from Miami, we're on the way."

"That has possibilities. What if bad guys intercept the message and show up?"

"You and the children are still safe."

"What about your family?"

"We've dealt with danger before, but in this case, given the number of children they kidnapped, I think it's remote the blackmailers would bother about three children and a judge. Are you sure you weren't the target?"

"I'm certain I wasn't. After a heated discussion, the lead thug decided not to mention I shot their driver. I got the impression the big boss wasn't the understanding sort. They didn't seem to know who I was; first time I've been grateful to be *some old guy*."

Judge sat in the nearest porch rocker. "Too many people in Miami are sick, and everybody's worried about an epidemic. Maybe it's just south Florida?"

"We heard something's going around, but it hasn't made it to our community yet." Major gazed into his empty cup. "Let's get a cinnamon roll before they're all gone."

As they walked to the house, Rosalie and the younger children dashed past them and headed to the garden. Shadow changed his direction and raced after them.

"Something's up," Major said. "I'm sure we'll find out later." When they reached the side door, he paused. "Your limp is about gone. You feeling better?"

"Much. A shower and a good night's sleep did the trick. And knowing Dolly was safe. What about your shoulder? Where's your sling?"

"My shoulder's still sore, but it was stiffening up on me. I gave the sling back to Stuart to put in his pack."

As they strolled into the kitchen, Sandra asked, "The second pot just finished perking. More coffee? How do you want your eggs?"

"Over easy for me," Major said.

"Same. What are the kids up to?" Judge asked.

"A secret mission. At least that's what Dolly said. I'd worry about what shenanigans they had in mind, but Rosalie was in charge. Scott's gone to check the goat pen, and Aimee Louise and Stuart are gathering the materials to repair the fences."

Major pulled out a chair next to the judge and sat at the wooden kitchen table. "If we eat slowly enough, Judge, those two will have finished the repairs."

Sandra laughed as she served their plates. "Isn't that the truth?" She joined them at the table with her coffee. "I expect the electricity to be on sometime this morning. It's been four days. It's never been off that long since the electrical co-ops got together and started the rolling wave of electricity last year." Sandra frowned and rubbed her forehead. "I'm eager to get started with the laundry, but while I wait, I can go through the clothes in the attic. After you eat, send in the young ones. They can help me, and I'll release Rosalie from secret mission duty."

After the men cleared their dishes, Major carried in the bucket of water from the side porch, and the judge left to fetch Rosalie and the children. Sandra poured water into a large pan on the stove to heat the water for dishwashing. As Major headed outside, Rosalie and the children rushed into the kitchen.

"Did you get run down?" Judge Rodney waited for Major in the yard.

"Close to it."

When the two men reached the goat pen, Scott said, "We're missing a goat, Major. If the judge and I gather our materials, could you look for her? One of her favorite places is the south pasture close to the neighbor's cows, but she'll head to the pen when she sees you." He chuckled. "She knows she's not supposed to run off and leave her babies."

* * *

Stuart and the girls loaded the trailer behind the tractor with fence boards, posts, wire, and tools.

Stuart glanced at the girls. "I'm glad you're following the Major's farm rule and wearing your pistols in your holsters for the day's work away from the house, but Rosalie, I'd feel more comfortable if you took along your rifle too."

Rosalie dashed to the house and returned with her rifle and a brown paper sack. "Ms. Sandra said we might need a snack. I think she packed sandwiches and cinnamon rolls."

Stuart chuckled. "That's my mom. Aimee Louise, you want to drive the tractor? I thought we'd start at the far southwest corner and go along the road to the driveway first."

Aimee Louise jumped onto the seat and started the engine while Stuart and Rosalie climbed into the trailer.

"Ready," Stuart shouted over the noise. When Aimee Louise turned to go across the field, Stuart asked, "You want to ride or run? The field will be bumpy."

"I want to run," Rosalie said. "Aimee Louise can drive faster if we're not in the trailer."

"Let's go then."

They jumped out and raced to the far corner, and Aimee Louise sped up.

Rosalie beat Stuart to the post and twirled as he ran the last few yards. "I appreciate my ball cap, Stuart. Won't be long before it's hot out here."

When Stuart reached her, he bent over to catch his breath and nodded. *No more racing Rosalie.*

After his breathing slowed to normal, he said, "The corner fence post is solid in the ground and straight; all we need to do here is find where the wire's cut."

Rosalie trotted along the fence line. "Found it."

The three of them began the repairs, and by midmorning, they had reached the driveway.

"Do we continue down the driveway?" Rosalie asked.

"We have only a few yards of fence to fix. Do you want to check along the north field to see if there are any sections we need to repair?"

"Water break first," Aimee Louise said.

The three of them sat on the back of the trailer and drained their water bottles then Rosalie grabbed her rifle and headed through the trees to the north field.

Stuart pulled a fence board off the trailer, and Aimee Louise held it in place while he nailed one side to the corner post. As he finished hammering the other side, Aimee Louise tapped his arm and pointed to the south. A mule-drawn wagon headed toward them on the road.

"Run find Rosalie, and the two of you stay hidden in the trees," Stuart said as he moved to the north side of the tractor.

Stuart narrowed his eyes as the wagon made its way to the farm.

"Danger," Aimee Louise called out from the trees behind him.

"Thought so. Thank you," Stuart said without turning.

The man slowed his mule and stopped at the driveway entrance.

"Hey there, neighbor. I live just up the road. You have anything to trade for some venison? Just shot and butchered a big ole doe yesterday, and the kids could use some milk, or maybe you have some ammo or old guns you could swap for some meat."

His forced smile revealed broken, stained teeth, and the bug bites on his face, torn shirt, and dirty hands hinted of a longer travel than his claimed up-the-road. "I'll carry it to the house for ya." He clicked his teeth and pulled on the reins to turn the mule at the entrance to the driveway.

"Stop right there, fella. Flip up the flap on the wagon and show me what's in the back."

The man's face reddened. "You calling me a liar? You can't talk to me like that. My kids are in the back of this wagon. I was trying to be neighborly."

He reached under his seat, pulled out a pistol, and waved it. "Get out of my way."

A shot rang out, the mule bucked, and the man screamed and clutched his hand as his pistol flew into the ditch. Another man jumped out of the back of the wagon with a rifle, and Stuart shot him in the right shoulder.

"Get out of here and don't come back," Stuart growled.

The driver smacked the reins. The man in the road abandoned his rifle and dived into the back of the wagon as the mule lurched forward then broke into a run. Stuart glared at the wagon until it was out of sight then strode to the road and picked up the rifle. He stopped at the ditch and kicked the pistol.

"Okay to come out?" Rosalie called.

"Yes," Stuart said as the girls stepped out of the woods. Rosalie wore her ball cap backward.

Stuart raised his eyebrows. *She's a natural.* "That was an amazing shot. He lost his pistol, and I bet the pain in his fingers will be around for quite a while."

"Dead Eye Red," Aimee Louise said. "That's what Josh says."

Stuart shook his head. "Josh is right. Let's get the fences finished up. I'll talk to my dad, but I think we'll fell a tree across the driveway before we leave in the morning."

After they finished the short section of fence along the driveway, Rosalie said, "North field is good. There's another section along the driveway closer to the house. Want us to check the south pasture fence line?"

"Go ahead. I'll move the tractor to the next section for repair."

Stuart shaded his eyes and shook his head as Aimee Louise and Rosalie raced across the field in front of the house toward the south field. *Amazing how they run in tandem.*

Stuart turned around the tractor and wagon and drove to the next section along the driveway. Major met him as he turned off the tractor engine.

"We heard two shots," Major said.

"We chased off some unwelcome visitors. First time I've seen Dead Eye Red in action. She's good. The other shot was mine," Stuart said. "I don't think they'll be back, but there will be others. We might want to drop a tree or two over the driveway before we leave in the morning."

"Sounds like a good idea. Think they had anything to do with the military trucks?" Major asked.

"No. They were low-level scum looking for a simple hit."

Major scanned the area. "Where are the girls?"

"They ran to check the south pasture." Stuart's mouth turned dry. *Was that a mistake? I should have gone with them.*

"Here they come." Major pointed. "Can you keep up with them when they run like that? They put the sleekest cheetahs to shame, don't they?"

"We win," Aimee Louise said as she and Rosalie slammed to a stop in front of Major.

"We saw you, Pops, and raced," Rosalie said. "All the fences around the south pasture are intact."

"Not even out of breath," Stuart mumbled.

"I'll be at the goat pen," Major said as he walked down the driveway.

"We've got these last two boards to replace," Stuart said as he knocked down the split boards.

Aimee Louise and Rosalie held a fence board in place while Stuart attached it to the fence posts. As they held up the second board, Rosalie asked, "What do we do next?"

"This is a shady spot," Stuart said after he attached the last board. "Let's have lunch then we can put the tools away. I want to tune up the tractor before I plow the field for Dad."

"No," Aimee Louise said.

Stuart stared at Aimee Louise. *No, what?*

He peered at Rosalie, and she shrugged. He frowned at the tractor and glanced up the driveway. "The field. You're talking about the field. I can disc the section that's east of the planted trees but not the west side that borders the road. Is that it, Aimee Louise?"

"Yes," she said.

"Brilliant." Stuart held up his hand, and Rosalie smacked a high-five then Aimee Louise copied Rosalie.

After they ate, Aimee Louise drove the tractor to the barn, and Stuart disconnected the trailer. Rosalie asked, "Is it okay if I leave? I want to finish weeding Ms. Sandra's garden."

"Sure. We can take care of things here," Stuart said.

"Thanks." Rosalie hurried to the garden.

Stuart and Aimee Louise carried the tools to the shop then put away the wire and lumber. Stuart jumped on the tractor and headed to the south pasture. Aimee Louise joined Rosalie at the garden to finish the weeding then they raced to the pasture. Stuart stopped the tractor and turned off the engine.

"We think you can work faster if you don't have to worry about anybody sneaking up on you. We'll be your lookouts. Aimee Louise will stay on the move where you can see her, and I'll be in the pines."

"Thanks. I can work much faster with you two on guard." Stuart continued to the south pasture and smiled. *I have formidable guardian angels.*

After Stuart finished the field, he headed to the barn, and the girls ran to the house.

* * *

Major waited for Stuart at the barn. He exhaled as the girls dashed to the house. *Makes it simpler without the girls here. I don't know how Stuart will take this.*

After Stuart dropped off the disc and parked the tractor, Major said, "Stuart, we've got a complication. Brandon has a cough and a spiked fever. Sandra wants you to move in with me. Scott is sanitizing all the cots. Sandra's planning to put Dolly and Henry together and the girls in the living room on cots. She says she wants to isolate us from any sickness. Another option we have that will simplify things for your folks is to leave after supper and travel all night. There's a full moon tonight, and the sky is clear. Might even be better than day travel."

"If Dad's comfortable with what we got done today then I have no problem with leaving tonight. Farm work's never-ending, but I'm not worried about them like I was before we got here. Dad's perked up, and they have the judge to help him."

"I needed to know what you thought. Sounds like we're in agreement. Let's go talk to them."

The two men strode to the house, and Aimee Louise, Rosalie, and Shadow met them outside.

"We packed," Rosalie said. "We're ready to go whenever you say."

Major shook his head. *Those two are always a step ahead of me.*

When Major and Stuart entered the house, Sandra said, "We need to talk. Scott will be down in just a second. Get yourself a glass of water and let's go into the living room."

Scott came down the stairs. "Rodney's getting Brandon settled then he'll be down with Henry and Dolly. Major, Sandra and I think y'all would be safer if you limited your exposure to whatever Brandon has. Sandra thinks it's a cold, but we're being cautious. If you could leave early in the morning or even today, we wanted you to know we'll be fine."

Rodney came down the stairs, and Henry and Dolly hopped from stair to stair behind him. Aimee Louise and Rosalie came into the living room.

"It sounds like we've all come to the same conclusion," Major said. "As long as we've done enough for you to get back on your feet, we'd like to leave as soon as we can pull our things together. But if it would make things easier for you if we stayed another day or even two, we're fine with that too."

"Scott and I have planned our week," Rodney said. "There's nothing you could do to make it easier for us."

"It's settled. I'll pack sandwiches for your evening meal and cookies for a late-night snack," Sandra said. "I'd love it if you would stay a few weeks, but your family at home might have something to say about that." She smiled.

"Are you going to stay, Rosalie?" Dolly asked.

"No, I have to get home. I have chores to do there too."

"I'm the expert garden weeder," Henry said. "Mama Sandra said so. That's my chore now."

"My chore is to sweep the porch," Dolly said. "I did it good the first time, didn't I?"

"You two did great today on your chores." Sandra beamed.

"Let's get busy then," Major said. "I'd like to talk to Brandon before we leave to tell him how brave he was. Coming, Judge?"

"Sure am."

"We'll help Ms. Sandra fix our supper and snack," Rosalie said.

"And me. I'll help, and Henry will too," Dolly added.

Scott stopped Major before he headed upstairs. "Major, I need to talk to you, Rodney, and Stuart after you talk to Brandon. Meet us at the barn?"

Major tapped on the bedroom door. "How you doing, Brandon?"

Brandon coughed into his elbow then reached for a tissue and blew his nose. "I'm okay. Just a little sick."

"Show me your hands." Brandon raised his palms then flipped to show Major the backs of his hands.

No rash. "We're leaving soon. I wanted to tell you how brave you were. You saved yourself and Henry in the tornado, handled the radio, and kept Henry calm. Few adults would have been able to do what you did. You are a genuine hero, Brandon." Major saluted Brandon, and wide-eyed Brandon returned the salute then sneezed into his tissue.

CHAPTER SIX

When Major and the judge arrived at the barn, Scott was sitting on a hay bale, and Stuart was organizing tools. Judge sat on a bale next to Scott, and Stuart stood next to Major who leaned against an old stall.

"I didn't want to say anything in front of Sandra or the kids, but there's something fishy going on with the electricity," Scott said. "Long story, but farmers and their families from all around received invitations to a free fancy dinner six months ago. No surprise, it was a well-presented sales pitch: convincing and slick. When we realized the revolutionary crop they were touting for everyone to grow, sunroot, was actually Jerusalem artichokes, several of us almost choked on our coffee. They claimed the government pays farmers out west to grow sunroot, and those farmers are desperate for the seedlings that grow only in the south. Their fancy graphs and charts showed sunroot has remarkable nutritional value and will save the starving people in the cities."

Major frowned. "From what I remember about the Jerusalem artichoke hype from thirty-plus years ago, none of that is true. Back then it was a version of a pyramid scheme, except worse. The meeting organizers sold the first seedlings, and they made a lot of money. The first few farmers who bought the seedlings made a hefty profit selling choke seedlings to other farmers, but the supply rapidly exceeded demand because there was no one to sell to except other farmers. The predicted swell of consumer demand never happened. The worst part was that the Jerusalem artichoke was an invasive tuber, and it was practically impossible to rid the fields of it to plant other crops."

"That's how we remembered it too. My dad told me about farmers who used herbicides then burned their fields trying to get rid of it. Some of them couldn't plant anything for two years. Farmers put their farms up for auction, but the glut of available farms drove down the price."

"I don't get it," Stuart said. "What does that have to do with electricity?"

"A group of us around the county got together after that hard-core sales meeting and decided we'd wait it out. Other farmers jumped in and bought sunroot seedlings. Our group met again right before I fell. One farmer had a brother who went with the sunroot crowd. The brother had what he called priority status for electricity as long as he grew sunroot and convinced at least three other farmers to grow sunroot each quarter. He wanted his brother to help him recruit more growers. Who wouldn't want to feed starving people and have guaranteed electricity?"

"And burned out fields and no income." Rodney shook his head.

"I think access to electricity is the punishment or reward, and it's not a coincidence that our times between outages increased. Not sure what we can do about it yet. Our group will meet later this week."

Rodney frowned. "Does this relate to the blackmail scheme?"

"I wouldn't think so, but there's no way to tell," Major said. "What do you think, Scott?"

"I agree. Hard to say. I know you need to get moving, but I have good news. Aimee Louise gave me her handheld radio," Scott said. "She's an accomplished teacher, did you know that? She explained how to use it and made sure I understood. Local hams will be at the meeting, and I'll talk to them about setting up a communication group for us. She said they'd be able to get messages to her. I've got all the information."

"Wow," Stuart said. "Aimee Louise doesn't talk to many people. I always knew you were awesome, Dad."

"Just an old dog willing to learn a new trick." Scott smiled. "That was all I had. Y'all need to load up and hit the road. Rodney and I can fell the trees after you leave. No need to slow down for that. Rodney needs the practice anyway."

"Sure do. I can deliver a verdict, but my tree skills need work."

"You sure?" Stuart asked.

"We'll be fine, Son. Thank you."

* * *

"You drive until dark, Aimee Louise, then we'll switch off," Major said as they finished loading the truck. After hugs and waves, Aimee Louise started the truck engine then they left.

"I feel like I'm leaving my family," Rosalie said. "If Dolly had red hair, she'd be my mini-me, wouldn't she?"

Major chuckled. "I thought the same thing more than once."

He glanced at Aimee Louise. "Scott said you gave him your handheld. I didn't think of it. Thanks."

"I won't worry about them so much. Thanks, Aimee Louise." Stuart leaned back in his seat and closed his eyes.

Shadow snuggled against Rosalie, and she stroked his back.

After Aimee Louise turned south, Major said, "Let's stay on this back road until we get close to a town. If there's no roadblock, let's travel as far as we can along the coast before we head east."

As the sun set, Major glanced at the sleeping back seat occupants. "When it gets dark, pull over when you see a wide spot, Aimee Louise. Might as well take advantage of as much daylight as we can. We'll take a quick break and switch drivers then eat as we go down the road."

After dark, Aimee Louise pulled over onto the shoulder, and Stuart and Rosalie sat up. "Shoulder's wide here," Aimee Louise said.

"We'll take a quick break then Rosalie and Aimee Louise can switch places. I'll drive for a while," Major said.

After everyone climbed back into the truck, Major headed down the road, and Aimee Louise passed around sandwiches and sweet tea.

"Ms. Sandra said we needed to remember Georgia sweet tea," Aimee Louise said. "She taught me how to make it so we could have her sweet tea whenever we like."

"I love my mom's sweet tea." Stuart took a big swig of his drink. He leaned over the front seat and squinted. "Is there something in the road ahead?"

Major slowed. "Might be a log?"

"You have room to clear it on the left shoulder, Pops," Aimee Louise said.

"Hold on, everybody, and stay alert."

Major drove straight toward the object then as he changed to the oncoming lane and headed to the left shoulder, it scampered off the road. Major continued in the oncoming lane then returned to his travel lane.

He shook his head. "Didn't expect that."

"What was it? An alligator?" Rosalie asked.

"I think it was," Stuart said. "At least it won't chase us down."

"What was it doing lying in the middle of the road?" Rosalie asked. "Warming itself on the asphalt?"

"I don't know, but I'm glad it ran off to the right and not in front of us," Major said.

After another hour, Aimee Louise said, "Lights in the sky off to the right."

"That's bizarre," Major said. "I'm not used to seeing that many lights. How close are we, do you think?"

Stuart stared out his window. "Not close enough to see what it is, but we may come across traffic leaving or going to it. Reminds me of a large feedlot or poultry farm. That couldn't be, though, could it?"

As they neared the property, the lights flickered, dimmed then went black. "That makes it even more puzzling," Stuart said.

"I'll pick up speed to get past it," Major said. "Let me know if you see any movement."

After they cleared the area, Major flexed his fingers to relax the muscles. *Sure had a grip on the steering wheel.*

As Major headed south, the moon rose from the east and the pale light cast eerie shadows on the surrounding countryside. He glanced across a field and stared at a tractor near a fence. "Keep a lookout. Anything could be in those shadows."

"Up ahead on the left," Stuart said. "Is that a truck in the ditch?"

Major lifted his foot off the accelerator and slowed the truck.

"Are you stopping, Pops?" Rosalie asked.

"Yep. Slide behind the wheel when I get out. Watch Stuart for the signal to drive past us." Major slowed and parked. "Stuart, you take the right. Aimee Louise, cover me."

When he eased out of the truck, Aimee Louise followed him, and Stuart headed to the ditch on the right side of the road. Major advanced along the left shoulder, and Aimee Louise kept her distance as she moved in the shadows of the trees.

Major assessed the truck as he approached. *Front end is in the ditch. Right tires are on the shoulder; left one has dug into the ditch.* He listened. *Engine's off.* When he reached the rear of the truck, he placed his palm on the exhaust pipe. *Still warm.* He examined the open bed of the pickup and peered into the cab. *No one visible.* He glanced at the body of the truck and tensed. *Two bullet holes in the passenger side door.* He crouched, approached the cab, and held his cap up at the window then rose to check the cab. *Empty.*

He continued around the front of the truck. The left front tire was deep in the ditch, and the soft dirt hid the buried front bumper.

"Here," Aimee Louise called out.

Major hurried to the tree line at the rear of the truck where Aimee Louise knelt next to a man. She helped the man sit up, and he said, "Hey, Major. An angel found me."

"What happened, Phil?"

"A truck with its headlights off came up behind me and slammed into me. I didn't even see it coming. I know it saw me because I had my headlights on. I climbed out to see what my damage was, but when they backed up and started shooting at my truck, I twisted my ankle as I dove for the ditch. I held my breath until they sped away."

"I think we can pull the truck out. Can you drive?"

"Yep. It's my left ankle. Any idea who they were? I was at the feedlot and dropped off a trailer there. They need to move animals on a small scale. They shut down their operation when the lights dim to keep from stressing their electrical system. Did you see their lights?"

"When we got close to them, their lights went off. I wasn't sure why, but now it makes sense."

Aimee Louise returned with Stuart.

Major smiled. *She's always thinking.*

"Stuart, I think we can pull this truck out. Signal Rosalie to bring the truck in front of Phil's then pull the tow straps out of the back."

After Rosalie positioned the truck, Aimee Louise climbed into the driver's seat. Rosalie and Shadow joined Phil to watch the operation. Major and Stuart attached the straps and assessed Phil's truck. Stuart cleared dirt to make a track for the front left tire then Major slid into Phil's truck.

"All ready?" Stuart asked.

Major turned on the ignition, and Stuart motioned for Aimee Louise to move forward to tighten the straps between the vehicles.

At Stuart's signal, Aimee Louise pulled straight ahead at a slow, steady pace and eased Phil's truck out of the ditch onto the shoulder. Stuart signaled for her to stop then Major moved Phil's truck forward. When the straps slackened, Stuart released them.

Phil leaned on Rosalie's arm as he limped to his truck. "That was slick to see. Thanks, Major."

"Glad we could help. Have you heard anything about that new crop, sunroot?"

"I received an invitation to dinner next week. Sounds like it'll be an opportunity for our local farmers to get out of the financial hole."

"It's a slick deal, but it's a scam. It's the old Jerusalem artichokes reinvented."

"Jerusalem artichokes? Thanks for the heads up."

After Phil climbed into his truck with Stuart's help, he said, "I'll meet you down the road. We've got a roadblock. I'll wave you through."

While Stuart re-wrapped the straps and tossed them into the back, Rosalie and Shadow jumped into the back seat, and Major climbed into the passenger's seat. After Stuart hopped in, Aimee Louise sped up.

"You think that was the military truck crowd?" Stuart asked.

"I hope so," Major said. "I'd hate to think there's another group of fanatics going around shooting at people."

Stuart snorted.

Major smiled. *Point for Stuart. He gets my humor.*

When they reached the roadblock, Aimee Louise slowed then stopped and lowered her window.

"Here she is." Phil leaned on the roadblock for support. "This is the angel who found me. Y'all be safe, Major. Remember Fred, who worked the roadblock with me earlier? He's not doing well. His wife's worried."

He waved them on, and Aimee Louise accelerated past the roadblock.

Almost forgot about the sickness. One more thing to worry about. Major rubbed his neck then glanced at the countryside. "We'll be home before light. Knock on wood. Or vinyl." He tapped on the dash then leaned back in his seat.

Major closed his eyes and relaxed. He woke when Aimee Louise said, "Plainview."

"I didn't know I was asleep until you spoke." Stuart leaned across the seat.

Major straightened his back and glanced at Rosalie, who yawned.

"Guess we all took a snooze. Thanks for driving, Aimee Louise."

She slowed as she approached the Plainview roadblock. Brad, another one of Sheriff's deputies, strolled to the truck when Aimee Louise stopped. "Didn't recognize the truck right off. What happened to you?"

"Which time?" Stuart asked, and Rosalie snickered.

"That good? Get some rest." Brad waved them on. "I'll expect stories."

"We've got two hours to catch some sleep before sunrise," Major said. "Stuart, want us to drop you off or do you want to sleep on our sofa?"

"I'll crash at your place. No sense in disturbing two households," Stuart said.

"Smart," Rosalie said. "No babies to wake up at our place."

When Aimee Louise turned at the farm driveway, Shadow whined and pushed against Rosalie. Major groaned as he opened the truck door and climbed out to open the gate. "Stiff from all the travel. Go ahead; I'll walk. Park the truck near the back."

Shadow yipped. Rosalie opened the door, and he leaped over her and joined Major at the gate. When Aimee Louise drove down the driveway, Shadow raced ahead and waited at the barn while she parked. Major locked the gate then gazed at the bright moon that had drifted across the sky to the west. A light breeze from the south brushed the treetops. *Good to be home.*

When Major reached the house, the sheriff was waiting on the back porch with the coffee pot and cups.

"We can unload in the morning," Major said. "You girls get some rest. I know you need it, Aimee Louise."

"Let's go, Aimee Louise. We can sleep in, or I'll watch the sun come up with you," Rosalie said.

"Stuart, there's a spare bed in the boys' room. They're heavy sleepers. You can sneak upstairs if you'd like to catch a nap," the sheriff said.

After the younger set left, the sheriff poured two cups of coffee. "How'd it go? What happened to the truck?"

"Hope I don't have to do it again." Major sipped his coffee and told the sheriff about the military trucks, the judge, Brandon, Henry, the sickness, Jerusalem artichokes, and the tornado.

"What are you going to tell your wife?"

Major gulped down his coffee and held out his cup for more. "Sandra's a talented cook."

"You're looking for trouble, aren't you?" Sheriff refilled their cups as his wife, Molly, stepped outside. Her curly dark blonde hair framed her round face.

When she smiled, her blue eyes twinkled, and her dimples dotted her cheeks. "Glad you're back, Major."

She peered at the pot in Sheriff's hand. "Pour me a cup, or is your pot empty? I have another one perking on the stove."

Sheriff poured the rest of the coffee into Molly's cup and took the empty pot inside.

She narrowed her eyes. "How did you hurt your shoulder, Major?"

"How did you know?" Major's eyes widened.

"You're favoring it." Molly pointed to his cup. "And you never drink coffee with your left hand."

"I injured my shoulder when the tornado hit."

"Tornado? Is that what happened to the truck? Anybody else hurt?"

"Nope."

"You better beef up your storytelling skills before Vanessa gets up. Your wife's a lawyer."

"I need more coffee," Major said.

"Stay put. You look exhausted. Sheriff's bringing the fresh pot, and I'll grab a cup for Mr. Young. His trailer lights are on. He and I have coffee together every morning before everyone else gets up. We call it our grownup time."

Sheriff carried the coffeepot and an extra cup outside. He handed the cup to Molly before she reached the door. "Here's Mr. Young's cup, Molly."

He refilled Major's cup and his own and set the coffeepot next to Molly's chair. "Major and I will take a walk."

Sheriff and Major strolled to the barn. On the way, Sheriff said, "I might have a problem."

They sat on the bench outside the barn. Major stared at the sky in the east. The sky had lightened on the horizon. *Aimee Louise will wake up soon to wait for the sun to rise.*

"A few weeks ago, Pete at the diner in town told me two guys he didn't know showed up at the swap table and talked about law enforcement cooperation. Their conversation caught his attention because it was a strange topic," Sheriff said. "He and I decided the strangers were talking about the sheriffs' network we have in our region. Then two days ago, I found a note under my cruiser's windshield wiper that said my family's health depended on my cooperation. Yesterday Josh found a piece of paper nailed to the driveway fence post. It said *Cooperate. Keep them safe.*"

Sheriff rose and paced then leaned against the barn door as he sipped his coffee. "I was angry because I thought it was a prank that was going too far, but now after hearing about the boys and the judge, I'm spooked. I'm bringing it up at our weekly sheriffs' network call this morning."

Major frowned and rubbed his chin. "We can tighten our security for the children. We need to make everyone aware of the threat. Let's have a family meeting after breakfast, and we can discuss our trip. Rosalie's our best storyteller and will jump in with details. We don't have to bring up the notes you've received unless you want to."

"I'd rather wait until after my discussion with the other sheriffs," Sheriff said.

Stuart wandered to the barn and paused at the door. "The boys stirred so I slipped downstairs. Molly and Mr. Young are on the back porch. She told me to find you. Am I kicked out?"

Sheriff chuckled. "Molly's not at her most subtle in the morning. She and Mr. Young have a chat every morning before the kids get up. She only kicked you off the porch. Now that you're here, we can talk security."

Sheriff explained about the threats. "After the family meeting, I'll talk to the other deputies."

"I want the local farmers to hear about the Jerusalem artichoke scam too," Major said. "I'll discuss the scam with Mr. Young. He may take the lead in getting the word out."

"I'll bring up sunroot on my call," Sheriff said.

"Aimee Louise, Rosalie, the kids, and I can unload the truck," Stuart said.

"We just developed our plans without Rosalie. Wonder what we left out?" Major joined Stuart at the door and squinted at the eastern horizon. "Suppose it's light enough that Molly has breakfast going?"

"Lead the way, Major," Sheriff said. "We're right behind you."

"Unless Vanessa's standing on the porch then you'll scatter, right?" Major asked.

Sheriff grinned. "Only to check the fields."

CHAPTER SEVEN

When they reached the house, the back porch was empty until eight-year-old Sara opened the back door. "I saw you coming." She brushed her unruly pale blond curls off her face and away from her pink- and silver-sparkled glasses frame. She was slender and shorter than her twin, Brett, who peered over her head then grinned and disappeared.

Major smiled at Brett's lopsided grin and brown hair with the recalcitrant cowlick. *He's a Sheriff miniature.*

"Daddy's here." Sara twirled on the porch.

Brett and Josh barreled out of the back door, and Penny, the Starrs' brown mixed-breed pointer, scrambled after them. Sheriff and Molly had adopted nine-year-old Josh and his eleven-year-old sister Annie a year ago after their parents were murdered. Josh was the tallest of the four Starr children. His dark-brown skin and dark-brown eyes that bordered on black were a contrast to Annie's paler brown skin and her light brown eyes. Penny loved all the children, but Josh was her boy.

Josh stopped short in front of Sheriff then sidestepped before Brett crashed into him. Brett tripped, and Sheriff caught him.

Brett hung his head. "Sorry. Couldn't stop."

Penny pushed Josh's hand with her nose, and he rubbed her ear and grinned. "Didn't think you could, so I got out of your way."

The boys elbowed each other, and Sheriff chuckled as he wrapped his arms around them and headed to the house.

"Is breakfast ready?" Sheriff asked when Sara met them at the porch.

"Mommy said to tell you *don't dawdle*. What does dawdle mean?" she asked.

Stuart held the door for Vanessa as she hurried out of the house then he followed Sheriff and the children inside.

Vanessa rushed to Major and wrapped her arms around his neck. He buried his face in her hair and breathed in. "Missed you," he said. "You smell good, and you're wearing your blue shirt I like so much."

"I'm glad you're home safe," she murmured. "I won't yell at you for anything until tomorrow."

"Might need to take you up on that."

"What? Why? What did you do?" Vanessa stepped away and gazed at his face. "Never mind. A promise is a promise. Let's have breakfast." She chuckled as she took his arm, and they strolled to the house. "Tomorrow will be here before you know it."

Molly stood at the stove in front of the griddle. She flipped pancakes, and Mr. Young served them to the three younger children who slid into their chairs at the table.

"Good to see you, Major." Mr. Young pushed his wire-framed glasses up as he set a stack of pancakes on the table. "The girls took over radio duty. They'll be here soon."

"Everything okay here?" Major asked as he smeared a dollop of Molly's canned blackberry jam on his pancakes.

Mr. Young glanced at Molly and Vanessa. "Ask them."

"Now Mr. Young, we agreed we wouldn't say anything until after breakfast." Molly waved her spatula, and Vanessa bit her lip.

"I forgot. Guess it's my job to spill the beans." Mr. Young covered his mouth.

"Let me tell," said Sara. "I can tell, right, Mommy?"

"Go ahead, Sara." Molly turned back to the stove.

"Mommy spilled the beans."

"What?" Sheriff asked, and everyone except Major laughed.

Molly wiped her eyes. "Yesterday afternoon I was carrying a pot of beans outside to can so the house wouldn't be so hot, and I tripped. It was a gigantic mess, and I had a terrible time keeping Penny away from the beans."

Vanessa fanned her face with a napkin. "We told bean jokes the rest of the day. Our best punchline was always *Who spilled the beans?*"

Major shook his head. "Sorry I asked."

Sheriff shrugged. "You beat me to it. I thank you for that."

"It was funny yesterday," Mr. Young said.

"You had to bean there," Josh added, and even Sheriff and Major laughed.

Mr. Young patted Josh on the back. "That's a new one, Josh. Well done."

Josh jumped up from the table and bowed then took his seat and helped himself to two more pancakes.

When Aimee Louise, Rosalie, and Annie came into the kitchen, Molly's eyes widened. "Aimee Louise, you have a black eye. Is anybody else hurt?"

Aimee Louise touched her cheek. "It doesn't hurt." She and Rosalie took their places at the long wooden farmhouse table that Major had hand hewn before Aimee Louise's dad was born.

Mr. Young peered at Aimee Louise's eye. "Yep, black all right. Here are your pancakes."

"Most of the discussion this morning was about the electrical power being off so much more now." Rosalie cut her pancake into bite-sized pieces.

"One ham said his area had almost continuous power. He said everyone else's outages were a maintenance thing, which made no sense to me," Annie said. "How could all the regional electric companies except one be undergoing maintenance? They would have coordinated when Daddy was Operations Manager."

"You're right, Annie," Sheriff said. "Your dad would have organized it."

Annie took her seat next to Aimee Louise, and Mr. Young served her a fresh pancake.

"I'd like to have a family meeting with everyone then we'll excuse the kids when we go into more discussion." Major mopped his plate clean of any traces of blackberry jam with his last bite of pancake.

"Glad we don't have to stay for the boring stuff, aren't you?" Josh poked Brett.

Brett opened his mouth to speak, and Molly raised an eyebrow. He closed his mouth and chewed as he nodded. After everyone had eaten, Stuart and Aimee Louise helped Molly clear the dishes, and Mr. Young refilled coffee cups.

"I'd like to see us step up our security. I think it's time to get everyone more involved with security," Major said.

"I'm ready to be dangerous," Sara said.

Major swallowed to keep from laughing. "That's what we'll work on then. Deputy Stuart and I will work on a plan. But for now, it's important that no kid goes anywhere outside the house without someone else along or an adult nearby; Aimee Louise and Rosalie count as adults."

Annie frowned. "What about chores? Sara and Brett take care of the chickens, Josh feeds the goats, and I'm building a new tool shed."

"Everyone will still have chores, but if you're going to the garden, for example, take Sara or one of your brothers with you or let an adult know where you'll be."

Josh leaned his head back and groaned. "Are we done?"

Molly rose and wiped down the stove and counters. "Before you disappear, we need to clean the upstairs. It won't take long if you're organized. We'll excuse Rosalie long enough to help you plan then she can come join us."

"Rosalie's a good planner," Josh said.

"Let's go," Rosalie said. "We can sit on the front porch to plan then you can get to work. It won't take long."

After the kids and Penny followed Rosalie out of the house, Vanessa crossed her arms. "What's this all about?"

"We sent our best reporter out of the room. You can get details when she returns, but there appears to be a move to blackmail law enforcement officers by kidnapping their children," Major said.

Molly dropped onto her chair. "What? Are you sure?"

"Yes," Aimee Louise said.

Stuart explained about finding the truck, Brandon, Henry, Dolly, and the judge, and tears streamed down Molly's face.

"We need to do something." Vanessa rose and paced. "What do we do?"

"For starters, we make sure our children are safe," Sheriff said. "I'm talking to the surrounding sheriffs later today."

"The children run to the house when we call *Inside*. What else do we need to do?" Molly asked.

"Annie and I have been working on her shooting skills with the twenty-two," Mr. Young said. "I can talk to Josh about gun safety."

The children stampeded up the stairs, and Rosalie came into the room and sat next to Aimee Louise. "We need an accountability process. Maybe we could keep an ongoing chart of who is tracking which kid."

"That would ease my mind," Molly said. "Thank you, Rosalie."

"We've got an old chalkboard," Vanessa said. "I'll put it by the back door so you can check it, Molly." Vanessa stepped into the pantry and retrieved the chalkboard.

"We have another critical issue," Major said. "We may lose electricity. We've adjusted to the rolling wave of electricity, but our service may drop without warning. What do we need to do today to prepare for no electricity tomorrow?"

"Water's the first thing that pops into my head," Sheriff said. "Our rain barrels are low, and we've quit storing extra water for household use."

Molly's eyes widened. "The freezer is full. We need to can everything in the freezer."

"We do laundry once a week. We'll switch to daily," Vanessa said. "I'll start the laundry. What about notifying Pastor John, the deputies, and our other neighbors?"

"I meet with the other sheriffs on our radio network," Sheriff said. "I'll stop by the deputies' house on my way to the office then talk to Pete when I get into town. He'll get the word out."

"Aimee Louise and I can run to Pastor John's," Rosalie said.

"You'd be gone too long," Major said.

"I can take Number 48. It's a utility vehicle and doesn't use much gas. I'll start a load of laundry then leave," Vanessa said.

"Not by yourself," Major said.

Vanessa's face reddened. "I'm not a—"

"We've always had the rule no traveling alone." Major's eyes narrowed. "Not negotiable."

"Fine. Aimee Louise can go with me."

"Good idea. Aimee Louise is our best driver," Major said.

"Perfect. Rosalie can help here, and I'll get the full story before you do," Molly snickered.

"You and Rosalie need to wait for me," Vanessa said. "After I gather up laundry, we can head out, Aimee Louise."

The children bounded down the stairs.

"Just in time," Sheriff said. "We're ready to double up on chores."

"I'll help Molly with the canning," Mr. Young said.

"I want to finish up my tool shed I'm building for our gardening tools and the supplies for the chickens and goats. Is that okay?" Annie asked.

"I'll help you if you'll help me fill the rain barrels and water the garden first," Major said.

"Deal."

"We're tracking everybody," Rosalie said. "Annie, write your name and Pops on the chalkboard."

"You know we'll never keep this up, right?" Annie asked as she wrote on the chalkboard. "We already have the rule *Nobody travels alone.* Can't we just apply that?"

"Josh, we can feed and water your goats and clean out their shed then I will help the deputies at their house," Stuart said.

Josh fist-bumped Stuart. "Thanks, Deputy Stuart. Will you tell me how you became a deputy? I might be one someday."

"You'll be a great deputy, Josh."

"Rosalie, will you work with me and Brett?" Sara asked.

"I'd love to. We'll do the chickens, weed the garden, and keep the laundry going until Aunt Vanessa gets back."

"We'll be important," Brett said.

"You always are." Molly beamed.

Annie filled in the board. "Do I have everybody?"

"Put me on the board with your mom, Annie," Mr. Young said as everyone else hurried to their tasks for the morning.

Molly stared at the board. "Annie, let's experiment and see how long this lasts. You don't have to worry about keeping the board updated. If anybody needs to be reminded about the travel rule, I'll do it."

Before he left the kitchen, Major said, "I need to get with you later, Mr. Young."

"I'll be easy to find." Mr. Young stepped into the pantry for his canning apron.

As Major and Annie strolled to the barn to pick up the wagon to haul the rain barrels, Annie asked, "Is something going to happen to our electricity again?"

"I think there could be a problem, and we won't get as much as we have been this past year; in fact, we might not have any power for a while. We're preparing, just in case."

Annie pulled the wagon then Major lifted two empty rain barrels into it. They headed to the garden to fill the barrels with the hose. Shadow followed them then dashed to the chicken coop.

"Shadow has a busy day today," Major said. "Looks like he plans to keep track of everybody."

"Rosalie told me a little girl named Dolly and two boys were in a truck, and y'all took them to Deputy Stuart's farm. Is that why we are doing extra security for my sister, brothers, and me? So nobody puts us in a truck?"

"Yes. That's it exactly. We didn't go into detail because we have work to do and didn't want to scare the younger ones. We'll talk about it more later."

Major placed the barrels inside the fence then Annie pulled the garden hose to fill the barrels.

Annie held the hose and peered at the water flow. "Josh has nightmares sometimes, but he wants to be brave. He's happy when he's brave."

When the barrels were full, they returned the wagon to the barn and collected the tools to finish building the shed.

"I need my gloves. I left them in my room," Annie said.

"Let's go," Major said.

When they reached the house, Shadow waited on the porch. Annie dashed upstairs, and Major leaned against the doorjamb while Molly and Mr. Young stood in front of the open freezer.

"Have any ideas for an approach?" Molly asked.

"The good news is we have a great freezer," Mr. Young said. "The bad news is this stuff won't thaw until tomorrow." He rubbed his chin. "We can turn the freezer off and leave everything in it except the ground meat and the chicken. Let's put the ground meat in the refrigerator and the chicken in tepid water."

"Don't mean to stick my nose into your business, but could you put a roast or two in a slow cooker?" Major asked.

"Brilliant," Molly said.

"I wish I could take full credit, but that's what Trish used to do," Major said.

"Another brilliant idea. I'll check Trish's notes on canning. I'll bet there are more gems in there. If the chicken isn't thawed enough when we're ready to can, we'll brown the ground meat, mix it with tomato sauce, and can it as our new multipurpose sauce."

Mr. Young ran water into the sink while Molly pulled out chicken and ground meat.

Annie dashed down the stairs and waved her gloves when she came into the kitchen. "Ready, Pops?"

Major opened the back door. "Let's go. Tell me what you had in mind for the tool shed."

"I planned to hang racks and shovels on the outside and have two shelves for garden supplies and tools. We could store spare chicken and goat feed in metal trash bins with lids. It's tall enough for you to walk in without hitting your head, and I built it on a skid so we can move it around. I've got it mostly done except for the roof, the outside hangers, and the shelves. I've got scraps from the chicken coop roof."

"Let's get the ladder and your roofing. Doesn't sound like this will take us long."

* * *

Aimee Louise ran upstairs and picked up her backpack. She stopped at the kitchen, grabbed her water tumbler, and filled it for the trip. When she reached Number 48, Vanessa sat in the driver's seat.

"Let's go, Aimee Louise." Vanessa started the engine. "I know you always drive, but I've never had the chance. Major always drives too."

Aimee Louise shrugged and jumped into the passenger seat. Vanessa pushed on the accelerator, but when it didn't move, she stomped on it. Number 48 lurched backward, and the sudden motion jerked Aimee Louise's neck. Vanessa slammed on the brake, but Aimee Louise had braced herself.

"How do I make it go forward?" she asked.

Aimee Louise pointed to the gearshift. "I should drive, Aunt Vanessa."

"No, no. I'll be fine. Just a little rusty. Hang on. Here we go." Vanessa pressed on the accelerator and Number 48 eased forward. She pressed the accelerator to the floor, and they zoomed down the driveway. Before she crashed into the gate, Vanessa slammed on the brake. "I'm doing better. Would you get the gate?" Vanessa adjusted her garden hat that had gone askew.

After Vanessa lurched through the open gate, Aimee Louise closed it then returned to Number 48. *I may run back.*

As Vanessa sped across the field, Aimee Louise held onto the strap by her door.

"This is too fast for the field. Slow down," Aimee Louise said.

Vanessa's body was tense as she stared straight ahead and leaned over the steering wheel with a tight grip. "You drive fast. I don't want anybody at the house to think I drive like an old lady. I'll slow down after we're out of sight."

That makes no sense. Nobody at the farm has time to watch.

Vanessa hit an animal hole hard, and the vehicle careened. She over-corrected, and Number 48 leaned over on two wheels then slammed to the ground as it righted itself.

"If you slow down, you can see the armadillo holes," Aimee Louise said.

"It won't be bumpy like this after we clear the field," Vanessa said.

No. It will be worse. Aimee Louise tightened her seat belt.

When they reached the fence, Vanessa stopped. "What do I do now? Drive along the fence line?"

I don't know why anyone would want to drive along the fence line unless we're supposed to check the fence while we're out here? Wouldn't that take longer? Didn't we bring Number 48 so the trip would be shorter?

"Oh, here. You drive." Vanessa climbed out of the driver's seat and strolled around Number 48 to the passenger's side. "When we get close to the road, we can take a break then I'll drive. I want Pastor

John's wife to see me at the wheel. I'm a farmer's wife. I should know how to drive tractors and farm things. I need to be good for something."

Aimee Louise slid over to the driver's seat, and after Vanessa sat in the passenger's seat, she drove Number 48 to the trail that led through the woods to the state road.

"I was at the top of my class in law school. I worked hard to be the best. Before the grid collapsed last year, I was one of the top, up-and-coming lawyers in the state." Vanessa chuckled. "It's funny, now that I stop to think about it. Top Gun. At my age."

Aimee Louise increased her speed through a curve.

Vanessa glanced at the ground as Number 48 glided along the path. "How do you know when to accelerate and when to brake? There's no Top Gun thing left for me. Molly's a daunting cook. Mr. Young is a remarkably patient teacher. Major can fix anything. Sheriff keeps the entire county safe. Rosalie's a crack shot, and you're brilliant at everything you do. What do I do? I'm a helper, that's all."

"Top Gun Helper," Aimee Louise said.

Vanessa stared at Aimee Louise. "I'll think about it."

Aimee Louise glanced at Vanessa then slowed. "Fasten your seat belt."

"Stop, stop," Vanessa said. "Isn't the state road coming up? I'll take it from here."

Aimee Louise stopped then Vanessa dashed around Number 48.

"Leave it in gear," Vanessa said. "After we get close to Pastor John's, do you mind getting out? Then Vicki can see me driving up by myself. I know it might be silly, but it's important to me to look at least competent if I can't be Top Gun."

Aimee Louise applied the emergency brake, climbed out, and remained at the side of Number 48.

"Not here. Climb in. I'm not sure which way to go. I'll need you to navigate." Vanessa clicked her seat belt.

I could run ahead, and Aunt Vanessa could follow me. No, she might run over me. Aimee Louise climbed in and tightened her seat belt.

Vanessa stomped the accelerator, but Number 48 didn't move. "Emergency brake. I forgot."

Vanessa released the brake and Number 48 lurched forward. "I can't drive wearing the seatbelt. It's too tight across my chest." She unfastened it.

Vanessa stopped at the rise when she reached the state road. "Do you want to check the road before I go across? Major always did that."

Aimee Louise stepped to the shoulder and checked both ways. "Clear."

"Come get in. I'll wait for you."

After Aimee Louise fastened her seatbelt, Vanessa revved Number 48's engine. "I can clear the ditch." She slammed the accelerator to the floor.

"No." Aimee Louise shouted, but Number 48 went airborne and crashed into the ditch on the other side of the road and rolled then slammed into the trees.

CHAPTER EIGHT

Aimee Louise put her hand to her head. *Head hurts*. She brushed her fingers across her forehead and felt wetness. She gazed at her hand. *Blood. We crashed.*

Number 48 lay on the driver's side, and tall grass and weeds brushed Aimee Louise's neck and face. Birds in the trees serenaded her as she struggled to unfasten her seatbelt. When she unbuckled the belt, she dropped to the ground but couldn't move because her seat pinned her foot to the floorboard. She wiggled her foot free and reached for the dash to pull up, but a searing pain in her shoulder stopped her. She pulled back her shirt and stared at the abrasion and swelling on her shoulder. *Seatbelt.*

She pushed herself up with her left arm and struggled out through the opening left by the missing windshield. When she turned and reached for her go-bag, her feet tangled in the vines, and she fell facedown into the dirt and weeds. She sputtered and spit as she rolled to a sitting position to unsnarl the vines, but froze at the sound of a rumble.

Truck coming this way. She scrambled to free her feet and pushed her go-bag in front of her to protect her face as she crawled through the brush and away from Number 48. When she reached higher ground, she peered at the road through the thicket.

The air brakes of the truck hissed as it stopped on the road, and a man stepped out. She shrank back. *Danger cloud.*

"Can you tell what that is in the ditch?" A man with a raspy voice asked.

"Might be a woman." A second man with a high-pitched voice answered.

"She alive?"

"Don't think so." The crack of a shot silenced the morning's songbirds.

"Whatcha do that for?"

"Creepy. Let's get out of here."

The man climbed back into the truck and slammed the door, and the truck roared away.

"Aunt Vanessa?" Aimee Louise called out and rose to her feet, but she had twisted her ankle during her drop to the ground. She grabbed onto a tree until the wave of pain passed then searched the surrounding ground until she found a dead branch to lean on. She limped to the road using the path cleared by Number 48.

As she crossed the ditch, her shoes sank into the mud, and the stagnant water filled her shoes and soaked her socks. As she reached the shoulder, a rat snake crawled across the road to the other side. An empty twenty-two shell was on the pavement. Her heart pounded when she glanced down the road at the splash of turquoise in the ditch.

"Aunt Vanessa?" She limped along the shoulder.

"Aimee Louise? Is that you?"

Aimee Louise paused in relief. When she reached Vanessa, she eased to the ground next to her. Vanessa sat in the mire at the bottom of the ditch. Mud covered her hair and face, and muck and weeds covered her arms and clothes except for her right shoulder where her turquoise shirt shone through the single clean spot.

"Is the truck gone?" Vanessa asked as she brushed her face with her muddy hand.

"Yes."

"I landed on the soft shoulder. I think I've used up all my guardian angel's patience. When I heard the truck coming, I flattened myself as much as I could in the ditch. Didn't think it through, but it seemed to be my best option. When the truck stopped, I held my breath and stayed as still as I could. Is the snake dead?"

"No."

"Good. I'm so sorry you were hurt. I should have listened to you." Vanessa struggled to her knees but fell back into the ditch. Her eyes filled with tears. "Can you help me up?"

Aimee Louise handed Vanessa her walking stick, and Vanessa pulled herself upright then lost her balance when she put her weight on her left leg. The stick kept her from falling as she eased herself down to a sitting position on the bank of the ditch.

"I think I can make it to the woods by myself, but it will take a while. Do you think you can make it to Pastor John's house?" Vanessa asked.

"Yes." Aimee Louise rose and struggled on the path to Pastor John's house. Her shoulder throbbed, and she stopped after each step to wait until the wave of pain from her ankle passed.

When Aimee Louise reached Pastor John's house, she waved to Vicki who tended the vegetable garden near the house. Aimee Louise stumbled and collapsed in the sandy driveway, and the pastor's wife rushed to her.

"John, Aimee Louise is here, and she's hurt." Vicki waved her hands toward the barn.

Aimee Louise struggled to her feet then relaxed when Vicki called out, "Just stay there."

"What happened, Aimee Louise?" Vicki was breathing hard when she reached Aimee Louise. Vicki held her hands on her chest for a few minutes then knelt on the ground next to her.

"We crashed Number 48, and it's on its side near the ditch at our state road crossing. The force ejected Aunt Vanessa, and she landed in the ditch. She has an injured leg."

"What about you?"

"I caught my ankle under my seat and twisted it." Aimee Louise rubbed her forehead. "I think I bumped my head."

"You sure did, darlin'," Vicki said. "You've got a cut on your head and swelling under your eyes. You may end up with two black eyes." She peered at Aimee Louise's face. "Your left cheekbone below your eye has a greenish tint. Did you have a recent injury?"

"Yes, Ms. Vicki."

"I'll clean the cut. Tell me how many fingers you see." Vicki held three fingers in front of Aimee Louise's nose.

Aimee Louise blinked. "Three."

"That's a relief. Let's get you inside." Vicki struggled to her feet then helped Aimee Louise up as Pastor John and his brother, Chuck, raced to the driveway.

"We were on our way here to tell you to expect the power grid to go down without warning," Aimee Louise said when Pastor John and Chuck reached her.

"That shifts our routine, doesn't it?" Pastor John frowned. "How were you hurt?"

Aimee Louise was a head taller than Vicki, but Vicki wrapped her arm around Aimee Louise's waist. "Lean on me," Vicki said. "Number 48 crashed and is on its side in the trees near the state road crossing. Vanessa has an injured leg. You can use the golf cart because it's charged and take the first aid kit that's on top of the refrigerator. Aimee Louise and I are going inside."

"If I take the tractor, maybe we can upright Number 48," Chuck said.

"Sounds good. I'll drive the golf cart and meet you there," John said.

"Don't let Aunt Vanessa drive," Aimee Louise said.

Vicki raised her eyebrows, and Pastor John said, "I won't. Thank you for the heads-up."

* * *

Pastor John took the lead on the path in Vicki's golf cart. When he reached the state road, he parked on the shoulder and called out, "Vanessa? It's Pastor John."

"This way," Vanessa said.

Pastor John grabbed the first aid kit and walked north toward her voice.

"Here. In the trees."

Pastor John peered into the woods. When Vanessa waved her arm, he glimpsed a flash of turquoise and hurried to her.

Vanessa picked at the dried mud on her arms. "This stuff is itchy," she said.

Pastor John's eyes widened. "You need to move, Vanessa. You're sitting in a patch of poison ivy. The mud's probably protecting your skin."

Vanessa scooted away from the greenery to the carpet of pine needles.

"Don't touch your face," Pastor John said. "Keep your hands away from your eyes and nose. I have a first aid kit."

"I know poison ivy when I see it, but I wasn't paying attention." Tears streaked through the mud on her face.

"Let's clean your hands the best we can." Pastor John handed her a bottle of hand sanitizer. "Scrub your hands then you can apply the anti-itch gel."

Vanessa squirted the sanitizing liquid on her hands and rubbed them together. "This isn't working. Now I have clean mud."

Pastor John donned a pair of bright yellow kitchen cleaning gloves and furrowed his brow. "Sorry, but maybe you scrubbed away the oils. The gloves might be overkill, but I'm not a fan of poison ivy. Aimee Louise told me you injured your leg. Which one?"

"The left one. It hurts below my knee."

Pastor John took out his pocketknife and slit her jeans from the bottom to above her knee along the outside seam line then folded the material back with care to inspect her leg. "We'll be careful. You have something sticking out—looks like a bone. It's hard to see much because there's a lot of blood. I'll bandage it, but I'll splint your leg before we move you."

As Pastor John dressed the wound, Vanessa flinched. "Hear that? Somebody's coming. We need to hide." She tried to push herself up, but Pastor John put his hand out to stop her.

"It's okay. Chuck's bringing the tractor. We're going to try to get Number 48 back on its wheels."

After Pastor John finished wrapping gauze around the bulky bandage, he wrapped above and below the wound site with duct tape and taped the gaping jeans leg back together. "I've never heard how Number 48 got its name."

Vanessa sniffed back her tears. "Rosalie named it. I don't know where it came from."

"Rosalie? Doesn't seem like she'd be a fan," he said. "I'll ask her."

"A fan of what?" Vanessa asked. "Can I move now?"

"Don't move until we have your leg stabilized. I'll see if Chuck needs a hand then I'll see what I can find for a splint. I may run back to the house for Vicki. She'll have something. Maybe we can get Number 48 upright, and maybe it will still run."

Vanessa smiled. "I'm fine. Can you pray for Number 48?"

"Wouldn't be the first time," Pastor John mumbled as he strode away to join Chuck.

* * *

Major inspected the newly installed roof then climbed down the ladder. When he reached the last rung, he froze.

"Did we forget something, Pops?" Annie asked as she paused in the middle of loading scrap lumber into the wagon.

"Something's wrong." Major stared at the driveway gate. "I have to go."

"Do you need me to help?" Annie asked.

"Finish up here then see how you can help your mom."

"Will do." Annie loaded the remaining scraps into the wagon.

He strode to the house and hurried into the kitchen. He inhaled the cooking aromas of garlic, onion, and herbs and enjoyed the sizzling sound from the pan on the stove. Mr. Young browned a batch of ground meat in a large cast-iron skillet while Molly stirred sauce and prepared jars for canning. Josh carried jars from the pantry and stacked them on a small utility table.

Major filled his water bottle with water. "Be back later."

"Where are you going?" Molly asked.

"They've been gone too long, haven't they?" Mr. Young asked.

"Yes." Major grabbed his rifle and backpack on his way out the front door. Shadow dashed after him as he headed to the gate.

"You stay, boy."

Shadow wagged his tail and trotted to his favorite shady spot then flopped down to guard the farm.

After Major locked the gate, he jogged across the mowed field. Before he reached the fence line, he glanced back. Rosalie ran toward him.

He crossed his arms and waited. When she reached him, he said, "We're leaving the farm short-handed."

"I know, but this is important. They should have been back by now. Aunt Molly and Mr. Young will divide up the inside and outside chores until we get back."

He glared. "Stay with me. No running ahead."

Rosalie grinned. "Busted."

Major snorted and strode to the fence line then jogged down the path toward the state road with Rosalie sprinting ahead then returning before she was out of sight.

"You walk almost as fast as you jog because of your long stride," she said the third time she returned. "You'll save energy."

"I'll walk then." Major stopped jogging and stretched his legs as he headed along the path. *She's right. I would have worn myself out.*

As they neared the state road, Major furrowed his brow, then held up his hand and whispered, "Sounds like a tractor. Wait here."

Rosalie stepped off the path and crouched in the brush as Major crept to the road. A tractor pushed through the brush across the road, and he exhaled in relief. "It's okay to come out, Rosalie."

"Hey, Chuck!" He shouted and waved as he crossed the road.

Chuck turned off the tractor and wiped his brow with his shirtsleeve, and Pastor John pushed his way out of the brush and through the knee-high weeds.

"You saved us a trip to your place, Major. Vanessa's up the road, and Aimee Louise is at the house." Pastor John said. "No major injuries, but we need a splint for Vanessa's broken leg before we can move her."

He glanced across the road. "Do you suppose we could send Rosalie to the house? We almost have Number 48 untangled so we can right it. Don't know if it will run, though."

Rosalie dashed across the road. "I'll go. Okay with you, Pops?"

Major nodded, and she raced to the path to Pastor John's house.

After he crossed the road, Major stopped at the tractor and examined the crash site. "What happened?"

"Not sure." Chuck scratched his head. "I suspect Vanessa lost control."

"Take a break, Chuck. We'll go check on Vanessa," Pastor John said.

Major and Pastor John headed up the road. "We need your expertise. It's a wonder we haven't rolled it on ourselves or had a snapped strap hit us. I need to warn you, so you don't look shocked— she's a mess. She's covered in mud."

Major picked up the pace. *Can't be that bad.*

When Pastor John stopped, Major scanned the area.

"Where is she?" he asked.

"Up here. You need glasses, old man," Vanessa said.

Major glanced at Vanessa and stared at the ground as he made his way across the ditch and up the bank to the stand of pine trees.

"Told you," Pastor John mumbled, and Major nodded.

"Are you okay, Honey?" Major knelt next to Vanessa and peered at her mud-covered face. *Thank goodness for her fiery blue eyes.*

Vanessa pursed her lips. "I'm fine except Pastor John, who is not a doctor, says I have a broken leg and won't let me move."

"Not exactly true," Pastor John said. "I suggested you—"

"Fine. He let me move to the pine needles."

"Looks like he did an expert job protecting your leg," Major said.

"Open fracture," Pastor John said. "Just guessing, but that's why we need the splint."

"I'll wait here with Vanessa until we can move her then we can work on getting Number 48 to the road," Major said.

"You'll do nothing of the kind. I'll be fine, and I assure you, I'm not going anywhere," Vanessa said. "And if I were, we'd need Number 48 to transport me."

"You're right. Do you have your whistle?" Major asked.

Vanessa glared, and he rose and cleared his throat. "Let's go, John. You and Chuck did the hard work. Shouldn't take us long to get it upright to see if it's operational."

On the way back, Major said, "I can't thank you enough for warning me. If I'd even smiled, I'd be in trouble for weeks. How did you have duct tape?"

"Vicki packs it in all our first aid boxes. It's come in handy more than once."

When they reached the tractor, Chuck said, "I repositioned the straps. Would you check them, Major?"

Major circled the vehicle and tightened the straps. "I'll stay by the vehicle to direct. John, if you'll stand where you can see me and where Chuck can see you then you can communicate the hand signals to him."

Chuck jumped into the tractor seat. "Let's do this."

Under Major's direction, the tractor eased the vehicle away from the trees then Number 48 rolled upright on its wheels. Major held up his hands with his wrists crossed to signal *stop*. Chuck moved backward to give the straps slack then John and Major removed them.

Chuck turned off the engine and hopped to the ground. "How'd we do?"

"I didn't see any damage underneath, and the tires look good. Key's still in the ignition." Major jumped into the driver's seat, and after three attempts, the engine roared to life. He backed up then drove forward across the ditch to the road.

Pastor John and Chuck cheered.

"I'll take the tractor back. See you later," Chuck said.

As Chuck headed home, Rosalie popped out of the woods with a splint and more bandaging material.

"Ms. Vicki said she wants Aimee Louise to stay with her until tomorrow so she can make sure Aimee Louise doesn't have a head injury," Rosalie said. "Aimee Louise has a minor laceration on her head and a reddish swelling under her eyes, an abrasion on her shoulder, and she twisted her ankle. I want to stay too."

"That's fine. I know Vicki will be happy to have your help. John, we need to talk." Major told John about the sunroot, electricity, the strange illness, and the threats to law enforcement. "Bottom line, we don't know exactly what's going on, but we're preparing for no electricity. When we discussed the possibility at the farm this morning, we realized how dependent we've become on our daily hours of electricity. Molly's canning everything in the freezer."

"Wow. We're in the same boat." Pastor John frowned. "What about people in town?"

"Sheriff's talking to Pete this morning. Pete will get the word out."

"That's a relief." John shook his head. "We need to get busy. I can't believe we quit keeping up with our water storage for the garden. I keep forgetting to repair the downspout that collects rainwater. I'm sure we'll think of more things we've dropped."

"I'll take care of Vanessa's splint, and we'll return home in Number 48. Why don't you and Rosalie go on back to your place? I know you want to talk to Vicki and Chuck and his wife so you all can get busy."

"You're right. Are you sure?" Pastor John asked. "I don't mind staying if you need help."

"No, I'm fine. Go on. I'll be back in the morning to pick up the girls."

Rosalie hugged Major then she and Pastor John hurried to the golf cart.

Major drove Number 48 the short distance to Vanessa. When he strolled to her with the splint, she smiled. "I can't tell you how thrilled I was when I heard the engine start up."

When Major knelt next to her with the splint, Vanessa bit her lip. "Wait a minute. Put on your work gloves. I accidently sat in a patch of poison ivy. We might have to treat my hands and maybe my face, but the mud might have protected the rest of me." She gazed at his face, and her eyes welled up. "Go ahead. You can laugh."

Major met her gaze. "I know this is awful for you. We'll laugh later. Right now, I want to get you home."

As Major applied the splint, she said, "I've been thinking—"

Major pinched his lips together and focused on the splint. *Oh Lord.*

"I can strip in the barn then Molly can hose me off. Except we'll be careful of the open wound. Maybe Molly will have an idea on how we can do all that."

Major finished the final wrap for the splint. "You're right." He rose to his feet. "Let's get you into the passenger's seat."

He stepped behind her and bent his knees then wrapped his arms around her torso. "I'll lift you to the vehicle. Ready?"

In one swoop, Major lifted her and set her at the edge of the passenger's seat. "You okay?"

"So far; so good. If I scoot my butt back on the seat, I can use my arms to shift."

"Don't use your legs. I'll manage them after you're situated."

"You're the boss," Vanessa mumbled as she broke into a sweat with the effort to shift herself with her arms.

"I'm not sure I understood what you said," Major said. "Repeat that, please?"

"No." Vanessa swatted his arm, and Major chuckled.

After Major moved her legs, she clicked her seatbelt, and he trotted to the driver's side. "I'll drive back on the paved road. It'll be a smoother ride."

"That's twenty miles of public road," Vanessa said. "Too risky. Let's go our usual route. You'll take it slow. I'll be fine."

On the way back, Vanessa said, "I've totally ruined the entire day. You had to stop what you were doing to rescue me. Aimee Louise is hurt. Rosalie won't be at the farm. I'll be useless. That's four people taken out of commission at a critical time because I was careless. And prideful. I pulled Pastor John and Chuck away from their families. Vicki has to take care of Aimee Louise. Molly will have to take care of me." She wailed and pounded her fist on the dash. After her tears dried, her sobs turned into hiccups.

"You done?" Major asked.

"Yes."

Good.

When Major stopped to unlock the gate, Vanessa said, "Thanks for listening to me."

He smiled. "Any time."

She snorted. "I went on a rant. I don't plan to make that a habit."

Major drove down the driveway and parked at the barn. "I'll get Molly then we'll lift you out of the vehicle. You can tell her your barn idea. Just let me know what you want me to do."

"Thank you." Vanessa's shoulders slumped as Molly and the children poured out of the house. "Sara will give me the third degree, won't she?"

"You know it." Major grinned. "Better you than me."

"Thanks for the support, Bud." Vanessa's eyes twinkled.

Major climbed out of the vehicle and smiled at Vanessa. "You are one beautiful mud-covered woman. You know that?"

He dodged the mud that she rubbed off her arm. then tried to fling on him.

When he laughed, Vanessa sighed. "I need to work on my mud-slinging skills too."

CHAPTER NINE

When Major drove Number 48 toward the house, the children swarmed to meet them.

"You're all muddy, Aunt Vanessa," Sara squealed. "Did you hurt your leg when you fell in the mud? Where's Aimee Louise and Rosalie? Did they fall in the mud too?"

"Back off, everybody," Molly said. "We'll get the full story later. Y'all go back and help Mr. Young. Shoo." She waved her hands. "Don't make me call *Inside*."

After the children left, Molly put her hands on her hips. "What's with the splint?"

"Open fracture," Major said.

"Ugh. That complicates things. We'll clean the mud away in stages."

"My idea was to strip down in the barn, and you could hose me off," Vanessa said.

"I was thinking more on the order of a sponge bath, but the barn's perfect. I'll need a chair that can get wet, a way to prop up the leg, and a set of fresh clothes."

On their way to the house, Molly said, "We need Heather. I'm worried about the open fracture. We need her medical expertise for guidance."

"After you're set, I'll leave for the deputies' house."

When Major reached the house, he said. "Annie, would you help me select clean clothes for Aunt Vanessa?"

"How can I help?" Josh asked.

"Take one of our plastic chairs from the yard and one of the folding patio tables to the barn."

"Can I help you, Josh?" Brett asked.

"Yeah. Let's go." Josh, Brett, and Penny dashed outside.

Mr. Young was loading the canner with jars. "Can I get a quick recap?"

Major stopped. "Annie, pick out a change of clothes. You know what she likes to wear."

Annie hurried to the master bedroom, and Sara followed her. "I'll help you, Annie. We need to find something sparkly."

"Vanessa was driving and flipped Number 48. She has an open leg fracture. Aimee Louise has a cut on her head, so Vicki is keeping her overnight for observation. Rosalie stayed to help Vicki. Vanessa is caked with mud, and Molly will clean her up. Molly wants Heather to check the open wound."

"Wow. Thanks. Annie and I will take over the canning until Molly's available again." Mr. Young chuckled. "We need to find a job for Sara."

"I might have an idea. I'll be back soon." Major filled his water bottle then headed to the barn. He stepped over the garden hose that stretched into the barn.

"We delivered the chair and table," Josh said as he and Brett raced past him on their way out of the barn. Penny trotted behind them.

Vanessa sat in the chair, and the table supported her leg. Molly had wrapped the splinted leg with an industrial-sized black trash sack. Vanessa's face, hands, and arms were clean, and she leaned back while Molly shampooed her hair.

"You work fast, Molly. I'm on my way to talk to Heather. Annie and Sara are picking out clothes. Anything else?"

"Thanks, Major. Tell Heather I'd like for her to inspect the wound." Molly brushed her hair away from her eyes with her wrist. "The boys pulled in the hose for me. I sent them for my scissors for the jeans, but I think I can salvage the shirt."

"Special request. I know it's your favorite color, Honey." Vanessa said.

Major bent over and kissed Vanessa's cheek. "Be back soon."

He hurried to Number 48 and sped to the deputies' house. Stuart met him at the end of the driveway.

"Everything okay?" Stuart asked.

"Bottom line, yes. Except for some complications. Where's Heather? It will be simpler if I tell the story one time."

"She's inside. Is Aimee Louise okay?" Stuart hopped into the vehicle, and Major sped down the driveway.

"She's—okay." Major parked. "Let's go inside."

When they walked into the house, Stuart shouted, "Major's here. Something's up."

Major raised his eyebrows. *Good assessment.*

Heather came out of the kitchen. "Brad's out back with our son, Stuart. They're running off some energy. Jim and I are canning."

Stuart rushed to the back door and returned with Brad, who held his three-year-old's hand.

Wally hurried down the stairs. "Kris is settling the kids down for a nap. Can we start without her?"

"Let's sit," Brad said.

After everyone grabbed a seat, Major recounted the details of the crash and the injuries. Heather dashed up the stairs and returned with her medical bag. "Let's go."

"I'm going too," Stuart said. "I can run to Pastor John's farm from your place, Major."

"Been thinking about that," Major said. "Might be better if you stay here and help finish up the preparations then come to the farm tomorrow. I'll be going to Pastor John's to pick up Rosalie and Aimee Louise in the morning. We could use your help if you can get caught up here. We've lost almost a full day's work with the diversion of the crash, and we'll be down two people."

"Makes sense," Jim said as he came from the kitchen, and Brad nodded.

"Unanimous," Wally said.

"But you didn't see Aimee Louise." Stuart narrowed his eyes.

"Rosalie is with her. If anything was wrong, we'd know," Major said.

Stuart frowned. "Okay."

"Let's go." Heather tapped her foot as she waited at the door.

On the way to Major's farm, Heather said, "You know Stuart's almost as protective about Aimee Louise as you are."

"I know. Not sure I like it much, but I know."

"It'll grow on you." Heather smiled. "Tell me more about Vanessa's condition. Did she hit her head? She was ejected, right?"

"I don't think she hit her head. She fell into a muddy ditch, so it was hard to assess her injuries. She was wearing sturdy jeans. Pastor John assessed her wound and bandaged it to protect it. He duct-taped where he'd cut her jeans and above and below the wound to keep it stable until we had a splint."

"Duct tape?" Heather snickered.

"Evidently, that's his go-to first aid tool because Vicki puts it in all their first aid boxes."

"Did you laugh when you saw your mud-caked wife with her duct-taped leg?"

"Are you kidding?" Major raised his eyebrows. "No."

"Good."

When they reached the farm gate, Heather said, "The treatment for an open fracture is surgery. Maybe you and I could go out to Doc's farm to see what he wants to do after I check her leg. He's still around, right?"

"Not sure. I heard he left, but our vet's still around."

"I know you think like a farmer and look at all the options, but don't say that to Vanessa. Ever. Trust me on this one."

Major shrugged and parked in front of the barn. "You need me?" he asked.

"If I do, I'll send for you," Heather said. "I need to scrub my hands before I do anything."

When Major and Heather walked into the kitchen, he said, "Heather needs to wash her hands."

"Water's warm at the sink. I just washed some pans," Mr. Young said.

After Heather washed and rinsed her hands, Major opened the door for her. "I'll send Annie to the barn with the clothes."

Heather hurried to the barn.

* * *

Molly met Heather at the doorway. "I've cleaned up most of the mud, but I was nervous about doing much around the wound. I waited for you until I cut off her jeans."

"Let's see what we have. How are you feeling, Vanessa?" Heather stared at Vanessa who was rubbing her hands together. "Your face is a little red. Have you been scratching it?"

"No. Just rubbing it a little. I might have gotten into a little poison ivy."

"Let me see your palms." Heather narrowed her eyes. "They're a little red too. Cut away, Molly, and let's have a look. Do you have any antihistamines? That might help the itch."

"I'm sure we do, but I'll check Rosalie's list of our medications."

Vanessa reached for her face, and Molly said, "No. We may have to put some socks on your hands to keep you from scratching. I'll cover you with a sheet as soon as I get these jeans off."

While Molly cut away the jeans, Heather asked, "What happened?"

"I was on our side of the state road and thought the best way to get over the ditches on both sides was to gun it. When I slammed on the accelerator, Aimee Louise yelled, but I wanted to make the jump. We left the first bank airborne and slammed into the one across the road."

She sighed. "It would have been a beautiful jump if I'd made it. I didn't have my seatbelt on. I remember flying and thinking, *this is not good*. I landed on my chest at the side of the ditch, and I think the force knocked the breath out of me. When I heard a truck coming down the state road, I panicked and tried to get lower in the ditch. I rolled down into the mud then lay there until Aimee Louise found me."

Molly dropped the jeans to the barn floor and tossed a sheet over Vanessa. Heather glanced up as Annie came in with Vanessa's clothes.

"Annie, would you get my bag out of Number 48 for me?"

When Annie returned, Heather said, "Thanks, now set my bag on a hay bale and open it." Heather knelt next to Vanessa's wound. "Annie, do you see the trauma shears? They're the ones with the lip near the tip."

Annie handed her the shears, and Heather snipped away the bandaging. After the dressing dropped to the ground, she said, "Annie, could you bring me the tea kettle?"

Annie dashed to the house and returned with the kettle. Heather touched it with her elbow. "Good. Lukewarm. Pour a small stream around the wound, but not directly on it."

Annie drizzled water where Heather pointed. Heather applied gentle pressure above the wound then sat back on her heels. "What do you see, Annie?"

Annie peered at the wound. "A stick?"

"That's what it looks like to me too. Give the tea kettle to your mom and bring my pack over close to me then put on a pair of gloves. They're in the side pocket."

"A stick?" Vanessa asked. "There's a stick in my leg?"

Molly stepped closer and peered over Heather's shoulder. "Looks like a bone to me but more like a chicken bone."

The corners of Vanessa's mouth drooped, and her brow furrowed. "I have chicken bone legs?"

"I've got gloves on," Annie said.

"Good. Go on the other side of Vanessa's leg across from me." Heather opened several packs of gauze pads and handed one to Annie.

"Wrap the gauze around the stick then pull slowly toward Vanessa's foot. While you pull, I'll hold pressure to control any bleeding."

Annie knelt across from Heather, wrapped the stick with gauze, and eased the stick back a half-inch. As Annie pulled, Heather packed sterile gauze pads around the wound to soak up the blood flow.

After she'd used a pack of pads, Heather said, "Stop a minute." She removed the top layers of gauze, blotted away blood, and examined the open wound. "Doing good. Feels like at least another two inches to go."

As Annie pulled, the wound bled more freely, and Heather used another pack of sterile pads.

Vanessa squirmed, and Molly held out two fingers. "Quit watching, and hold my fingers, and squeeze."

Vanessa's eyes welled up, and she held Molly's fingers in her fist.

Heather blotted the blood with gauze pads. "Keep going."

Annie pulled until she removed the stick.

"It's out. Good." Heather applied pressure to the bleeding wound.

"Thank you." Vanessa released Molly's fingers.

"I should have squeezed yours. Trying to get the feeling back." Molly wiggled her fingers.

"I'll hold pressure for a bit. Hold the stick where I can see it." Heather inspected the stick as Annie held it in the flat of her hand and turned it slowly. "What does it look like to you?"

"It's about a half-inch in diameter, and four inches long. Hardwood. Maybe pecan? Both ends look broken off. Not clean-cut."

Heather squinted at the stick. "I'm not sure I could have identified the wood, Annie. Well done. If there's a splinter left, we'll need Doc to cut it out." Heather shifted to a more comfortable position. "I felt the piece of wood close to the surface, but from the angle it came out, it might have been fairly deep." She reached for antibiotic cream, gauze, and tape then dressed the wound.

"You're missing something." Vanessa smiled.

Heather snorted. "I'm fresh out of duct tape."

"Let's get you dressed and inside." Molly's eyes widened when she picked up a sheer blouse.

"Here's a T-shirt to wear under the shirt Sara picked out," Annie said.

"Thank you, Annie," Vanessa said.

"Give your leg a chance to heal." Heather packed her bag. "Stay off it for at least three days then use a stick for balance to be sure you don't fall. Molly, change the dressing three times a day, and watch that wound for redness and swelling. Send for me if you need me to look at it, but I trust your judgment. If y'all don't need me for anything else, I'll head home."

While Molly and Annie helped Vanessa dress, Heather left for the house to find Major.

Major met Heather on her way to the house. "Ready to go see Doc?" he asked.

"Don't need to. It wasn't an open fracture, but we couldn't really tell until we cleaned it up a bit. Pastor John did the right thing. Vanessa's supposed to stay off her leg for at least three days. Molly will monitor her, and I'm ready to go home."

As they drove to the deputies' house, Major asked, "No broken bones? Does she have just a cut?"

"I don't think she has a fracture, but it wasn't a simple laceration; it's more of a deep puncture wound. She had a stick embedded in her leg. I can't tell you how it happened, but her injuries could have been much more extensive. We don't know if there is a splinter left. Molly will watch for signs of infection or swelling."

Major shook his head. "What a mess. We're down one, maybe two, depending on Aimee Louise's condition."

"You mean three. Molly will need to take care of Vanessa."

"I may have that covered."

When Major pulled in front of the deputies' house, Stuart strode out to meet him. "How's Aimee Louise?"

"I'll pick her up in the morning. Come to the farm for lunch. Clear it with Brad, first. It's his call, not mine or yours."

As he turned at the end of the driveway, Major glanced back at the house. Stuart was still on the porch with his arms crossed. *I might understand more than you think, Son.*

After he parked, Major strolled to the hen house where he knew he'd find Sara and Brett. "How are the chickens doing?" he asked.

Sara held out the egg basket. "They like the warm weather. This is the best day all week."

Brett came out of the coop. "I replaced the straw in one of the nest boxes. Sometimes they scratch the straw out. I think they are looking for bugs."

They came out of the run, and Brett locked the gate. Major strolled along with them.

"Sara, do you suppose you could take on an extra chore? Aunt Vanessa needs someone to look after her. She's injured and needs a nurse. Could you could do that?"

"Yes. I could be the nurse for Aunt Vanessa. I'll be the best nurse she's ever had. I'll be the best nurse the farm has ever seen. Except for Aunt Heather. I could never be as good as Aunt Heather." Sara shoved the basket at Brett and raced to the house.

Brett held the basket and gazed up at Major. "What about me, Pops? Do I get a special project too? I'd like a special project."

"You sure do. You'll have double the work because Sara will be busy. Can you do the work of two? I know that's a lot. Can you handle it?"

"I sure can. Thanks, Pops." Brett strutted to the house.

Shadow trotted to Major then flopped down at his feet. Major knelt and stroked Shadow's back. When he rose, Molly came out of the house and strolled down the path to meet him.

"Sara said you assigned her to look after Vanessa. She and Mr. Young are making a nurse's cap. I had to come out to tell you because I laugh every time I think about it. You are brilliant." Molly burst out laughing and wiped her eyes.

When she regained control, she said, "I have lunch on the table for you. While you eat, we'll catch you up on what we've done so far.

We won't get everything done, but if we all push, we can finish in the morning unless you want us to work after dark."

"We should stop after supper. The kids can take their baths and read or relax before bedtime. I have a feeling Stuart will be here for breakfast and will want to pick up the girls, so I'll be able to get some of my things done."

"Mr. Young and Annie got a lot of canning done. We'll finish by lunch tomorrow, but we're not as dependent on utility power as we were this morning."

When they reached the porch, Molly stopped. "Are we going to have Stuart here on a semi-permanent basis?"

"Depends on whether Brad can get by without him, but I suspect we will."

"He's welcome to stay here, and we have the room. I just hope he knows what he's getting into. Our Aimee Louise is different."

"He knows. It's hard for me to mind my own business though."

"Understandable. Ready to see Sara's nurse's cap? Remember, no laughing and don't look at me."

Major washed his hands then sat at the table. He peered at his sandwich. "Chicken salad? My favorite."

"We're eating the more perishable items first. Just like old times."

Mr. Young stirred a pot of stew on the stove. "About ready to can, Molly."

"Sounds good. What's on our schedule for the rest of the day?"

"From the kitchen side, canning." He lowered the burner and filled a quart jar to go into the pressure canner.

"Major, Mr. Young and I will focus on the canning if you don't mind checking the kids' tasks then you can work on what you had planned."

Sara strutted into the kitchen. She wore a white handkerchief tied in the style of a motorcycle rider's bandana. On the front of her headgear, she had painted a pink cross and sprinkled it with silver and gold glitter.

"Hi, Pops. I'm Aunt Vanessa's nurse. She needs water and a snack. She said she wanted to rest, but she needs to eat, or she'll be cranky. Mama says I get cranky when I'm hungry." Sara pulled out a cookie sheet and put a dinosaur placemat on it. "It's important for a snack to be pretty."

"Maybe she can have her snack later, Nurse Sara," Molly said. "She might be tired right now. You can put a glass of water on her table where she can reach it."

"Okay, Mommy. I'll pull a chair next to her door so she can tell me if she needs anything."

"Sounds good. Just remember, don't ask her if she needs anything. We need to let her rest."

Sara marched out of the kitchen with the full glass of water.

"Vanessa owes you, Molly." Mr. Young chuckled.

"I'll make sure she knows."

After Major polished off his sandwich and glass of water, Molly picked up his dishes and handed them to Mr. Young.

"Assembly line," she said. "You go on. Sara will tell me if Vanessa stirs. We've got this."

Major strolled to the shed. Annie, Josh, and Brett were putting away their buckets and supplies. "I need to repair fences. Josh and Brett, you can pull the wagon, and Annie, you can help me nail the boards in place. We may end up needing four wagonloads of lumber. We've got that entire section along the road to repair."

Josh and Brett saluted, and Annie giggled then the four of them loaded the wagon with lumber and tools.

After the second load of lumber, Major said, "Bring water back with the next load, and we'll take a break. This is going faster than I expected."

"We're an excellent team," Josh said.

"We sure are." Major and Annie set the next board in place then secured it while Josh and Brett hurried to pick up the last load of lumber and water for a break.

Sheriff pulled over at the shoulder and stepped out of his truck. "Looks good. Anything I can do to help?"

"We'll take a break when the boys get back. Won't take us long to finish after we hydrate."

"See you at the house." Sheriff turned at the driveway and waved to the boys who headed to the fence.

* * *

After their water break, the boys raced back to the house, and Major and Annie continued to repair the fence with new boards.

"Pops, I wish Aimee Louise was here." Annie nailed the last board to the fence post.

Major paused as he set his tools into the empty wagon. "She'll be here tomorrow. Why?"

Annie added her hammer and the leveler to the tool collection. "She needs to look at Mr. Young. I don't think he feels well."

"I'll talk to him."

"You can try. He's cagey." Annie smiled, and Major chuckled.

After they reached the tool shed, Major said, "I need to find your dad. I think he wants to talk to me."

"I think so too."

Sheriff met them at his truck, and Annie hurried inside. "Let's walk. Wouldn't mind seeing Annie's shed."

CHAPTER TEN

When they reached the shed, Sheriff's eyes widened. "Annie did this? By herself?"

"Sure did. The only thing I helped with was a few panels on the roof to save time. It's all her design and her work. Go around back."

Sheriff strolled around the shed, and Major followed him.

"A potting table?" Sheriff shook his head. "Amazing. She's talked about a greenhouse."

"I'm sure we'll have one by fall. Heather gave her some heritage seeds. Annie's hoping to keep us in vegetables year around."

Sheriff leaned against the table. "I had a visitor in the office today. He said he worked for Charles McNeil."

"What? I thought Charlie was in prison." Major narrowed his eyes.

"So did I. After my visitor left, I did some checking. McNeil must have had high-powered contacts we didn't know about because the prison released him three months ago, and he's back in his old position at the agency office. No paper trail of any charges, conviction, or prison time exists. Wiped clean." His face reddened, and he slammed his fist on the table. "He ordered the murders of Josh and Annie's parents, Russell and Margo Gaston, and he's free."

"I can't believe he's out and in charge of the agency again." Major frowned. "What does he want?"

Sheriff snorted. "My cooperation with the sunroot project. Turns out it's my honor and patriotic duty as a law enforcement officer to enforce the new federal directive for farmers to plant sunroot to feed our country's starving children."

"Bull crap. We should have permanently stopped McNeil when we had the chance. How wide is his reach, do you know? Any threats?"

"Best I can tell, he's in charge of the agency for the southeast. For sure Florida, Georgia, Alabama, and Tennessee. No threats this visit, but I'm sure this was just the first shot over the bow. He'll ramp it up."

"I think we have our priorities straight. Protect the children and be ready for the electricity to go off permanently then go after Charlie."

"Right. The other sheriffs in our region know about the scam now. Some were skeptical, but most will be on their toes. We'll have resources to tap."

"I'll bet you haven't had lunch. Molly made chicken salad." Major chuckled. "We need to eat it up before the electricity goes off."

As the two men strolled to the house, Sheriff said, "I thought after we empty the freezer, we could fill containers with water and put them inside it, so we'll have blocks of ice when we lose power."

"That's an outstanding idea. I may have some containers in the shed we can scrub and use."

When they reached the porch, Major said, "Almost forgot to warn you. Nurse Sara is on duty, and her patient is Vanessa."

"Oh, boy." Sheriff chuckled as he opened the door.

"There you are," Molly said. "Annie told me you were here. Your lunch is on the table. The boys are helping us can."

Sara bustled into the kitchen. "Mommy, Aunt Vanessa needs lunch. She's washing her hands first. I already washed my hands so I can make her sandwich. Would you make her hot tea? She said she likes sweet tea. I thought hot tea would be better for sick people, but if she's hurt not sick, can she have sweet tea?"

"I'll make her sandwich," Molly said. "You could pour her some sweet tea. It's good for injured people," Molly said.

"If you don't mind, Molly, I could use Annie's help with another project at the equipment shed unless you've got something else in mind for us to do," Major said.

"I'm all about the canning and sandwiches," Molly said. "Be my guest."

Sheriff said, "Molly, I have an idea for the freezers after you empty them."

"Let's go, Annie," Major said.

Annie skipped along to match Major's long stride to the shed. "What's our project?" she asked.

"We'll find buckets and bins that don't leak and clean them up to hold water. We'll put them in the freezers to make blocks of ice."

"That's brilliant," she said.

"Your dad's idea."

"I told Mr. Young he looked flushed, and he told me canning does that to an old man."

"You were right. Cagey."

When they reached the shed, Major said, "I like your idea of getting Aimee Louise and Rosalie back earlier. If Stuart shows up this afternoon, I'll send him."

"That's good because he'll be here before supper." Annie smiled and picked up a bucket. "I'll fill buckets with water, and we can see if they leak."

After they tested buckets and scrubbed the ones that didn't leak, Major said, "Let's take these to the house. We can leave them on the porch upside down until your mom is ready for them."

Annie picked up the two small buckets, and Major grabbed the three large ones.

When they reached the porch, Vanessa was in her chair with her leg propped up. "We have the most remarkable weapon here against self-pity. Sara told me to get out of bed because it was time for lunch, and my hair was messy." Vanessa laughed. "Molly helped me to the porch, and Sara brought my lunch."

After Annie placed her buckets upside down near the door, she hurried inside.

Major kissed the top of Vanessa's head. "Your hair is always messy." He sat next to her and grinned.

"You are such a stinker," Vanessa said. "What's next on your agenda?"

"Test the generators. We test them once a month, and while they aren't due until next week, it's simpler to fix any problems today."

Sheriff joined them on the porch. "I was thinking the same thing. We should also start up the tractor and the chainsaws. The gas station was open when I left town. I stopped and filled my tank and the one can I carry. I'll check the rest of the cans to see what our status is. I can make a quick run back to town if we need refills. Nobody goes much of anywhere anymore, so there are no lines for fuel."

"Why don't you check the gas, and I'll make sure all our tools are ready."

Annie returned from the house. "Sara told Mr. Young he needed to sit so she could take his temperature. Mom stood behind Sara with her arms crossed. You should have seen his face. He told Mom he couldn't take them both on, and Sara took his temperature. Mom checked. It was normal, but she made him take a break. What are we doing next, Pops?"

"We'll run all our equipment. Let's start with the generators."

"I'll grab the boys and take them to town with me," Sheriff said. "Molly and Mr. Young can work faster alone, I'm sure."

* * *

"You might as well learn how to start up the generators," Major said. Annie started up the first generator with coaching. Major explained how to troubleshoot if it wouldn't start then they moved to the next generator. The second generator was the oldest, and it sputtered and wouldn't start. After the third try, Annie stepped back and put her hands in the air. "I smell gas. I flooded it, didn't I?"

Major chuckled. "At least you didn't keep going. Give it a minute: you forgot about the choke."

By the third generator, Annie started without a hitch then they discussed the quirks and differences in the generators.

"What about moving them closer to the house? How do I do that if you aren't here?" Annie asked.

"Good question. We need to be thinking contingencies. Why don't we…" Major paused. "Let me ask you, what would work for you?"

Annie stared at the generator then stared at the house. "If the generator was on a skid, I could hook it up to the riding mower and drag it over."

Major nodded. "Just what I was thinking. Let's check the spare lumber to see if there's enough for you to build a skid for the largest generator. What other projects do you have in mind?"

"I want to build a greenhouse. Mr. Young said there might be some plastic at his old farm that I could use if Pastor John doesn't already have something in mind for it."

"That can be your next project. We'll ask Stuart to check on the plastic to see if that's an option when he goes to Pastor John's. Let's check the chainsaws and the rest of the equipment."

After they tested all the equipment and made minor repairs, Major said, "We're set. Let's take a break."

When they reached the back porch, Sara was sitting in Major's chair next to Vanessa. Sara was reading aloud, and Vanessa's eyes were closed. Sara waved, and Vanessa opened her eyes.

"I'm reading my favorite book to Aunt Vanessa." Sara held up her book.

"I'm getting a refresher on fairies," Vanessa said. "It's been a while since I've taken the time to relax, and Sara is an excellent reader. We've got another book picked out for tomorrow."

"It's about fairies," Sara said.

"We'll clean up and see what else we need to do," Major said. "You need anything?"

Vanessa shook her head, and Sara continued reading.

Molly and Mr. Young were sitting at the table when they walked into the kitchen.

"You two have been working hard," Molly said. "I reached a wall with canning. Take a break with us. Help yourself to the goat cheese and crackers."

Major poured two glasses of water and sat at the table next to Annie.

"Vanessa, Sara, and I talked about the garden earlier," Mr. Young said. "We want to plant tomato and pepper seeds in pots next week."

Josh and Brett burst through the back door. "We're starved," Josh said.

"Wash your hands then sit at the table and have a snack," Molly said. As the boys rushed to the sink, she said, "No. Not here. Go to the bathroom."

When Sheriff came inside, Molly handed him a glass of water, and he gulped it down. "Annie, I found some lumber in town. Check my truck after your snack. Molly, we owe Pete strawberry jam and four jars of canned beans. Major, let's go out to the porch. Mr. Young, join us?"

"I'll be there in a minute too," Molly said. "Send Sara in for a break too."

After the adults were out back, Sheriff said, "I've got news. First, Stuart will be here later this afternoon. The deputies decided if Stuart was here then Jim can move out of the bachelor trailer that has been next to the house. They can save the trailer's propane as a contingency for heating water or even providing a warm place to stay if things are rough. Heather liked the plan to designate a place to isolate someone who is sick."

Vanessa smiled. "I suspect Nurse Sara would approve."

Sheriff chuckled. "Second, McNeil's organization is moving fast. The town south of us lost all their electricity yesterday, and the electric company told the mayor the farmers who stole electricity off-schedule caused a technical glitch. Charlie needs to research his targets better. The mayor's a farmer, and the electric company spokesperson admitted they had no evidence of a technical glitch or of anyone stealing electricity."

"He's expanding ways to put pressure on the farmers," Mr. Young said. "If the farmers were cheating the system, the ham community would talk about it. Nobody's said anything."

"Dividing the communities into *us* and *them* categories isn't new, but it can be effective," Major said. "How can we stop Charlie?"

"I don't see how we can," Vanessa said. "I don't see any definitive evidence for criminal charges against McNeil. A civil suit might draw some publicity, but it also may backfire as a trivial suit."

"That takes care of that," Molly said. "Not up to us."

"You're right," Mr. Young said. "Case closed. Break's over." He winked at Major and headed inside.

* * *

Later in the afternoon, Major and Josh set up a rain barrel next to the barn with Penny and Shadow's supervision.

Shadow yipped, and Josh pointed. "Stuart's coming down the road. Can I meet him?"

"Go ahead," Major said.

Josh and Penny ran to the gate. Stuart wore his backpack and carried two over-sized duffle bags. His guitar case was slung over one shoulder, and his rifle on the other.

Major frowned. *I hope this doesn't backfire.*

He shook his head and attached the downspout to the barrel.

When Stuart and Josh reached the house, Major waved. "Welcome, Stuart. Check in with Molly."

Mr. Young joined Major at the barn. "I have some thoughts about McNeil; however, none of them would technically pass the Vanessa lawyer-test of legal."

"It makes sense for me to go after him because I don't want him coming to the farm. What I need is a trap." Major picked up his scraps and tools and dropped them into the wagon.

"My farm could have been an option if Pastor John and family weren't there," Mr. Young said.

"Right." Major paced. "If we need a location to set a trap, the county building opens only twice a week. Pete's Diner isn't being used except for the informal gatherings at the swap tables outside."

"When the electricity's cut off, people will revert to getting water from the diner's well. What are you thinking?"

"Not sure. There's got to be something that would bring Charlie out of hiding. You said you had some thoughts."

"I have to rest my feet." Mr. Young limped into the barn and sat on a hay bale. Major leaned against the door.

Mr. Young propped his feet up on a smaller bale. "The mayor that was a farmer got me to thinking. That was a misstep. What if there are other miscalculations where he's being stopped? For example, word is getting out through the sheriff's contacts and the amateur radio system about the sunroot scheme. You and the sheriff know him better than I do, but I know his type. He's blinded by his own ego. When do you think he'll decide it's time for him to make personal appearances to smooth things over with his self-perceived charm?"

"You might have an idea there. We just need to know when and where."

"Maybe there's a way we can help that along." Mr. Young rose. "Don't ask me how right this second."

Major gave Mr. Young his arm for balance as they returned to the house. "Did I make a mistake letting Stuart come here?"

Mr. Young paused at the porch. "No. We need the extra security, and the deputies needed to tighten their base. It was the right thing to do. If it's any consolation, I understand your concerns about Aimee Louise. I have two daughters."

When Major went into the house, Sheriff and Annie sat at the kitchen table, and Vanessa had stretched her legs out on the sofa. She rubbed her hands, but when she glanced at Major, she stuck them under her arms.

"My reader left me to go watch Stuart unpack. Stuart may not have realized the scrutiny he'll be under." Vanessa smiled.

"Not all bad." Major grinned.

"Major, come look at Annie's design. I'm not sure we have enough lumber, but we can get a start. See what you think," Sheriff said.

"Looks good. I like how you're managing the ventilation. What's your timeline?"

"If I can build the skid for the generator tomorrow, I can start on the greenhouse. We think full time would be three days, but with our normal chores, a week," Annie said.

Stuart came downstairs followed by his new entourage: Sara, Josh, and Brett.

"I'm set upstairs. Molly said to check with you, Major," Stuart said.

"I'd send you to pick up the girls at Pastor John's, but I realized Vicki will argue about Aimee Louise leaving. I need to go. Sorry."

Stuart nodded. "Number 48 seats two. If I ride with you, I could run back with Rosalie, so she doesn't have to run alone."

Sheriff mumbled, "Touché," and Vanessa snickered.

Major glared at Vanessa, and she shrugged.

"Grab your stuff. I'll hook up the small trailer then we can go," Major said.

Stuart met Major at Number 48 with his backpack, and they headed to Pastor John's house.

On the way, Major said, "I'm glad it worked out for you to come to the farm. I need to stop Charlie McNeil, and I'll feel better with you there."

"You going after him?" Stuart asked.

Major glanced at him. "I think I have to."

"I'm willing to go with you, Sir."

"I know that, but I may ask you to stay at the farm. I don't have a plan yet, though." Major caught up Stuart on his conversation with Mr. Young.

"Sounds like things are moving fast. We'll just have to move faster," Stuart said.

"My thoughts exactly."

As they headed down Pastor John's driveway, Stuart asked, "What are you going to say to Ms. Vicki?"

Major chuckled. "I have no idea, but it better be good."

Stuart nodded. "Give me a sign when you're ready to run."

Major burst out laughing. "It could come to that. Did you know that sweet pastor's wife shot at those three highway robbers that attacked Jim last year? Winged 'em. Pastor John tells the story better."

Vicki stood on the front porch with her arms crossed. Major smiled, and she glowered.

Here we go. Game on.

"I knew you'd be here this afternoon, Major. What do you have to say for yourself?"

Major cleared his throat. "We're hot and weary travelers…"

Vicki threw her head back and laughed. Pastor John and Chuck peered around the corner of the house.

"Major, you are full of surprises. I expected a long-winded string of excuses." Vicki wiped her eyes with her apron. "Come inside and have some sweet tea before you head back. We've been waiting for you, and the girls have their things pulled together. Aimee Louise is fine so far. I know Molly will check on her, and y'all are closer to Heather than we are if any problems arise."

Pastor John strode up to Major and followed him into the house.

"That was genius," he whispered. "Where did that come from?"

"Fear. Pure, icy fear."

Pastor John choked. "My wife was right; you are definitely full of surprises."

When Major stepped inside, he hugged the waiting girls.

"How's Vanessa?" Pastor John asked.

"After she cleaned Vanessa's wound, Heather discovered an embedded piece of wood in Vanessa's leg and supervised as Annie removed it. Vanessa's still under orders to rest, but it looked far worse than it turned out to be."

"I can't tell you how relieved I am." Pastor John dropped into his recliner. "We looked up open fracture in Vicki's medical book..."

"After we read the treatment was surgery, I worried about Vanessa all night," Vicki said. "I don't know if there are any doctors around since the hospital closed. We need to know what our options are before we have a medical emergency."

"You're right. I'll look into that," Major said.

"How are we all going to pile into Number 48?" Rosalie asked.

"I'll tell you if you'll tell me how you came up with its name," Stuart said.

Pastor John leaned back. "You mean you don't know, Deputy? I know."

"Really?" Major asked.

"Yep. My dad was a stock car racer in Tennessee before he went into the Army. I'm an expert in two things: The Holy Bible and the history of stock cars and infamous drivers." Pastor John grinned.

"My mom's dad knew everything about stock cars," Rosalie said. "When we'd visit Grandpa, he'd take us to races. He had a story about every car and driver. Mom said she grew up around stock cars and had car exhaust in her blood."

"That's awesome," Pastor John said.

"Now I'm wondering," Vicki said. "What does all this family nostalgia have to do with Number 48?"

"Jimmy Johnson was a legend, and his car was Number 48. Mom would be thrilled if she knew we're honoring Jimmy Johnson," Rosalie said, and Pastor John beamed.

Vicki shook her head and left for the kitchen.

"Did you know, Aimee Louise?" Stuart asked.

"Yes."

"Why didn't you say so?" Major asked. "Never mind. Nobody thought to ask you, did they?"

"No."

"Here's your sweet tea." Vicki handed glasses to Major and Stuart.

Stuart held up his glass. "I salute Jimmy Johnson." He took a long drink. "My turn. Rosalie, you and I will run back."

Pastor John smiled. "Simple. Always the best."

"Stuart's idea," Major said. "Before we go, I wanted to ask if you have any plans for the plastic and extra lumber Mr. Young stored in his barn."

"No plans at all. You need it?"

CHAPTER ELEVEN

"Annie's building a greenhouse and doesn't have enough wood or any plastic to speak of. If you won't be using it, I'd like to take some."

"Help yourself," John said.

When Major and Stuart returned from the barn, Vicki handed each one a fresh glass of sweet tea.

"I'm ready." Rosalie donned her backpack. "Let's go."

"Thanks for the tea." Stuart gulped it down and rushed out with Rosalie.

"You ready, Aimee Louise?" Major asked as he finished his tea.

"Yes."

On their way to the farm, Aimee Louise asked, "Are we ready to lose power?"

"We're in a little better shape, but I'm worried we've forgotten something. When we get back to the farm, I'd like for you to see what you can find."

"Rosalie too," Aimee Louise said.

"Of course."

Major passed Rosalie and Stuart at the state road and continued on to the farm. Aimee Louise leaned back in her seat.

"I've been thinking about how to contact the judge's son," Major said. "Could you ask the hams about any Amber alerts from Miami?"

"Yes. I'll tell them to contact the northern Florida sheriffs."

"That's easy." Major pulled up to the gate. "I'll unlock it."

After he opened the gate and climbed back in the driver's seat, he said, "But they won't, will they? They'll use the ham radio."

"Yes, but word will circulate beyond the ham community."

Major chuckled as he closed the gate then drove to the house.

* * *

After supper, Aimee Louise, Rosalie, and Annie settled in at the ham radio, and Stuart wandered to the computer room to listen. Vanessa returned to the sofa, and Sara, Molly, and Sheriff went for a stroll to check the garden, chickens, and goats. Josh and Brett raced to the goat pen and climbed onto the fence to wait. Shadow and Penny stayed on the back porch.

Major and Mr. Young relaxed in their rockers as the sun dipped into the horizon in a blaze of fiery orange, and a light breeze from the west cooled the air.

"I look forward to the sunrise in the mornings, but there's nothing more relaxing than the sunset," Mr. Young said as he rocked. "You have any more thoughts?"

"I have a feeling that things are not going well for Charles McNeil. I just need to be ready when the opportunity pops up."

"Seems like we might want to stage supplies for you, so you can take off at a moment's notice. My trailer might be the best place."

"Good idea." Major narrowed his eyes. "Annie said your face was flushed earlier. You running a fever?"

"No, I'm fine. The kitchen got too hot for me, and I didn't have the good sense to take a break. Molly sent me outside to cool down. She said if I don't take breaks and drink water, she'll fire me." Mr. Young shook his head. "It's been a long time since I've had a woman fussing over me. I'd forgotten how cranky a woman is when she's worried."

"Kind of nice, isn't it?" Major smiled when Mr. Young snorted.

Stuart, Aimee Louise, and Annie came out of the house.

"Rosalie will be here in a minute. She's organizing her notes. Where's the sheriff? Did they go check the animals?" Stuart asked. "He needs to hear this."

Josh and Brett raced to the porch and slid to a stop at the first step. Sara and Penny caught up with them, and Molly and Sheriff strolled along behind.

"All four of you beat us," Molly said. "We'll try again tomorrow."

"You can't win if you don't run, Mommy." Sara posed on the porch with her hands on her hips.

"Spitting image of her mother," Mr. Young whispered, and Major smiled.

Rosalie came out of the house. "Good. Everybody's here."

"You'll want to sit." Stuart motioned toward Sheriff and Molly's chairs.

When Rosalie sat on the steps, Aimee Louise and Annie sat next to her; Stuart stood behind Aimee Louise. The twins leaned against Molly's chair, and Josh leaned against Sheriff. Penny flopped down at Josh's feet.

"Aimee Louise asked about Amber alerts in the Miami area. Nobody knew anything, but the hams will check. She told them the inquiry came from the sheriffs in the north part of the state." Rosalie swallowed hard. "Then a ham reported the ambush and murders of the sheriff and his three deputies two counties over from us."

Sheriff rose. "What? When?"

"Early this morning at shift change right before daylight," Stuart said. "Details are sketchy, but a speeding military-style truck with men in the back hit and badly injured the animal control officer as she ran toward the shots. She'll be okay." Rosalie scooted toward the end of the step, and Stuart squeezed between her and Aimee Louise.

Stuart rubbed the back of his neck. "The county assessor found the sheriff and deputies. They didn't even have time to draw their weapons."

Rosalie cleared her throat. "The hams said the mayor claimed it was a group of farmers that the sheriff was about to arrest because they were stealing the town's electricity."

"Propaganda spreads fast," Mr. Young said.

"Some hams are farmers," Stuart said. "They were angry at the mayor and said nobody would believe such hooey."

"Rosalie told me what hooey meant," Annie said. "Handy word to know."

"You'll tell me later, right?" Sara asked.

"Next. Savannah," Aimee Louise said.

"Right," Rosalie said. "In the discussion about farms, a ham from Georgia mentioned somebody told him there's a big meeting for farmers near Savannah this coming weekend. Some bigwig will be there to talk about a revolutionary crop that's guaranteed to make them money."

"What does this mean for us?" Molly asked as she glanced at the younger children.

"Means that everything we're doing is right. We're sticking together and preparing for no electricity, and our neighbors are doing the same," Sheriff said.

"Our town and our farmers support our sheriff," Major said. "We don't have to be afraid."

"You're right. I feel better," Molly said. "It's almost bedtime. Who needs a snack? I might have a few cookies looking for friendly mouths to eat them."

The younger children jumped up and raced inside. Molly followed them. "Wash your hands first."

Annie raised her eyebrows at Sheriff, and he smiled and nodded. Annie rose and brushed off her jeans then sauntered inside.

"She's growing up," Major said.

"Not me. I'm getting a cookie," Sheriff said. "Anybody else?"

Mr. Young rose from his chair, and Sheriff held the door for him.

Vanessa went to bed early. After the four Starr children bathed and were in bed, the girls showered, and Shadow followed them to their bedroom. Mr. Young left for his trailer, and Molly and Sheriff relaxed on the sofa.

Stuart accompanied Major on his nightly security check.

Major stopped at the gate lock when he came to it. "I've learned if I touch a lock, I'll remember I checked it; otherwise, I'd have to come back out for a second check in the middle of the night when I woke up worrying about it."

"You're still going after McNeil, aren't you?" Stuart asked as they strolled from the driveway gate to the goat pen.

Major paused and gazed at Stuart. "You asking as a deputy?"

"I might have said yes before our trip to the folks' farm." He shook his head. "Times are different."

"You're right." Major pulled on the pen door and the lock.

"I want to go with you." Stuart paused on the path to the chicken coop.

"I know you do, but the farm has to…" Major held up his hand and whispered, "Something moved in the stand of trees on the other side of the house. Take the back of the house to the southwest corner. I'll go along the front of the house. After we reach the corners, back me up."

Stuart headed to the back, and Major strode toward the front of the house. He waited at the southeast corner until he heard Stuart's signature cardinal whistle.

Major stepped two yards then stopped to listen. He held up his hand at the sound of rustles in the woods. Stuart sounded the low coo of a mourning dove. When Major glanced back, Stuart pointed at the west end of the tree grove as a doe leaped the back fence and disappeared in the high grass then two figures on the east end crashed through the brush. Stuart raced past Major, but the roar of an engine filled the night air before he reached the fence.

When Stuart returned, he asked, "Do you think the deer spooked them?"

"Maybe, but they might have seen me move. Glad you were along."

Stuart stared at the road. "It will be hard to sleep tonight."

As they headed to the house, Major said, "It's hard to sleep every night."

When Major went into his bedroom, he eased the door closed so he wouldn't disturb Vanessa.

"I'm awake," Vanessa said. "Are you okay?"

"Stuart and I flushed out two intruders that took off before Stuart caught up to them." He pulled off his boots. "Complicates things. Sheriff will stick closer to the farm and coordinate a twenty-four-hour watch."

"You're going after Charlie McNeil, aren't you?"

Major went into the master bath and brushed his teeth.

"Well, are you?" Vanessa asked when he returned.

"What makes you think so?"

"I know you. What can I do to help?"

"I expected a huge argument. Are you trying to keep me on my toes?" He chuckled and pulled off his shirt then sat on the bed. "I'm not sure when I'm leaving, but I'm thinking soon. I need to gather supplies for the trip, and I don't know where I'm going."

"Mr. Young's helping you, right? Leave it up to us. We'll have you ready to go by the end of the day tomorrow."

Major shook his head. "You're amazing."

"I know. Get some rest."

* * *

When Major tiptoed into the kitchen before daylight, Shadow and the aroma of coffee greeted him.

"Good morning, Major. I poured you a cup," Mr. Young said.

After they stepped outside with their coffee, Shadow raced after a rabbit, and Mr. Young said, "There was some commotion last night. Did you flush a varmint?"

"We did. Like you said, it's moving fast."

"There wasn't any power when I got up an hour ago, but it's on now, so I started a load of laundry. I've been thinking about the sickness that's going around. Molly and I found facemasks in the storage closet a while ago, and I added them to the laundry. I'll pack two of them for you." Mr. Young rocked and sipped his coffee. "You know we really should have Rosalie make a list for us."

"Any way we can make it theoretical? Otherwise, I'll have the two girls tracking me because I wouldn't take them along."

Mr. Young snorted. "There is that. I'll make an attempt at a list then you can add to it."

"Since we have electricity, I'm going into town as soon as I finish my coffee to see if I can fill up the empty fuel cans and my truck. I plan to take off the topper and repair it this afternoon." Major rose. "Maybe Stuart can help. That should distract him. He wants to go with me, but I can't take him. I can't ruin his career."

"Can I ride along? I'd enjoy getting away." Mr. Young rose. "I'll take your cup inside and leave a note on the kitchen table for Molly."

Major waited for Mr. Young then they strolled to Major's truck.

"I don't think anybody will hear the engine start up, but Aimee Louise watches for the sunrise every morning. She'll know we left." Major shook his head. "Hard to do anything sneaky around here."

Mr. Young chuckled and pointed to the sack at his feet. "I lifted a few jars of Molly's strawberry jam in case there's something good on the swap table. I didn't have time to rearrange the cupboard, but it doesn't matter. Molly has radar and would have known something was missing."

As Major drove toward town, the eastern sky lightened. "Vanessa will help you gather supplies for the trip. She had figured out I'm leaving, and we talked. She was calm and didn't yell or even forbid me to go."

"It is hard to be sneaky. I put a jar of beans and a small box of crackers in a bag while she napped on the sofa. She must have peeked and figured out what was going on," Mr. Young said.

When they reached the outskirts of town, Mr. Young said, "Drop me off at Pete's. I'd like to see if Doc's around, and maybe I'll hear something."

Major parked at Pete's. "After I get fuel, I'll stop by any open stores to see what I can find."

"If you see candy, pick up some for me because I'm running low. The kids and I have gone to rationing, and we're down to one piece a day for each of us."

Major pulled up to the pump at the gas station and set his two gas cans on the ground to fill.

A farmer at the adjacent pump closed his truck's tailgate. "No diesel, Major. I filled three five-gallon cans with regular gas for my tractor and generator, but the regular is low too because the pump is running slow. It takes a while." He waved as he drove away.

While Major filled his gas cans, he glanced around. None of the surrounding businesses were open. Weathered and warped sheets of plywood covered windows and doors, weeds poked through sidewalk cracks, and dirt streaked the windows. *Been a while since I was in town.* He frowned. *It's really deteriorated.* After he filled the three cans, he strolled into the station and scanned the empty shelves.

"Haven't seen you in a while," the station owner said. "I'm almost out of gas. I expected a truck two weeks ago. Now, I don't know. Truck's never been more than a few days late. I hear the truckers don't want to leave home."

"I heard that too. I was hoping it wasn't true. You have any candy or gum?" Major pulled out his wallet to pay.

"No. Wish I did." The owner slid the money into the till. "I hear the farmers have around-the-clock electricity. Is that true?"

"Not here. Why?"

"Somebody said it's the farmers' fault our electricity goes off because they have priority, and some folks are getting riled up. My wife and kids are at her folks' farm in Alabama. I hope they're okay. If I don't get any gas by the end of the day, I think I'll head out and join them."

"You got everything you need?"

"I thought I did until you mentioned candy." He shook his head and smiled.

"They'll be glad to see you. Have a safe trip."

"Thanks, Major. And watch yourself. Might want to tell Pastor John to be careful when he comes to town too."

On his way to pick up Mr. Young, Major swung by Sheriff's house and narrowed his eyes. *Broken window.* He pulled into the driveway and grabbed his rifle then stepped to the side porch and tried the knob. The door swung open, and he peered inside. *Ransacked.* He swept each room and checked closets as he went. *All clear.*

The intruders had tossed drawers and smashed furniture. Major removed the remaining leg from the coffee table then hurried to his truck to pull out his tool chest. After he secured the broken window with the tabletop, he locked the door and left.

When he pulled into Pete's Diner, Mr. Young and Pete stood shoulder-to-shoulder against the swap table as they faced three men who had their fists clenched. Major jumped out of his truck with his rifle and positioned himself behind the men.

"How's everybody doing?" He lifted his rifle.

When the three men jerked around, Pete grabbed his shotgun that had been on the swap table under a stained, once-white bedsheet.

"Why don't you three move on?" Major asked as he aimed his rifle.

"You'll be sorry," the man in the middle growled and raised his fist.

Major narrowed his eyes at the rash on the man's hands. "Really? Who's your boss? I bet he and I are old friends."

"Let's go," the man on the right said, and the three men rushed to the parked blue truck that blocked the front of the diner.

After they peeled out, Major asked, "What was that all about?"

Pete grabbed a chair from behind the table and positioned it next to Mr. Young. "Sit."

Mr. Young dropped into the chair. "Thanks, Pete."

Pete leaned against the table. "When those three showed up, they said they were looking for farmers. They said they needed to teach the farmers a lesson."

"Pete told them he was a dentist, and I was a gynecologist." Mr. Young chuckled.

"First thing that came into my mind." Pete shrugged.

"You doing okay, Mr. Young?" Major asked. "Did you see Doc?"

"Doc says I'm getting old and need to take it easy." Mr. Young glowered and crossed his arms.

Pete nodded. "And he said you have to take your blood pressure medicine."

"Did you run out of your medicine?" Major asked.

"No. I was taking it every other day to make it last," Mr. Young mumbled.

"But Doc gave him enough to last a year," Pete said. "And if he dies, he's supposed to give back what's left. I suggested that."

Major cleared his throat. "Pete, I'm not sure it's safe for you to be here by yourself. Is there anybody who can be with you?"

Pete rubbed his chin. "A dental assistant? I think I can come up with somebody."

Mr. Young rose and patted his shirt pocket. "Got my meds. I'm ready to go."

On their way to the farm, Major said, "I noticed one guy had a rash on his hands."

Mr. Young nodded. "I think they meant to sneak up on us, but he ruined that with a coughing fit. When Pete stepped toward them, I pulled him back. I hope we stayed far enough away. How contagious is this thing? Do we know?"

"Somebody might, but I haven't heard." Major drummed his fingers on the steering wheel. "I'm not sure I should leave. We don't have any evidence that Charlie McNeil is behind all this. Am I letting my intense dislike of a crooked federal agent cloud my judgment?"

"Maybe. But wouldn't it be unusual for someone else to pull together a large organization in our area without McNeil stepping in long before now?"

"True. This doesn't feel like a power struggle. It appears he's lost his key lieutenants though and has second-rate talent doing his dirty work."

"Vanessa and I will have everything ready for you before this evening."

Major chuckled. "You're right. I'm going."

When they sauntered into the farmhouse, Molly said, "My spies told me you were on your way in. Your breakfast will be up in a minute."

Sheriff strolled into the kitchen. "The girls have news for you. Eat then come out to the porch. We'll meet you there."

Molly set Mr. Young's plate in front of him, and he placed his bottle of pills in the middle of the table.

"Told you so," she said.

"Good. You got a refill." Vanessa patted Mr. Young's shoulder as she headed to the porch.

While they ate, Mr. Young said, "No privacy around here at all."

"You're right."

They hurried through their breakfasts and stepped out to the back porch where everyone waited.

Rosalie tapped her notebook. "Several hams with contacts in the Miami area reported that children of law enforcement officers have disappeared the last week or so. An FBI agent from Miami will be at a sheriff's office in north Florida today or tomorrow." Rosalie looked up from her notes. "That's all the information we have. The hams speculated the agent caught a ride with an eighteen-wheeler on its way to a distribution center in Atlanta and will go to the county where the murders occurred."

"Could show up at mine. Depends on which direction the truck driver goes," Sheriff said. "I'll leave for my office after lunch and check in with the sheriffs' network."

Major leaned forward in his rocker. "It's getting rough in town. Three thugs showed up at Pete's Diner, and somebody broke a window at your house. I covered the window, but you might want to check it out for yourself."

"Can I go with you?" Josh asked.

Sheriff frowned. "I don't think…"

Molly broke in. "I agree with you. There's no reason Josh can't go; after all, our latest rule is that nobody goes alone."

"I'll think about it, Josh," Sheriff said. "Molly, can we talk in private?"

CHAPTER TWELVE

"Anything else, Rosalie?" Major asked.

"Farms," Aimee Louise said.

"Right. A ham said that someone has been setting farmhouses and barns on fire in south Florida. Another one said there was some kind of bounty for every barn burned."

"Payoff doubles if the farm belongs to law enforcement," Aimee Louise added.

"That's the rumor," Rosalie said.

"No encouraging news?" Molly asked.

"There is. It's supposed to rain tonight or in the morning—just in time to plant seeds. That's all we have," Rosalie said.

"May I be excused?" Annie asked. "I'd like to build my skid for the generator."

Major rose to go with Annie.

"Major, would you stay for a minute?" Sheriff asked.

"Sure. Annie, I'll see you soon. You can go on."

Annie jumped off the porch and skipped across the yard to the barn.

Molly sat in her chair, and Josh lingered at the door until Sheriff patted the chair next to him.

"What do you think, Major?" Sheriff asked after everyone else left.

"Josh, what were you thinking when you asked to go along?" Major leaned forward.

"I can be a second pair of eyes and ears. I can follow orders and run fast. I don't want Dad to be by himself." Josh straightened his back and glanced at his dad.

"What will you do if someone shoots your Dad?"

"Whatever he says."

"If I'm shot, I'd want you to get away safe. Leave me. Could you do that?" Sheriff asked.

"I'm supposed to say yes, but if there was another way, I'd stay."

"Honest answer. Thank you, Josh. Go help Mr. Young. We won't be long," Sheriff said.

After Josh left, Sheriff said, "Molly, he's only nine years old."

"You understand boys better than I do, Jack. I'd be perfectly happy if he stays with me, but it's important to him to be with you."

"Do you think he wants to be with me because he wasn't with Russell and Margo when they were murdered? Does he think if he'd stayed with them, he could have saved them?"

"I don't know. Maybe, but you aren't going to town to be in a gunfight. I know every time you leave, you walk toward danger. Just take him; he needs to be with you. I can't explain why, and I'm not staying out here to argue with you. I have canning to finish up." Molly rose and slammed the door behind her as she went inside.

"Other than I'm in trouble, what do you think, Major?"

"Two things: you're looking only at the worst case, and times are different." Major stepped off the porch and headed to the barn.

When he reached Annie, he examined her handiwork. "You're almost finished. Looks sturdy. I'm just in time to load the generator, right?"

She wiped the sweat off her face and grinned. "It's a simple design, so it didn't take long."

They loaded the generator onto the skid then Annie hooked it to the riding lawn mower and drove it to the house.

Major trotted along behind her. "Excellent test run."

"Needs some straps then I'll put the generator in the barn." Annie said.

After Major tightened the straps and parked the generator, he asked, "What's your next project?"

"The greenhouse. I'll unload the trailer; maybe I can get some help."

As they strolled to the house, she said, "I've been reading about hydroponic gardening, and I found some irrigation pipe in the shed. I might change my design, but I'm not clear on how to handle the water. I can set up the pump with solar, but I need to talk to Aimee Louise. She knows everything."

"Let me know if you need me."

When Major neared the house, Sheriff and Josh waved as they headed to the farm range with the twenty-two rifle. *Good for Josh to get some dad-time.*

Mr. Young and Brett sat at the kitchen table. Brett's chin was at the same height as the canning jars filled with chicken that covered the table. Brett wiped the tops of the jars then Mr. Young wrote the contents and date on the lids. Rosalie added each jar to her list then Aimee Louise put them on the pantry shelves with the most recent date in back.

"You've got an efficient assembly line here," Major said.

"This is the last of what we had in the freezer. Feels good to get this finished." Molly wiped her face with her apron.

"What's next on your agenda?" Major asked.

"Finish up the laundry then plant the garden after lunch. You need help with anything? Vanessa and Sara are in your bedroom. I think Sara's reading."

"I could use some help at my trailer after lunch," Mr. Young said. "Annie recruited Stuart to help her unload the trailer."

Major strolled into the bedroom. Sara sat cross-legged on the king-sized bed while Vanessa packed a gym bag with clothes. Sara was reading another book about fairies.

Vanessa rolled up one of Major's long-sleeved T-shirts and placed it into the bag.

"Aunt Vanessa's packing while I read," Sara said.

"I'm setting aside some of your winter clothes to make room for summer shirts." Vanessa smiled at Major.

"Don't overdo," he said.

Major lifted three ammo cans out of the closet. "I can move these. Does that help?"

"Sure does," Vanessa said.

Major carried the ammo out the front door to his truck.

"Need some help, Major?" Stuart strolled to the truck.

"Help me get the topper off? I want to see if I can pound out the dents."

After they lifted it off, they laid it on the ground and examined the damage. "Maybe we can knock out some of these dents from the inside," Major said. "I'll find two mallets."

When he returned, Stuart had the topper on its side. They started with the deepest dent and pounded it back.

Major examined the outside of the topper. "Much better. Won't take long."

They pounded the rest of the dents until the underside resembled its original shape.

"This is great. Let's put it back," Major said.

After they secured the topper, Major said, "Looks like its old self with just a few wrinkles. Perfect."

"Your ears still ringing?" Stuart asked. "Mine are."

Major laughed. "I'll put the mallets away then check on Annie."

"See you at the house." Stuart strode away.

Annie met Major on his way to the barn. "I found a pump for the reservoir. I don't know if it works. I'll bet Stuart could get it working. Aimee Louise says Stuart can do anything. I laid out the pipes, but I'm missing a few connectors and don't have a reservoir. Do you have any ideas?"

"We've got five-gallon buckets, but you probably want something closer to twenty gallons, right? Nothing here. Ask Mr. Young if there might be something on his farm." Major inspected her layout. "I'm sure we've got more connectors. So, you need how many now? By my count, you'll need five more. What's your first crop?"

"Aimee Louise suggested lettuce to start. Mama was excited about salads year 'round. Did you know Grandma Trish had a book on hydroponic vegetables? Aimee Louise gave it to me to read. I thought hydroponics was new."

Major smiled at the enthusiasm in her voice. "I didn't remember the book, but I knew Grandma Trish was interested in hydroponics. She talked about solar. She said it was too expensive, but the price would come down, and everyone would have solar. She'd be proud of you. I'm proud of you."

Annie stared at the pipes. "Thanks, Pops."

"After lunch we can check the equipment shed for connectors, and Stuart can test the pump. Let's talk to Mr. Young."

While they ate, Sheriff said, "Josh is going with me to my office to check in with the sheriffs' network. Anything else anyone can think of?"

"Annie needs a fifteen- or twenty-gallon container with a lid that she can use as the reservoir for her hydroponic garden," Major said.

"Might check with Pete," Mr. Young said. "If he has nothing, I might have a thirty-gallon container at the farm. Have you modified the design for your greenhouse, Annie?"

"I'm working on it. I'll show you what I'm thinking after lunch. Aimee Louise, I have some questions about hydroponics too."

"Sara and I would like to sit in on the discussion," Vanessa said.

"We'll swing by and see Pete while we're in town," Sheriff said.

"Take off your deputy cap at the table, Josh," Molly said.

"Oops. Forgot." Josh pulled off the cap and held it on his lap.

"I loaned it to him," Stuart said. "I forgot to remind him to take it off."

"You look like a deputy with the hat on," Sara said. "And that's not hooey."

Sheriff chuckled, and Sara leaned toward Annie. "Did I use *hooey* right in the sentence?"

"Yes, you did," Annie said. "Excellent choice."

After everyone had eaten, Josh jumped up from the table and crammed his borrowed hat on his head. Aimee Louise handed him his backpack.

"We're heading out," Sheriff said.

"Wait a second. Take some strawberry jam to Pete."

Molly returned from the pantry with two jars of jam.

* * *

"We going in the cruiser, Dad?" Josh asked as they headed outside. Penny followed Josh.

"No, let's take my truck. The cruiser could draw attention." Sheriff stopped at the truck and opened the back door. "Okay, girl. You can go too."

After they left the farm property, Josh asked, "Does Stuart's cap draw attention?"

"I didn't think of that. Both of us should leave our caps in the truck."

"Are we undercover?" Josh asked.

"I think we are. Undercover Josh and Undercover Dad are on duty."

"And Undercover Penny." Josh giggled.

When they passed the deputies' house that had belonged to Josh's parents, Josh said, "I always think of Mom and Dad when I see our house."

Sheriff nodded. "Miss them?"

Josh sniffed back tears. "Yeah."

"I think you always will."

When they reached Pete's Diner, Josh said, "Mom would be happy with Annie's new garden."

"You're right."

Josh shoved his cap under his seat when Sheriff parked the truck in front of the diner. Pete peeked out of the diner then came outside.

"Nice to see you, Sheriff. Hey there, Josh. What brings y'all to town?"

"I've got a meeting with the sheriffs' network, and Molly sent you some jam."

Josh opened the door for Penny then held up the two jars.

"Molly's strawberry jam is the best in the county. Tell her I appreciate it." Pete slipped the two jars into his overalls pocket.

"We're looking for items for Annie's newest gardening venture. She needs a twenty-gallon water reservoir. Mr. Young thought you might have something."

Pete slapped his knee and laughed. "I've got just the thing. I've got a thirty-gallon pickle barrel that was just too good to throw away. I'm glad somebody finally came up with something. Let's go inside."

When they reached the diner kitchen, Pete pointed to a large black container with a top. "Isn't she pretty? Food grade. Might be a shade bigger than what she was thinking, but I suspect she'll make it work. Annie putting in a hydroponic garden? Don't know why we all didn't think of that. I've got some heritage seeds that I pulled off the swap table: tomatoes, squash, and cucumbers. She can use what she wants and share the rest."

"I think it's perfect, Pete, and I know Kris and Vicki will be happy for the seeds too."

"Glad you can help me share them. I don't get out that far these days. I stick close to home and the diner."

Josh examined the pickle barrel.

"Pick it up," Pete said.

Josh bent his knees, wrapped his arms half-way around the barrel, and lifted.

"It's light, but I can't see around it." Josh grinned and shuffled his feet as he walked the barrel to the front door.

Pete chuckled and opened the door.

"Guess we'll be going, Pete. Thanks for everything." Sheriff held onto the barrel to guide Josh to the truck then opened the cab door, and Penny jumped in. Sheriff helped Josh lift the barrel onto the back seat.

"Next, we'll check the house. I'll make sure it's all clear then you can see if there's anything we can take to the farm. Major said somebody broke in, so most of the house might be messy."

"I smell pickles," Josh said. "Is it still okay for Annie's garden?"

"It'll be fine. She might rinse it out a bit or just leave it if it won't hurt the plants. She'll know what to do."

On their way to the house, Josh stared out his window. "Looks creepy. Nobody's around."

"Most of the people in town left to join their families. There are a few neighborhoods where folks got together in groups, but not many."

When Sheriff pulled into his driveway, he said, "There's the board Major put up. I don't see any more broken windows. Stay here while I check the house. If you see anything, honk the horn."

Sheriff locked the truck door after he got out. Josh climbed over the center console to the driver's seat, and Penny moved to Josh's seat. Sheriff pulled his gun from its holster and unlocked the door.

Sheriff scanned the room and the broken furniture. *Glad Major warned me.* He moved from room to room then stepped out back and examined the back yard. When he went back inside, he locked the back door.

He stepped out front and waved Josh inside. Josh and Penny jumped out of the truck. "There's a laundry basket in the utility. Let's put it in the living room and gather up what we can find."

Josh carried out the basket with a new bottle of cleaning spray and cleaning cloths inside it.

"Where do you want to start? Kitchen or bedrooms?" Sheriff asked.

"Kitchen," Josh said.

The two of them scoured the house and filled the basket with cleaning supplies, kitchen utensils, and pantry items. Sheriff found a duffle bag in his closet and filled it with sheets, towels, and toys.

"Pretty good haul," Sheriff said. "You and Penny can be lookouts while I load the truck."

"Come on, girl." Josh headed to the front door, and Penny followed.

Sheriff slung the duffle bag over his shoulder then picked up the basket. He loaded the items into the truck bed then locked the house.

"Now the office," Sheriff said as he pulled out of his driveway.

"Still creepy that nobody's around," Josh said.

"I agree." He stopped in the parking lot. "I'll check the building. You honk if you see anyone."

While Sheriff checked the outside of the building, Josh and Penny assumed their positions in the truck. Sheriff returned to the front, unlocked the door, and scanned the lobby. *Smells musty.* He checked each office and the jail cells then returned to the truck.

"Let's go inside." Sheriff opened the passenger's door, and Penny jumped out. Josh grabbed his backpack, and Sheriff locked the door.

"Building's creepy too," Josh said after they were inside.

"It's quiet like this at night. Come to my office. I'll get on the radio, and you can make yourself comfortable."

Josh sat cross-legged on the floor and unzipped his backpack. "Aimee Louise put two books in here." He scooted back against the wall and opened his book. Penny flopped on the floor next to him.

Sheriff turned on his radio and grabbed a book off his shelf.

After an hour, the radio crackled and startled Sheriff. "You there, Jack?"

Sheriff grabbed up the microphone. "Right here."

"FBI agents…outside of Orlando. Your way…two hours."

"You kind of broke up, but I'll be at my office."

"Next item is…" The radio cut off, and the office was dark.

"Hey, Dad." Josh said.

"Right here, Josh. Give me a second." Sheriff pulled a flashlight out of his desk drawer and clicked it on.

"What happened?" Josh asked.

"Electricity went out. Here's a flashlight for you." Sheriff pulled out a second flashlight and handed it to Josh.

"I'm taking my handheld radio outside to see if I can pick up the transmission. Will you be okay?"

"We'll be fine."

Sheriff strode out the back door with his handheld radio. He stepped away from the building and listened. When he didn't hear anything, he signed on and waited.

"Was that you, Jack?"

"We lost power. I've got my handheld."

"You weren't the only one. I'm outside with mine. I think it was region…" The voice faded then was strong again. "…reconvene tomorrow. If there's…we'll be on mobile."

Sheriff went back inside to Josh and Penny. "We need to hang around for about two hours. Got any preferences?"

"Something outside?"

"Long time since we've checked the river."

Sheriff pulled into the tree-lined park south of town and next to the river, and Penny whined. Sheriff chuckled, "This is her favorite place to run."

"Mine too," Josh said. "Can we run?"

"Sure can. I'll run with you."

Josh set the pace as they ran the two-mile trail along the river and around the park. When they returned to the truck, Sheriff pulled out their water, and they drained their bottles.

"Good run, Josh," Sheriff said. Sheriff held up his hand at a rumble. "Stay here." He stopped near the road as an eighteen-wheeler sped north into town.

He strode back to the truck. "Maybe it's our visitor. Let's go."

Sheriff caught up with the eighteen-wheeler near the edge of town at Pete's Diner. The truck slowed as it drove through Plainview then pulled to a stop in front of the sheriff's office. A passenger jumped out of the cab, and the truck idled.

"Do we put on our sheriff and deputy hats?" Josh asked.

"It's time."

Sheriff slowed as the passenger approached the front door. When Sheriff parked near the building, the passenger spun and faced the truck. She had pulled her long, black hair into a ponytail that flipped to the front when she turned. Her deep brown eyes narrowed, and she had her hand on her right hip.

"It's a lady," Josh said. "She's pretty."

"Sure is. Stay in the truck and be my backup. Honk if you see anyone try to sneak up on me." Sheriff stepped out of the truck.

"Can I help you?" he asked. He maintained a relaxed stance but scanned the area.

"I need to talk to the sheriff." She narrowed her eyes and glanced from him to the truck.

"You're talking to him."

"Right."

Sheriff glared at her, and she met his gaze.

"If that's all you've got, I'll be going." Sheriff stepped backward to the truck. When he opened the door, Penny bounded out, wagged her tail, and trotted to the woman who offered her hand to Penny to smell.

"Penny, wait." Josh jumped out of the truck but froze next to his door.

The woman glanced at Penny and Josh then laughed. "I don't know who you are, mister, but you aren't a dangerous guy. I'm Peyton from Miami."

"The FBI is a lady, Dad," Josh said.

"You have ID?" Sheriff asked. "I'll pull mine out of my pocket." Sheriff flipped open his wallet to his ID and badge.

She squinted. "I can't see it from here. I'll toss you mine if you toss me yours." She reached into her pocket then pitched a folded wallet that landed near his feet.

He flung his wallet, and it landed on her boot.

CHAPTER THIRTEEN

"You got closer, Dad," Josh said, and Peyton laughed as she picked up his badge and ID.

"Well, Sheriff Jack Starr, you've got one of the sharpest deputies I've ever met." She hopped on the running board of the waiting truck then tapped on the window and held a thumb up. After she backed away from the truck, it lumbered away.

"Thank you, Agent Peyton Romero. What's your plan?"

"I need to find the sheriff who has information about the missing Miami boys."

"You've found him. I've got a question. Have you been around anyone who was sick?"

"Three guys from the office who went home with a bad flu bug, but I've been in the field. Surveillance. Funny you should ask. My driver pulled into a truck stop for us to take a bio break then pointed at a man at the pump who was scratching at his hands. When he drove away, I asked why, and he said the man was contagious."

"Good to hear word is getting around. This isn't a fit place to talk." Sheriff rubbed his chin. "I take it you don't have dinner plans.

Let's go to the farm. We'll be safe, and you can talk to the retired state trooper who has first-hand information."

Josh climbed into the back seat and Penny dashed around the truck then jumped in next to him.

Peyton frowned. "I don't know. I should stay here. Is there a motel close?" She scanned the deserted area then picked up her duffle bag. "Okay. Although I can't see how an empty town could be unsafe."

She tossed her duffle bag into the bed of the truck and climbed into the passenger's seat.

"Here's your ID and badge," she said when Sheriff closed his door.

"Here's yours." He turned on the engine and headed to the farm. "I heard two agents were coming."

"There are some agency problems. My partner, Agent Cabello, is on a temporary assignment and couldn't get away as quickly as I did. I couldn't wait for him. My brother-in-law is a trucker and called in a favor."

"I've never ridden in an eighteen-wheeler," Josh said.

Peyton turned and smiled. "It was fun. You remind me of someone I know. Are you ten?"

"I'm nine, but I'm tall."

"The boy I know is eight, and he's tall too."

Josh hugged Penny, and she licked his face.

"You weren't kidding when you said farm." Peyton peered out her window. "Not much concrete around here. Sure makes me feel like a city girl. Tallest thing I saw after we left the Orlando area was a cell tower."

When Sheriff pulled into the driveway, Josh and Penny jumped out.

"We'll close the gate then run to the house," Josh said.

After Josh opened the gate, Sheriff drove to the house but peered at his rearview mirror.

"He's a good kid," Peyton said.

"Thanks. He has his moments, but you're right, he is."

Mr. Young and Brett waited for the truck next to the house.

"Hi Dad," Brett said. "You're just in time to help me haul water to the kitchen for Mom, Josh."

"Can I be off duty, Dad?"

"Yep. Your assignment's completed. Well done."

Brett and Josh raced to the well.

When Peyton climbed out of the truck, Sheriff introduced her to Mr. Young.

"Welcome, Agent Romero," Mr. Young said. "We've got a large crew here."

"That's right," Sheriff said. "I forgot to warn you. We have two families and Mr. Young living here. The farm belongs to Major. Grab your bag, and we'll go in."

"I won't stay long. I need to be in town in case my partner got away quicker than we expected."

When they stepped into the family room, Sara squealed, "We've got company."

After Sheriff introduced Agent Romero to everyone, Molly said, "You have great timing, Sheriff. Supper is almost ready."

At the end of the meal, Annie and Mr. Young cleared the table while Molly heated water on the stove to wash dishes.

"Let's sit on the porch, Peyton," Major said, and Stuart joined them. A cool wind gusted from the northwest.

"My husband, Troy, grew up on a farm in South Carolina. He's a general contractor and an accomplished carpenter. Now I understand why he wanted to move back home." Peyton rocked in her chair and gazed at the darkening clouds. "Sheriff said you could tell me about the missing Miami boys."

Major told her about traveling to the Newtons' farm, the tornado, and the crashed truck.

"We found only two survivors inside the truck." Major said. "A judge and his granddaughter."

Peyton stared at Major.

"And two boys in a nearby field," Stuart added.

"Judge Cabello?" she asked.

"You know him?" Major raised his eyebrows.

"Agent Nathaniel Cabello is his son. Nate hoped to travel with me, but he waited for travel approval. When our supervisor denied his request, he planned to use vacation time, but our supervisor told him he couldn't leave his temporary assignment then claimed the main office canceled all leave. Any way that we can get word to him so he can meet me in town?"

"Let's talk to Aimee Louise and Rosalie. Aimee Louise checks in with the ham radio community every morning and evening. So how did you get approved?"

"I lied. Nate has more dedication to the big bosses than I do. Aimee Louise seemed so quiet. She's a ham operator?"

"One of the best," Major said.

"I'll get Aimee Louise and Rosalie," Stuart said.

When the girls joined them on the porch, Stuart caught them up on the discussion.

"How do we let Agent Cabello know?" Major asked.

"Dolly," Aimee Louise said.

"That's perfect," Stuart said.

"It's the only logical way," Rosalie added.

Molly slipped outside and relaxed in her chair. Annie joined her.

Peyton stared at Aimee Louise then rubbed her forehead. "I am exhausted. I'm having trouble processing everything. Dolly's okay?"

"Yes. The judge, Dolly, and the two boys are at my folks' farm in Georgia," Stuart said.

"Two boys?" Peyton asked. "I missed that too."

"Peyton, you're practically dead on your feet," Molly said. "Let the smart folks figure this out. We've got more important things to do like get you some sleep. I'll set up a mat for Sara in my room, and Annie will put fresh sheets on her cot for you. Come with us. Annie will show you the girls' room and the bathroom and how to flush the toilet."

"You're right, Molly. I'll be smart tomorrow." Peyton followed Molly and Annie into the house.

"We need to go inside too. It's radio time," Rosalie said.

After Aimee Louise and Rosalie left, Major asked, "What do you suppose Aimee Louise will say?"

"Something smart." Stuart chuckled and followed the girls.

Major coaxed Shadow and Penny off the porch for a stroll then he and the dogs ran to the back door when the light sprinkle turned to heavy rain.

* * *

Major slipped out of his bedroom and eased the door shut then waited a moment for his eyes to adjust to the dark. When he reached the kitchen, the pilot light on the stove guided him to the coffee pot. He poured a cup and headed outside, and Shadow followed him.

"Good morning, Major. Have you changed your plans?" Molly asked.

His chair creaked as he sat. "Does everybody know my business?"

Molly sipped her coffee. "Sheriff might not, if that helps you feel better, but that's only because he and Josh were away from the farm most of the day."

"I'll delay at least a day." Major glanced at the camper trailer parked near the house. "Trailer lights went on. Mr. Young will be out soon. I'll refill my coffee then check the barn and animals."

"Before you go, Major, how did Vanessa sleep? She's had trouble with a lot of pain in her leg. I check her wound three times a day. No signs of infection, which is good."

"She was not near as restless as she was the night before as far as the pain, but the itching is driving her crazy."

The door opened, and Shadow rose and wagged his tail.

"Care for some coffee, Peyton?" Molly asked.

"How did you know it was Peyton?" Major stared at Molly.

"I'm a mom and have eyes in the back of my head, you know; besides, Shadow told me."

Major chuckled. "I'll grab you a cup, Peyton. I was about to get myself a refill."

When he returned, Molly said, "All we have is black coffee. We save the sugar for the tea, and milk for the kids."

"I'm in luck. That's how I take my coffee," Peyton said as she held the cup while Major poured.

When the trailer door slammed, Major said, "I'll check the animals. Care to go along, Peyton?"

The morning sky in the east had lightened to a pale blue-gray, and the birds sang a promise of clear skies.

As they strolled along the path to the barn, Peyton said, "I abandoned my career after we heard in Miami that an overturned truck had been found, and…" She pursed her lips and ran her fingers through her hair. "I realized who had kidnapped my son. I walked out and came here. Brandon was…"

Major grabbed her arm. "You said *Brandon*. Do you have a picture?"

Her eyes widened, and she raced back to the house. Major hurried behind her.

"What's going on?" Mr. Young asked.

"Not sure." Major leaned against the railing as his heart pounded.

Stuart came out of the house with a cup of coffee. He dropped his cup, and it shattered as he rushed to Major. "Are you okay?"

"Fine. We may have…"

Peyton hurried out of the house and shoved a picture at Major. "Brandon."

Sheriff followed her outside.

When Stuart leaned to peer at the photo, he smiled. "Yep. That's our Brandon."

Peyton grabbed onto Molly's chair and sank to the floor. "He's alive? You found him?"

"Catch your breath then you'll hear a story about the bravest kid we've ever known," Major said. "I'll make another pot of coffee. Stuart will tell you about Brandon."

Major whistled under his breath as he waited for the coffee to perk. Vanessa hobbled into the kitchen and dropped on a chair. "You're annoyingly cheerful this morning. There should be a rule: coffee first then whistle."

"Peyton is Brandon's mother. I can't think of a better way to start off a morning."

Vanessa raised her eyebrows. "Definitely whistle worthy."

The children thundered down the stairs.

"I stand corrected. The sound of happy feet is another one." He winked.

"Where's Ms. Peyton? She was in a hurry to find something. What did she find? Can I see?" Sara asked.

"She's out back," Major said, and Sara and Annie bounded out the door. Major picked up the coffeepot.

"Pour me a cup before you head out," Vanessa said. "I'll sip mine in here. I'm sure I'll get the full story later from Sara."

Major poured a cup for Vanessa, grabbed extra cups, and headed out with the coffeepot. Peyton had tears running down her face, and Molly brushed her cheek.

"Brandon's okay? He wasn't hurt?" Peyton gazed at Stuart.

"He's fine. My mom said he has a cold." Stuart said.

Major patted Peyton's shoulder. "We've seen the sickness. Brandon doesn't have it."

"I need to see him. How long will it take me to walk there?"

"I know," Sara said. "Can I say, Mommy? It's okay, right, because I know. I can tell you, Ms. Peyton."

"How do you know?" Stuart asked.

Sara waved her hand. "Everybody knows. Can I say?"

"Go ahead," Sheriff said.

Stuart whispered to Major, "Does everybody know my business?"

Major nodded. "Yours and mine."

"Ten days," Sara said. "If everything goes right, which it will because you're a mom."

Molly rose. "This mom says time for breakfast. Everybody's that not dressed needs to get dressed." She glared at Josh and Brett who listened at the door. The boys disappeared.

"What happened to you?" Molly frowned and pointed at the bandage on Mr. Young's right thumb.

"Kitchen accident. Don't fire me."

"No such luck. We'll talk about a plan after breakfast." Molly headed to the kitchen.

"Kitchen helpers, let's go." Mr. Young followed Molly, and Annie and Sara fell in behind him.

"I'll see if Aimee Louise needs me to do anything," Stuart said.

* * *

As Mr. Young began serving plates, Aimee Louise, Rosalie, and Stuart took their seats at the table.

Rosalie set her notebook on the table and stared at the blueberry pancakes Mr. Young set in front of her.

"You can eat first," Molly said. "We'll wait."

Rosalie rushed through her breakfast then picked up her notebook.

"First," Stuart said, "Aimee Louise is brilliant. Last night she told the hams there was a genealogy connection to the Amber alert, and the experts located Ms. Madison through the family tree. The hams got into a lengthy discussion about DNA and genealogy.

Before he signed off, the Miami ham asked Aimee Louise if she had new boots, and she said yes. He's a sharp guy."

"And that was last night, right? When he asked about new boots do you think that is like boots on the ground, which what we called our troops back in the day?" Mr. Young said.

"Yes," Aimee Louise said.

Rosalie tapped her notebook. "Two hot topics today. The first was the mysterious illness. When one ham mentioned a rash was a key symptom, several others said they'd seen people with rashes on their hands. The second topic was the controversy that resulted in attacks on farmers and the claim that farmers were stealing electricity. That set off a loud, heated discussion. Many of the hams are farmers, and several of the non-farmer hams quoted sources that said the diverting of power was true. It's becoming a wedge between the two groups. A ham asked Aimee Louise if she lives on a farm."

"She asked *why?*" Stuart chuckled. "The hams were all silent for a few seconds. I thought our transmission had dropped."

Rosalie smiled. "Her reply resulted in a topic change. We're not sure how long that will last. Hams reported more power outages that are lasting longer each time. Our Miami ham missed the daily check-in, but we hung around and waited. When he came on, he said the experts released the DNA family tests and Ms. Madison was on the list. He also said he'd be offline with his wife and maybe her brother for no more than two days. We interpreted that to mean Nate will be here today or tomorrow. That's all we have."

Molly glanced around the table. "You children have finished eating. You don't have to sit around; you can be excused."

"Sara, we can read or draw, you can choose. We can sit on the back porch, but I need to elevate my leg," Vanessa said.

Annie jumped up to work on her construction. "Going to my project," she said.

The two boys left to check on the chickens and goats.

"Seems like we've got a potential for conflicting plans," Sheriff said. "When are you planning to leave, Major? Who is going with you?"

"Let's start with Peyton and Nate," Major said. "If Nate shows up in a vehicle, could we give them clear directions and send them to the Newtons' farm?"

"I journaled our trip," Rosalie said. "I have explicit directions and information about what to look for as far as what we ran into."

"Why do you think the ham mentioned family, his wife, and maybe her brother?" Aimee Louise asked.

Stuart stared at Aimee Louise. "You have a theory. Do you think he was saying Nate is bringing his wife and Peyton's husband?"

Sheriff shook his head. "That's a stretch."

"It is," Molly said. "But why would he say that? Do hams make idle conversation, Mr. Young?"

"Hams like to talk and sometimes they ramble, and sometimes a detail gets changed in the retelling, but my interpretation is Nate, his wife, and another man."

"If that's true, then they are driving," Major said. "What do you think, Peyton?"

"It's exactly what Nate would do. With Dolly and his father out of Miami, he'd leave and bring his wife and offer to bring another parent."

Sheriff sipped his coffee. "What if we're wrong? Does that change your plans, Major?"

"Not that I see." Major tapped his cup with his finger.

"When do we leave?" Rosalie asked.

Major's face reddened. "I'm going alone."

Mr. Young cleared his throat. "From the sound of your last trip, the four of you made an impressive travel team, and as a member of the home team, I can attest that our operation was smooth. Think about it, Major. You'll have an experienced deputy, the best shot in the state, and a brilliant mind with you. Sounds perfect to me."

Major rose and stomped out the back door.

Sheriff stared at the door. "Meeting adjourned."

"Let's get busy," Molly said. "We've got a lot to do before y'all leave."

* * *

Major slowed his pace as he reached the fence at the west pasture near the power line. Memories of the first power outage washed over him, and he shook his head. *Stuart is right. Times are different.* He stared at the blue sky with the high white wisps of clouds. *Could I really pull this off without Aimee Louise?* A male cardinal flitted along the fence then perched on a fencepost while his mate pecked at the grass and weed seeds. *Rosalie had my back when we went to Georgia.* He headed to the farmhouse and smiled when he spotted Sheriff waiting for him at the fence. *I worried about ruining Stuart's career as a deputy, but his career has changed to farming.*

When Major stopped at the fence, he said, "Times are different."

"Yep, and I don't like it either."

As they strolled to the house, Major chuckled. "If I tell the Terrible Three they have two minutes to load up, they'd do it, wouldn't they?"

Sheriff snorted. "You know it."

"I'll be in trouble for this, but I need to have a lean team. I'm taking only Stuart."

"You're right. You'll be in trouble, but for what it's worth, I agree it's best all around."

Major cocked his head. "Did you hear that? Was that Number 48?"

Sheriff frowned. "It's going away from us. Something's wrong."

They jogged across the field, and Josh and Brett met them at the barn. "We been looking for you," Josh said. "Mr. Young is sick. Aimee Louise and Rosalie left to get Heather."

When Major and Sheriff burst through the back door, Molly, Vanessa, and Peyton knelt on the kitchen floor next to Mr. Young who was on his side.

Molly's eyes were wide. "He pulled off his gloves, stopped talking mid-sentence, and grabbed onto a chair. I eased him to the floor. I put him on his side because I learned once that's the recovery position. That's the full extent of my medical training."

"He's breathing." Vanessa's face was tight as she knelt at his head. "It's ragged, but he's breathing. Aimee Louise and Rosalie raced out of the house then we heard Number 48. We think they went to get Heather. We sent the boys to look for you and Stuart, and Sara went out front to watch for the girls to return."

Stuart opened the back door then held out his hand to stop Annie.

"What do you need for us to do?" Sheriff asked.

Major scanned the room. "We don't need everybody in here. Let's clear out. Josh and Brett can stay on the porch to come get us if you need help, Molly."

When they congregated on the porch, Major said, "We can't help by standing around."

"I have a few more things to do then I need to straighten up my work area," Annie said.

"I'll be your assistant," Sheriff said.

"Stuart, can you help me at the barn?" Major asked.

CHAPTER FOURTEEN

As they strolled away from the house, Major said, "Stuart, I'd like to leave after lunch, but I might wait until this evening. Depends on whether I'm needed to help with Mr. Young. I decided not to take the girls, and this confirms it's best for them to stay here."

Stuart halted in the middle of the path. "You're not asking me to tell them, are you?"

Major chuckled. "Now that would be a test of your negotiation skills, wouldn't it? No, I'll tell them. Aimee Louise will see the logic, and Rosalie will argue."

Major sat on a hay bale. "What about you? Do you think it's better for you to stay here too?"

Stuart narrowed his eyes. "No. I need to go with you."

"I agree. I assume you're packed and ready. Let's check the truck to see what Vanessa and Mr. Young gathered."

When they reached the truck, Major picked up the folded paper stuck between the trailer hitch and bumper. He snorted then read aloud. "Pops, we know we aren't going. This is a list for you and Stuart. AL&R."

Stuart laughed. "I'll climb into the pickup bed, and you can check off our items."

As Stuart climbed out of the truck, the roar of Number 48 announced its arrival at the driveway.

"There are a few critical items missing," Major said.

"I'll take care of them, if you want to go inside." Stuart held out his hand for the list.

Major strode to the back door. "How's he doing?"

"No change. Still unconscious, but breathing."

Major stepped to the front door and waited for Heather as she hopped out of the vehicle and hurried to the front porch.

"How's he doing?" Heather asked as he opened the door.

"Breathing. Unconscious. In the kitchen." Major followed her inside.

Molly and Vanessa were still kneeling next to Mr. Young. Vanessa moved away from him to make room for Heather, but Heather froze at the door. "How long has he had the rash on his hands?"

"I didn't notice it," Vanessa said. "He's been wearing gloves in the kitchen since he cut his thumb."

"What rash?" Molly asked as she peered at his hands. "Oh. That wasn't there earlier."

"I can't stay in here. Come outside where we can talk."

Molly stayed with Mr. Young while everyone else followed Heather out the front door.

"Don't get close to me or to each other if you can manage it," Heather said. "You all need to consider yourself under quarantine. I suggest you mask up and be diligent in washing your hands. Sanitize the kitchen, and isolate Mr. Young. His trailer is the perfect place. Designate one person for his care, and treat that one person as contagious too. I don't know what he has, but there is a virus going around with the symptom of a rash on the hands and feet. Right now, he's dehydrated and appears to be suffering from exhaustion. I think getting him out of the hot kitchen will help. Put wet cloths on the back of his neck to cool him down. As soon as he rouses, give him sips of water. Keep him well hydrated and give him broth to drink. I'll walk back."

Heather grabbed her medical bag out of Number 48 and jogged to the road. Major watched her until she was out of sight. When he turned, Peyton waited on the porch. Tears slipped down her face. "Does this mean I can't see Brandon? What happens if Nate shows up? Will we turn him away?"

"It would be safer until we know more about Mr. Young's condition if they don't stay here. We have the option for them to use the Sheriff's house in town, and we could give them basic supplies and food. Another option is they could continue on to the Newtons' with Rosalie's directions, but I'm afraid it would have to be without you."

Peyton brushed her cheeks. "You're right. We have options. Keeping Brandon and Dolly safe is my number one priority. When are you leaving? Anything I can do to help?"

"We'll be down four people when I leave. Your help is critical, especially with security. I'm not sure I could leave if you weren't here."

"Four? So, Stuart is going with you, and you aren't worried about infecting Charles McNeil." She snickered.

"I'm looking forward to the opportunity to shake his hand." Major smiled.

When Major went into the house, Sheriff and Stuart were rolling Mr. Young onto a sheet with Molly's help.

"I sent the children outside until I can sanitize the kitchen," Molly said. "Vanessa is at Mr. Young's trailer. We decided if she needs anything, she can post a note in the window."

"Vanessa?" Major frowned.

Molly rose and put her hands on her hips. "It's done. Not your decision."

After Mr. Young was in position on the makeshift litter, Sheriff and Stuart grabbed the head and foot of the sheet, respectively, then Major and Molly each held onto a side.

"Count of three." Sheriff said. "One, two, three." The four of them carried Mr. Young to the trailer then Sheriff and Stuart carried him inside.

"Lunch," Molly said. "Maybe we'll picnic on the back porch."

When they reached the house, Peyton and Annie had moved a table to the porch and set a bucket of water near the steps.

"We guessed, Mama," Annie said.

"Good guess, Honey. Everybody wash your hands. I'll pull lunch together in two shakes."

As they ate, Major said, "Stuart and I planned to leave after lunch, but I bet everybody knows that. Didn't seem right to take off without saying good-bye."

"Good-bye, Pops," Aimee Louise said. Rosalie bit into her apple and waved.

"Bye," Josh and Brett said in unison.

After everyone else spoke, Stuart said, "Y'all are awesome."

"We had a secret family meeting," Sara said. "We each picked the time we thought you'd leave. Who won, Mommy?"

"You had a secret meeting?" Major asked. "I didn't know about it. How is that fair?"

Molly laughed. "I won't tell you who organized the secret meeting, but it was particularly well executed, don't you think? Rosalie, who won?"

Rosalie pulled her list out of her pocket. "Annie. She said, *after lunch.*"

"Well done, Annie. Here's your trophy." Molly presented Annie with the alarm clock that no longer kept time.

Annie accepted her award and bowed. "I'll cherish this always, or at least until someone else wins our next contest and steals it from me."

Peyton laughed. "You all are hilarious. Love your prize, Annie."

Major pointed to the truck, and Stuart waved to Aimee Louise.

"Do you think we're contagious?" Stuart lowered his window as Major pulled out of the driveway.

"My gut says no, but I agree with Heather. It's easier to isolate now than wish we'd isolated later."

No one was in sight as the truck rolled through Plainview, and the smell of old garbage permeated the air. The owner had boarded up the gas station windows with used plywood. *He hopes to return.*

"Looks like a ghost town or a hurricane's about to hit," Stuart said.

"No roadblocks," Major said when they reached the edge of town. "Everybody's hunkered down."

As they neared the vet's farm, a sudden *pop-pop-pop* sounded, and Major slammed on the brakes.

"Shots," Stuart said.

A black truck careened down the vet's driveway and sped north. Stuart held his rifle on his lap, and Major pulled into the driveway then leaned on his horn. When the truck was halfway to the house, Major stopped his truck but not the continuous sound of the horn.

"There." Stuart pointed to the far corner of the house. The vet peered around the corner then headed to Major's truck. Her left hand clutched her right arm, and she stumbled. Stuart jumped out and raced to her. Major turned off the engine and grabbed his rifle then followed.

"Varmints thought they'd get drugs here. I need to take down the veterinarian sign," she said. "I don't think they expected anyone to be here."

"I'll take down the sign," Stuart said.

"You take a bullet?" Major asked.

"They grazed my arm. I can take care of it. I heard their truck coming down the driveway, so I at least had time to grab my pistol." Jody pointed to Major's holster. "Lesson learned. I will wear my pistol."

Major grabbed a facemask from his truck then helped her inside.

"They were trying to break in the back door, but it was unlocked. I was outside and ambushed them, but I guess I'm a little rusty. One of them got off a shot."

As she sat at her dining table, Major poured water into a glass from the jug on the counter and placed it in front of her.

"Thanks." She pushed her curly black hair behind her ears. "I hit both of them. Not fatal unless they don't get their wounds taken care of. My first aid box is on top of the refrigerator. Mind wrapping this for me?"

Major opened the box and put on the gloves sitting on top then pulled out shears, gauze and a triangular bandage. He cut off the arm of her shirt, rinsed the wound, applied the antiseptic ointment, a dressing, and bandage then crafted a sling from the triangular bandage.

Jody patted her sling. "I'm left-handed so this doesn't slow me down so bad. Why are you two out and about?"

Major told her about Mr. Young, seeds, farmers, kidnapped children, and Charles McNeil.

"What can I do to help?" she asked.

"Can't think of anything," Major said. "I don't think you should be here alone though."

"My brother's been after me to join them on his farm. His wife and I have never gotten along, they don't have any room for me, and they're in South Carolina. Might have to, but it isn't a trip I'd like to make."

Stuart tapped on the back door then carried in the sign and leaned it against the wall.

Major said, "Pastor John and Chuck are at Mr. Young's farm and have an extra room. Why don't you go there?"

She stared at him. "It's outside my nature to barge in on folks; I've always lived alone, but times are different. I could do that. I packed up most of my things earlier this week in case I decided to go to my brother's. Could I trouble you and Stuart to load the boxes into my truck? My boxes are in the living room. Most of it is vet stuff. My suitcase is upstairs in my bedroom."

Stuart carried boxes to the truck, and Major grabbed her suitcase.

"Okay if I empty your medicine cabinet into this backpack?" Major asked.

"Thank you. Maybe you can grab a box or two and empty the pantry too. I loaded my spare ammo and guns into my truck yesterday."

After Stuart loaded all the boxes from the living room, he carried boxes of food as Major emptied the shelves.

"Case of wine here in the pantry," Stuart said. "We can't leave that."

"Heavens, no," Jody said. "I can't count on the pastor for my evening libation."

Major scanned the living room for any missed items then returned to the kitchen. "You've got a lot of books in your bookcase. Don't you want them?"

Jody smacked her forehead. "I can't believe I overlooked my books. Yes, thank you. I do need them."

As Stuart loaded the books, Major asked, "Do you have any medical books you could loan us? I realized we have a real gap in our knowledge when Mr. Young took ill."

"The best book I have for you is a wilderness medical survival handbook. Okay if I dig it out after I get settled?"

"That's perfect. Anything else we can do?" Major asked. "Do you want Stuart to drive your truck, and I'll follow?"

"No, I can make it to Mr. Young's farm in thirty minutes on these deserted roads. Sure beats a trip to South Carolina, and I like Vicki and Diane."

She made a last trip through her house then locked it. Major helped her into her truck, and she waved as she turned south at the road.

Major and Stuart continued their travel north on the highway.

"Do you think those two characters will come back?" Stuart asked.

"If not them, others will," Major said. "Her house was perfect for a business, but now being on a major road is a genuine disadvantage."

"Are we going to crash McNeil's meeting?"

"That's my plan," Major said. "We're taking back roads. It'll take an extra hour, assuming we don't run into any problems. If we do, we'll be traveling all night. When we get close to Savannah, we'll find out where the meeting is."

Stuart peered at the road ahead. "How are we going to figure out where we're going? We can't roll up to a farmhouse and ask where the meeting is."

Major hung his arm out his window, glanced at Stuart, and smiled.

Stuart sighed. "Don't tell Aimee Louise that I forgot about the ham radio."

The occasional shade from the trees that lined the west side of the road provided intermittent relief from the intense sunlight. Major pulled his arm inside. "I don't know which is worse: driving in the heat without using the air conditioning or having the window down and getting a one-arm sunburn."

Stuart gazed at the fields as they passed farm after farm. "Have you seen any livestock out in the fields?"

"If I lived this close to the road, I'd have moved my herd to a field hidden from the road. Farmers learn to adapt to change early on, or they aren't farmers their second year."

"Dad's always been a fixer. Mom said…"

"Roadblock up ahead." Major slowed the truck and peered at the old logs that obstructed the left lane and the rusty pickup truck that blocked their right lane. Four trucks lined the shoulder.

"I don't like the looks of it." Stuart leaned forward. "There's only one guy. Where are the rest?"

As they approached the roadblock, Stuart said, "Truck's tires are flat. They've been there a while."

Major slammed on the brakes, whipped the steering wheel into a controlled turn, and accelerated away from the roadblock. Stuart coughed as the acrid odor of burning rubber filled the cab. They ducked instinctively as shots cracked behind them. Major steered a zig-zag pattern when the back window of the topper shattered.

After they had traveled south five miles, Major slowed to ten miles an hour over the speed limit, and Stuart unfolded the map Rosalie had given him.

"We have an alternative, but we'll be backtracking," he said. "We'll end up forty miles from home before we turn north again."

Major glanced at the map. "Doesn't look like we have a choice."

Stuart pointed. "We'll turn east in six miles."

"Whoa." Major reduced his speed and clutched the steering wheel with both hands. "Got a wobble." He pulled onto the shoulder. "Feels like a flat."

Stuart jumped out and checked the tires. "You're right. Front tire on the driver's side is flat from what looks like a piece of embedded metal from road debris, but the other three are fine."

"At least it's on a hard surface." Major turned off the engine, and the two of them headed to the back of the truck for the lug wrench, jack, and spare tire.

"I've got this, Major."

Major grabbed his rifle and stood guard while Stuart changed the tire. After thirty minutes, Stuart wiped his hands on his jeans and rolled the flat to the back of the truck, and Major returned the lug wrench and jack to their compartment as the sun sunk lower and the sky turned from a pale blue to a brilliant orange.

"This road makes me nervous." Major glanced to the north. "Let's stop for our dinner break later."

After they turned east, Stuart said, "Aimee Louise would have seen his cloud."

"I know," Major chuckled. "She won't say anything when we tell the story, but Rosalie and Sara will."

When they turned north, a gust of wind rocked the truck, and Major stared at the sky as he held tight onto the steering wheel. "We've got a decent side wind. Turn on the radio. Let's see if we pick up anything."

The mobile radio scanned the repeater frequencies until it stopped on a repeater where hams were talking.

"I'll pull over after we cross the bridge ahead then we won't outrun our reception and can eat while we listen." After Major parked, he stepped out and stretched his back then opened the cooler for their supper.

When he slid into his seat, Stuart turned up the volume, and they ate while they listened to a discussion about the weather, farmers, and electricity.

"Somebody set my neighbor's barn on fire last night. Dogs woke him, or it would have been a total loss. We're getting together in the morning to see if we can help with repairs," one man said.

"Might have to wait until the afternoon. We got a storm coming," a second man said.

"Hear about that big meeting south of Savannah? It's about that exclusive cash crop. I'd like to get in on it, but I'm not sure about leaving the farm with all these fires," the first man said.

"Go to the one tomorrow at noon near Live Oak," a third man said. "What are these jokers that set barns on fire thinking?"

The discussion changed from arsonists to running wells without electricity then to the gas shortage.

Major turned down the volume. "We're not that far from Live Oak. If we can't find the noon meeting in Florida, we'll still have time to make the Georgia meeting." Another heavy gust rocked the truck, and Major scanned the sky. "We've got a front moving in. I'd planned to sleep in the pickup bed, but with our shattered window, guess we'll spend the night in the cab."

Stuart peered at the map. "There's a small town not too far ahead. Maybe we could park in a parking lot. Post Office might be an option."

When they neared the town limits, Major said, "I expected a roadblock, but if most of their folks have left, they might not have the manpower to staff it around the clock."

They passed a building with a busted-up church sign in front, a gas station with the windows boarded up, a combination grocery and bait shop, and the post office then came to the other edge of town. High weeds that surrounded the few houses fluttered as they passed,

"Looks abandoned," Stuart said. "Kind of creepy."

Major headed back to the post office that faced west and parked in the back. "Maybe we'll get a little protection from the storm here." He turned off the engine. "I'd prefer the company of ghosts to that crowd of hoodlums we ran into. I need to get out and stretch before any rain hits."

Major strolled to the edge of the parking lot and examined the surrounding neighborhoods. *Abandoned is right.* He continued his walk around the post office, and as he reached the truck, he heard a vehicle as it sped south. By the time he glanced over his shoulder, nothing was there.

"Did you see that?" Stuart rushed to the truck. "Four guys in a blue car. They were really hauling."

As they carried their sleeping bags to the truck, lightning flashed with a simultaneous crack of thunder.

"Better pull everything we need tonight," Major said as fat raindrops smacked them and bounced off the truck.

"Ouch. Hail." Stuart snatched up the rest of their gear, and Major slammed the tailgate shut.

Stuart jumped into the back seat, and Major climbed into the front. The hailstones grew to nickel-sized and pummeled the truck. Major winced at the relentless pounding on the roof. The hailstorm stopped.

Ears still ringing. Major opened his mouth to pop his ears.

CHAPTER FIFTEEN

"Do you suppose that car was trying to outrun the storm?" Stuart asked.

"Might have been."

Major squinted at the windshield through the heavy rain. *Can't see past the hood.*

"We're not going anywhere tonight." Major spread his sleeping bag out on the seat and put his pillow against the driver's door. After he pulled a light blanket over him, he closed his eyes.

* * *

When he opened his eyes, the sun peeked over the shed behind the post office. He stirred and moaned. *Too old for this.* "You awake, Stuart?"

Stuart yawned. "When I woke up, it was dark. I waited for the sun."

Major glanced around the parking lot. "Wonder how much rain we got last night? We're in a pond back here."

"Ready for breakfast?" Stuart opened the cooler. "Molly packed tortillas and oranges."

"Wouldn't you love to drop into Pete's and grab a cup of coffee?" Major chuckled and turned on the engine. "When Trish bought this little heater, I made fun of her. I'll bet she's laughing at me."

"You still miss her?" Stuart pulled on his boots.

"Sure do. Always will." Major cringed as a wave of his old melancholy swept in then shook it off and plugged the heater into the old lighter outlet.

Stuart stepped out of the truck, and Major stirred instant coffee into the hot water in his metal cup. When Stuart returned, he rubbed his hands together, and Major handed him a cup of coffee.

"Thought I got a whiff of smoke." Stuart peeled his orange, and the citrus smell filled the cab.

"Mmm. Sweet," Stuart said after he'd popped an orange segment into his mouth. "Mr. Young's an awesome trader. Wonder how he's doing?"

After they finished their breakfast, Major lowered his window and sniffed. "You're right. Faint, but it's smoke."

They repacked their gear and loaded it into the back. As he climbed into the truck, Major said, "Before we leave town, I'd like to see if we can find water. I wouldn't mind washing my hands and face, and I hate to waste our drinking water."

As the truck crept around the gas station, Stuart said, "There. An outside faucet." He jumped out and turned on the spigot, and muddy water trickled onto the ground.

"Couldn't be that easy, right?" Stuart asked as he opened his door.

When they approached the bait shop, Major pointed. "Truck in back. That wasn't there yesterday."

A man in overalls stood at the front door. He crossed his arms as the truck approached and nodded at a shotgun that lay on the bench next to him.

Major lowered his window and eased the truck into the parking lot but stayed near the road. "How ya doing? You open for business?"

The man glared. "Nope."

Major nodded. "Have you heard about a farmer meeting near Live Oak today? We were hoping to go."

"Meeting's at noon. Not sure where it is, but I suspect it's in the American Legion fifteen miles up the road." The man stepped away from the door and pointed north.

"You need anything?" Major asked.

The man raised his eyebrows and cocked his head. "You got any coffee?"

"Sure do." Major held out a packet of instant coffee.

"Toss it down. You need anything?"

"Wouldn't mind some water to wash my hands and face."

The man went into the shop and returned with a gallon jug of water. He set it on the ground between the truck and the store. Major tossed out two more packets of coffee. The man snatched up his packets and resumed his position at the door.

As Stuart picked up the water, the man saluted Major. "Nice doing business with ya. Stop by anytime."

"That was a good trade," Stuart said as Major drove away.

"I learned from Mr. Young. How's our coffee supply?"

Stuart peered into the sack. "We've got a month's worth." He picked up a packet and read it. "Expired two years ago."

"Tasted like the instant coffee I remember: burnt coffee-flavored water, one step from dirt, and it hit the spot."

Five minutes later, Major said, "We've got a driveway ahead, but I don't see any buildings. I'll pull in there."

After he parked, Stuart lowered the tailgate and pulled out a wash pan. Major poured an inch of water, and they washed their faces and hands.

"Up ahead. See that?" Stuart pointed to a charred barn and the surrounding burned field. The light breeze stirred up the few remaining embers.

As they continued on the road, Major said, "Hand sanitizer's fine, but it felt good to clean up."

Stuart nodded. "Must have caught fire and burned yesterday. I'm surprised the storm didn't put the fire completely out."

"Maybe it knocked down the field fire and kept it from spreading. Doesn't look like anybody was here."

When Major started up the truck, Stuart turned on the ham radio.

"That storm hit me bad. I've got trees down. When's the meeting?" a ham asked.

"Been moved up to ten," another man said. "I hear the bigwig likes to start early to avoid any of them townies showing up and trying to stir up trouble."

The discussion changed to weather, the storm, and hail damage.

After everyone signed off, Stuart said, "Doesn't sound like anybody knows about the barn fire."

"Interesting strategy to shift the meeting two hours earlier," Major said.

"Did you expect that?"

"No. Dumb luck on our part. We're getting close." Major pointed as trucks appeared on the road in front of him. He slowed and matched the pace of the trucks ahead.

When they reached the American Legion, they followed the trucks to the field to park.

Major glanced at the farmers who headed alone or in pairs from the field to the building. Most of them wore a holstered gun or carried a rifle. "This is good. They must know about the illness. Look at the distancing they maintain as they walk."

"I'm surprised how many are armed," Stuart said.

"It's probably natural to them now. Look at our farm." Major stepped out of his truck and nodded at the farmer who parked next to him.

Stuart wore a Florida feed store ball cap when he climbed out.

"You got a cap for every occasion?" Major asked.

"Pretty much. I even have a church hat. My grandpa gave it to me when I was eight, but Mom wouldn't let me wear it. Dad said nobody could get Mom's goat like her own dad."

When they entered the hall, Major followed the farmer in front of them to a side wall near the exit even though there were seats available.

Major scanned the room. There was no stage, but three men scooted two tables together at the front with four chairs facing the crowd. A podium was in front of the line of tables.

We're in the back and right by the exit. Couldn't have picked a better place.

Major returned the nod of the farmer next to them.

"Just like home where it's natural to leave the chairs for older folks," Stuart whispered.

"Yep. Save our spot. I'll be right back."

Major strolled down the short hallway and passed the men's and women's bathrooms and a locked door that appeared to be a small office. He peered out the window to the front as three black sedans pulled close to the door. *Show time.*

Major made his way to Stuart. *Hall's filled up.*

When two muscular men in black suits with bulges under their arms appeared at the doorway, Major snorted, and Stuart rolled his eyes. Three more men filed into the hall, and each one nodded to the door guards then they marched in formation to the front of the room.

The man next to Major grunted. "This better be good."

The small group chuckled.

The three men positioned themselves across the front and glared at the crowd.

Major glanced at Stuart, who examined the crowd. Stuart stretched then hooked his thumb into his belt near his holster.

He's a natural cop. Major inspected the men lined along the walls as everyone stared at the men up front who preened under the undivided attention. Major glanced at the entrance where more men had gathered.

A nearby man elbowed his neighbor and pointed. "Remind you of a wedding?"

The man snorted. "If music starts up, I'm out of here."

Four men entered the hall. Two of them strode to the right, and the other two strode to the left. They moved to the front and positioned themselves behind the three other men.

An overweight man with a ruddy face stepped into the hall. He nodded to men as he hurried to the front, and they returned his nod. His face reddened as he faced the crowd then Charles McNeil strode in. Stuart's eyes widened, and Major nodded. *Ole Charlie's put on weight.*

McNeil wore jeans, a plaid western shirt that stretched across his abdomen, and cowboy boots. His hair had grayed, and his face had fresh lines carved around his eyes. As McNeil strode to the front, he nodded and waved to the crowd, but no one returned his wave. When he reached the front, he stood next to the man with the ruddy face. McNeil signaled a man who sat on the front row. The man stood and announced the ruddy-faced man as the first speaker.

"We skipping the Pledge of Allegiance?" A man near the back spoke out.

McNeil raised his eyebrows and nodded at his man in the front row who said, "Rise."

The man designated as speaker led the group in the recitation. After the crowd resumed their seats, Major slipped toward the front then scanned the crowd as he returned to find a seat. He picked out men who didn't appear to be farmers. After he resumed his spot, he held seven fingers low, and Stuart nodded.

The man with the ruddy face coughed then read an introduction from a sheet of paper. When he finished, a few men clapped, and he beamed. One of the black-suited men behind him cleared his throat and pointed to a chair, and the speaker rushed to sit.

"You know he's hating life, right?" a man in the back row said, and the nearby men chuckled.

McNeil spoke of dire times and droned on about the economic collapse, failing farms, loss of electricity, attacks on farms, and growing animosity of people who live in the city toward farmers.

"People are hungry," he said. "They aren't thinking right. But we can feed them."

McNeil expounded the virtues of sunroot: ease of planting, resistance to disease, low cost to plant, self-seeding, high profit margin, and the health benefits of sunroot to the consumer.

"We just need to load up the trucks and send them to the market, and the cash will roll in." The man on the front row applauded and rose, and most of the audience joined him.

McNeil swept his arm toward the local speaker who rose with the assistance of two of the men in black suits. They accompanied him to the podium as McNeil slipped out the rear emergency exit.

Slick.

Stuart elbowed Major. "Do I follow?"

"Go to the bathrooms. There's a window where you can see the front of the building."

Major took a forward step and joined in the applause while Stuart sauntered to the bathroom. The audience settled back in their seats. The speaker read instructions from his sheet on how to sign up, and one of McNeil's men lined up sheets and pens on the front tables. The man in the front row rushed to a table and grabbed a pen, and men lined up along the tables and behind each other.

When Stuart returned, he said, "The black cars lined up in front of the building. McNeil and another man headed to a silver car and left."

Major and Stuart left with the first wave of farmers.

"What now?" Stuart asked as they reached the truck.

"Pull out your Georgia farmer cap. We're going to Savannah."

Major turned north while Stuart examined the Florida and Georgia maps.

"We're about four hours away from the Savannah area. Maybe we could make it by five, but we'd never get there by three o'clock." Stuart scratched his head. "McNeil isn't that far ahead of us. How is he going to make it?"

"He'll either reschedule for later today or postpone until tomorrow. Let's head that way to see if we can pick up anything on the radio." Major pointed to a sign. "Rest area three miles ahead. Might be a good spot to stop for lunch."

"Or a perfect place for an ambush."

"There is that."

When they pulled into the rest stop, Stuart peered out his window. "No vehicles around. That's a good sign."

Major slammed into reverse and sped backward onto the ramp, backed onto the highway, and accelerated away.

Stuart stared at the rest area as they passed the exit. "I didn't see those brown barrels at the exit until now. I'm not sure I would have seen them if I wasn't looking for something. Did you think they are sand-filled barrels?"

"I couldn't tell what they were. All I saw was something at the exit. I'll pull off down the road in a bit, and you can grab the cooler out of the back. Let's eat on the road."

After Major pulled onto the shoulder, Stuart grabbed the cooler and positioned it in the back where he could reach it.

"We have sliced homemade bread, strawberry jam, and peanut butter," Stuart said. "Guess I'm the chef."

"Molly's amazing," Major said. "I'm glad we have bread though. Don't tell her I'm tired of tortillas."

"I've put jam on my tortilla. Didn't think about peanut butter. I'll try that."

After they finished eating, Major said, "Show me the route you have planned."

"I'm assuming we avoid interstates." Stuart pointed to the route he'd planned.

"If he's not going all the way to Savannah, he could still have an afternoon meeting," Major said. "Let's head in that direction and keep the radio on to scan."

After two hours of crackles and static, Major said, "I need to stretch, and my eyes are drooping."

Major pulled over. "When we get back to the truck, you drive. Sometimes I forget to switch off."

Major strode a few hundred yards ahead of the truck and rounded a curve then paused at the sight of a roadblock ahead. He jogged back to the truck.

"How close are we to the next town ahead?" He leaned against the front of the truck while he caught his breath.

Stuart spread the map on the hood and pointed. "We're here. The closest town is here. Quick estimate is that the town is maybe nine or ten miles away. What's up?"

"There's a roadblock ahead. Too far away to be townspeople. Let's head back the way we came."

Stuart took the driver's seat and Major climbed in. As Stuart headed south, Major leaned back to clear his mind.

"We're going the wrong direction," Major said.

Stuart braked. "What? I thought we were supposed to go south."

"Sorry. Keep going south. I spoke mid-thought. We've been chasing McNeil and running into one roadblock after another. We've been lucky an ambush hasn't caught us. My original idea was to wait until he came to us, but I became impatient. It's time to go back to my original plan. McNeil's operation is crude and effective in its simplicity. He's repeating the meeting as he goes from town to town. Snake oil salesman."

Stuart's brow furrowed.

Major chuckled. "An old term; older than me. It means somebody super slick. It won't take him long to get to us, or at least to a community near us."

Stuart resumed his speed and nodded. "We can be ready."

"How long until we get home?" Major pulled off his boots and leaned back.

"An hour and a half or three days."

Major laughed. "That was a joke worthy of Josh. Well done." He leaned back and closed his eyes.

* * *

After an hour, Stuart asked, "Major? You awake?"

Major opened his eyes and straightened his back as he peered out the windshield. "What's that ahead?"

"I think it's a herd of cows. What do I do?"

"Turn around and go back two miles then we'll pull over and wait. We can drive back this way in fifteen minutes to see if they've moved on."

Stuart changed direction. As he drove away, he asked, "Why didn't we just pull over and wait where we could see them? Or go shoo them off the road?"

"That's what a normal person would do, right?" Major asked. "What normal people do sounds like a trap to me, and I'm sure I'm wrong here, but we have a history of too many dangerous things happening."

"It's not paranoid if they're really out to get you, right?"

Major snorted. "That could be our farm motto. While we wait, I'll check the map." Major unfolded the map and frowned. "Did we pass a county road not long ago?"

"We passed one about two miles back." Stuart leaned to see the map then pointed. "There it is."

"This goes to Red Springs, near Mr. Young's farm. It's not a shortcut, but it's home territory. Let's go back."

Stuart continued to the county road then turned. "In theory, we're less than an hour away from home."

"I'm glad we're going this way. We'll be going past Pete's diner."

Stuart slowed as he drove through Red Springs. The telltale signs of boards on windows confirmed the permanence of the closed shops, but someone had trimmed the bushes in front of the post office.

"Nobody around, but it looks better maintained than other towns we've driven through," Stuart said.

"Red Springs has three master gardeners. I suspect this is their handiwork."

When they reached Plainview, Stuart pulled into Pete's Diner and gave the horn two quick taps. Major lowered his window, "Hey, Pete."

Pete opened the door and held onto the jamb. His face was pale, and his voice was weak. "Major. Good to see you back."

"You okay?" Major frowned and stepped out.

"I'm sick. Don't come any closer. I have an old friend who checks on me. Take care of your family." Pete closed the door.

Major climbed into the truck. "This sickness is making its way into the small towns. Let's get home."

Major felt his old melancholy creep back, and he rubbed his forehead.

"You okay?"

Major heard the concern in Stuart's voice and shook off his mood. "I think I need a night's sleep in a bed."

When Stuart pulled into the driveway, Major moaned as he eased out of the truck and opened the gate. Shadow yipped and raced to Major who waved Stuart on.

Major knelt to rub Shadow's face and hug him while Shadow licked his face. When he rose, Aimee Louise and Rosalie had raced to meet him. He put his arms around each girl, and the three of them strolled to the farmhouse.

"Mr. Young's not doing well," Rosalie said. "Vanessa posts updates in the window: ten is great, and one is not good. She posted *two* at lunchtime."

CHAPTER SIXTEEN

When they neared the house, Aimee Louise hugged him. "I'm glad you're home."

"No more leaving us behind," Rosalie said. "You needed us, didn't you?"

"Always." Major returned Aimee Louise's hug. "Let's help Stuart unload the truck. He has lots of stories for you."

The four of them set all the gear on the back porch. When Molly stepped outside, she said, "The girls and I will take care of your things later. Annie and I have supper on the table. Wash your hands and sit at the table. Rosalie, let Vanessa know they are back."

Sheriff stood on the porch surrounded by his children "Glad you're safe."

He turned to his entourage. "Go wash your hands. Remember, no asking questions during the meal."

When the children trooped inside to wash, Sheriff asked, "Successful trip?"

"No, but it was worthwhile." Major stopped in the doorway and inhaled. "Ah. Coffee. Real coffee."

Molly and Peyton had set each plateful of meat, beans, and rice with a side salad on the table. "Just a little less passing around," Molly said when Major raised his eyebrows. "We're seeing how it works out."

Peyton dished up a plate for Vanessa, and when Rosalie rose to take it to the trailer, Major said, "I'll go with you."

When they reached the trailer, Vanessa was at the window. She waved and held up a three. Major put his fist on his heart, and Vanessa blew a kiss. Rosalie set the plate inside the box near the door.

When they returned to the house, Rosalie said, "Aunt Vanessa was at the window. She waved and put up a three."

"Small improvement," Sheriff said. "Thank you, Lord, for our food and the small things."

"Dig in. Let me know when you're ready for seconds," Molly said.

After he had eaten his fill, Major sipped his coffee. "Fine meal."

"I'll refill your cup, and you can relax on the porch. Peyton and I will be out after we wash dishes."

Major rose, and Aimee Louise rushed to his side then they strolled to the porch. Wisps of cirrus clouds swept the sky, and the horizon displayed a brilliant orange that faded to pink. The evening crickets sang the song of the approaching cooler night air, and the light breeze carried the sweet fragrance of honeysuckle.

Major inhaled the evening air and relaxed in his rocker as he scanned the farm. "Did you get any hail?"

"No, and no rain." Aimee Louise sat cross-legged next to his chair.

After everyone was on the porch, Major said, "Stuart, why don't you tell about our adventure. I'd be interested in hearing about how much fun we had."

The four younger children gathered around Stuart. He began with the vet then told the farm family a tale about roadblocks, a hailstorm, and chasing meetings across two states.

When he finished, Brett asked, "What about giants? Did you see any giants?"

"We didn't see any, but I heard them push the storm toward us. I'm pretty sure they threw the big hailstones too."

"What about fairies?" Sara asked.

"The fairies sparkled and danced when the man gave us water."

Sara nodded. "Fairies like people who are nice."

Josh crossed his arms. "You left out the part about pizza."

"Did I? I didn't mean to. I forgot to tell you about the roadblock of pizza boxes. Pops aimed the truck at the boxes and slammed down the accelerator. We held our breath when we crashed into them and boxes flew everywhere, but no pizza was harmed. The boxes were empty."

Everyone laughed then Aimee Louise, Rosalie, and Annie rose to go inside, and Stuart joined them.

"Radio time," Rosalie said as they left.

"What about here? What's your news?" Major asked.

Sara twirled and bounced on her toes. "Annie's greenhouse is almost done. Annie let me watch her, but I had to be quiet so I read to Peyton so she wouldn't be lonely. A chicken is pecking holes in eggs, but we haven't figured out which one."

"Penny and Shadow caught a possum, but it played dead and ran away," Brett said.

Josh scratched Penny's back. "We let the boy goat into the girl pen. Mom said we might have baby goats."

"The boy goat should have had a bath first. Now all the girl goats smell stinky too," Sara said.

"Thank you for the best story I've ever heard, Stuart." Molly rose. "Let's get ready for bed, kids."

After Molly and the three younger children left, Major said, "We stopped by the diner. Pete's not well. He said he had a friend checking up on him."

Sheriff shook his head. "Somebody who came to town must have exposed Pete and Mr. Young about the same time. So, what's the scoop on McNeil?"

"He moves the times and places of his meetings. I think it's to be sure only locals show up, and it's effective. Seasoned farmers attended the meeting we went to. I expected them to scoff at McNeil, and they did at first, but they bought into it. There was a rush to sign up for the sunroot program." Major narrowed his eyes. "He's a charmer."

"Old-time snake oil salesman." Stuart winked at Major.

"McNeil did a professional job of wiping his record, but he couldn't erase the memories," Peyton said. "There are a lot of us who haven't forgotten his original conviction. I can't tell you how disheartening it was when he reappeared in his old job. Our boss? Really? It was like he'd gone on vacation. Slimy…never mind. Sends me into a rant when I think about him."

"What's your plan now?" Sheriff asked.

"He's covering two states with his meetings. We'll wait for him to come here or close to here. I don't think it will be long."

"It wasn't a wasted trip because you saw his operation," Peyton said.

"Exactly. Have you heard anything from Nate?"

"Nothing, I'm hoping the hams have an update from him on the call this evening," she frowned. "Is there a link between the missing children and McNeil?"

"My instinct says yes, but I don't have any evidence."

Annie and Rosalie rushed out of the house. "We have news," Rosalie said.

Annie tapped her notebook, and Major smiled. *Rosalie's mini-me.*

"People are leaving Miami and there are reports of roadblocks and robbers. FBI agents left Orlando this morning to investigate."

Peyton frowned. "Didn't you say that's what you heard before I made it to Plainview?"

"Not exactly," Sheriff said. "I got the message about you on the sheriff's network. This is the hams and the first mention of the FBI and roadblocks."

Peyton rose and paced. "I want to go stand at the gate. How will he know how to get here? Nate doesn't have a ham radio. We can't get in touch with him."

"You're right," Sheriff said. "Let's go into town. If we're lucky, they're camped at the sheriff's office. Otherwise, we'll wait. We'll load my truck for an overnight adventure."

"Okay, but I'm hoping for fairies, not giants."

Sheriff chuckled as he and Peyton headed inside. "The good news is that we have room in the sheriff's office to stretch out."

"Where are Aimee Louise and Stuart?" Major asked after Sheriff and Peyton left.

"Still on the radio," Annie said.

"There's more news so they stayed to listen." Rosalie smiled. "You did a good job with your report, Annie."

Annie beamed.

"Where'd everybody go?" Stuart asked when he opened the door for Aimee Louise.

"Molly took the three younger ones to get ready for bed, and Sheriff and Peyton are going to the sheriff's office. They're packing for an overnight at the office while they wait for the FBI agent," Rosalie said.

Aimee Louise sat in her rocker, and Stuart scooted Mr. Young's rocker close to her.

"This is what we've got," Stuart said. "There's a meeting scheduled for farmers in the Mickleton area. You were right, Major." Start glanced at his notes. "It's scheduled for Monday at noon. One ham asked about the sponsor and the agenda. The newest information is that the sponsor is the US government. By implication that's the US Department of Agriculture, and the purpose is to help farmers who are losing money to shift to a profitable crop. There's more. The meeting organizers want to get in touch with Sheriff Starr, a supposed old friend of the key speaker. Aimee Louise said we could get in touch with Sheriff Starr through our sheriff."

Major rubbed his chin. "Remember the local speaker from the meeting? Maybe that's what McNeil has in mind. He must think the supposed award he presented is much-revered by Sheriff."

"Sheriff hasn't left yet." Rosalie jumped up and returned with Sheriff and Peyton.

"Rosalie gave me a quick rundown. That's an unexpected twist. What do you think?" Sheriff asked.

"See what the other sheriffs know and come back in the morning. If Nate hasn't shown up, Peyton can stay at your office," Major said.

"That's what we'll do. We're loaded up. If they show up, I'll lead them to my house. Peyton, how long has it been since you've seen Nate?"

"Two weeks. I've been in the field."

Major nodded. "Peyton, it's best for everyone if you come back here. You're fully exposed to us, and he isn't."

Peyton narrowed her eyes. "What about Brandon?"

"We've been exposed to Brandon, but we hadn't been exposed to Mr. Young when we saw him. Sure am glad I never wanted to be an epidemiologist. This is complex, and we have only three groups in the mix. Four, if you count Pete and Mr. Young," Major said.

"I could pick up Brandon, but Nate couldn't pick up his father and daughter," Peyton said.

"From our limited understanding, yes, but we may want to discuss with Doc first. She'll know."

"Too much to think about. I'll wait for Nate in the sheriff's office with the fairies." Peyton's shoulders slumped.

"Have a good night, Peyton," Major said.

Stuart helped Sheriff and Peyton finish loading up.

After they left, Major said, "I'm beat. I'll see if Vanessa has an update. See everybody in the morning."

Major strolled to the trailer and stood near the window. He reached up to tap but pulled his hand away. *She might be sleeping.*

* * *

When Major woke, it was dark. *I'm missing something.* He rolled over, and his hand dangled at the edge of his bed. He chuckled when Shadow licked his fingers.

"Hello, boy. What time is it?" Major stretched then dressed.

Shadow followed him as he tiptoed into the kitchen. A candle flickered on the table, and Molly sat alone. Tears ran down her face, but when she glanced up at Major, she brushed them away.

"Something wrong?"

"I'm worried about Mr. Young, and the kidnapped children, and what McNeil wants with Jack. Everything is wrong." She rose and picked up the coffeepot. "Coffee perked. Want some?"

"I'll never turn down a cup of coffee again. Have you tasted the instant?"

"Don't ruin it for me. I might like it," she said. "What are you doing up at whatever time it is?"

"I don't know. I woke up thinking we'd missed something. What do you think?"

Molly refilled his cup. "Have some brain juice. It's an unproven fact that people who drink coffee are smarter than anybody else."

Major sipped his coffee. "We talked about blackmailing the parents, didn't we? Might be something to discuss with Nate and Peyton."

"Is the illness a coincidence?"

Major stared at her. "What are you thinking?"

"If McNeil had a cure or vaccine that he could spring on the public, would he be a hero?"

Major drummed his fingers on the table. "You must drink a lot of coffee."

"I'm a mom." Molly flipped her short curls with her fingers. "Moms know everything. I do have one more thing. Is McNeil taking advantage of the electricity going down and the failing infrastructure, or is he controlling it?"

"McNeil is using access to electricity to pit the cities against the farmers."

"Why?"

"Control is the only thing I can think of. The only farmers in business will be under McNeil's control. Sunroot will ruin a farm in a single season. Quickest way to put an entire region of farmers out of business and force them to move to the cities. Control the electricity to the cities, and you control the people."

Molly nodded. "Peyton and Nate are key."

Major rose. "I feel better. I'll stalk the trailer."

Molly put on another pot of coffee. "I feel worse. I need to stalk McNeil."

"He's done it now," Major said. "McNeil crossed a mom."

Molly smiled. "And don't you forget it, bud."

Major stood on the porch and stared at the trailer. *No lights on.*

He strolled to the garden and glanced east then smiled. The sky had turned to pale gray with a thin line of pale yellow at the horizon. *Aimee Louise and Rosalie are up.*

His step had spring on his way back. When he went inside, Molly refilled his cup, and he strode to the front porch to watch the sunrise. As he rocked, he heard the door creak behind him and smiled. *No talking.*

Aimee Louise and Rosalie slipped out and sat on the porch with him.

"Sun's up?" Rosalie whispered.

"Yes," Aimee Louise said.

The girls jumped up and hurried inside. *They're going up the stairs to get dressed. They're quiet.*

He and Shadow strolled to the gate then he scanned the surrounding area. *Movement in the woods.*

He remained motionless then a young four-point buck appeared near the edge. The deer flipped his tail and disappeared into the trees.

"Let's check the trailer, Shadow. Molly will have breakfast soon."

They sauntered around the house to the trailer. Major stepped closer to read the paper in the window. *Three.*

When he returned to the kitchen, Molly and Annie were cooking breakfast.

"The sign still says three this morning," Annie said. "Rosalie checked."

"Are Aimee Louise and Rosalie at the radio? I'll take Vanessa her breakfast," he said.

Molly handed him Vanessa's plate. "Wave to her for me."

After he left her plate in the box, he paused at the window again, but Vanessa wasn't there.

When he walked into the house for breakfast, he scooted into his chair at the table. "I'm officially tired of this."

Molly set his plate in front of him. "Welcome to my world. I hit that point almost two years ago."

Molly walked to the foot of the stairs and shouted, "Breakfast."

Rosalie rushed to the table. "Lots on the radio this morning. Stuart and I are taking turns for breakfast."

"What about Aimee Louise? Should I fix her a plate?" Molly asked.

"She won't eat until she's off the radio."

The four children thundered down the stairs and darted to their seats.

"Trish loved the pounding sound of little feet on the stairs. She'd get a kick out of your crew, Molly."

Molly set plates in front of everybody. Rosalie and Annie rushed through breakfast and hurried to the computer room so Stuart could take his turn to eat.

Annie returned to the doorway. "Stuart wants to wait and eat with Aimee Louise." She rushed back to the computer room.

"No surprise," Major muttered.

After the children finished breakfast, they vanished to do their morning chores. Molly set her plate on the table and sat to eat.

"It's a little more hectic with Mr. Young out of commission," she said. "He needs to keep getting better."

When Aimee Louise, Rosalie, and Stuart came into the kitchen, Molly rose to prepare two more breakfasts.

"I've got this, Aunt Molly. Enjoy your coffee," Rosalie said.

Molly sank back into her chair while Rosalie cooked.

Stuart flipped back in Rosalie's notebook. "McNeil is desperate to talk to Sheriff, according to the hams. Aimee Louise replied with Sheriff's message he'd meet McNeil at the sheriff's office on Monday at noon."

Stuart frowned at the notebook. "Having trouble reading my handwriting," he mumbled. "Word is getting around that sunroot is a scam. There were questions because not all the hams are long-time farmers and some have never farmed. Aimee Louise and another ham fielded all the questions."

Rosalie set plates in front of Aimee Louise and Stuart and took back her notebook.

"Aimee Louise asked about the roadblocks across the highways. Four or five of the hams had seen them, and at least three groups plan to check them out. Everybody agreed to approach a roadblock in groups." Rosalie jumped up and refilled the coffee cups. "There's a lot of sickness going around, but no one knew anyone who has died from it. The hams reported people are very sick but recover anywhere from three days to two weeks later."

"Their reports counter the previous rumor, but we'll see." Stuart stabbed his sausage patty. "I don't think we want to change our precautions yet."

"Right. I want to check on Pete this morning," Major said.

Rosalie gave her notebook to Annie. "Why don't you share this part?"

Annie cleared her throat. "There was interesting news about the electricity. Some former utility engineers will look into the sources of the outages because, according to them, the outages are too controlled to be random."

Annie handed the notebook back to Rosalie who said, "That's it from this morning. Aimee Louise and I will take care of the dishes, Aunt Molly, unless there's something else you want us to do."

"I'd love it," Molly said. "I'd like to spend the morning helping the children with their chores."

After Molly left, Rosalie said, "I'll collect Aunt Vanessa's dishes. Aunt Molly washes them separately then boils water to rinse them."

"I'll walk with you," Major said.

When they reached the trailer, Rosalie opened the box for the dishes, and her eyes widened. "Pops, she hasn't touched her breakfast."

"What?" Major grabbed the plate and stared at it then pounded on the door and shouted, "Vanessa. Vanessa!"

Vanessa threw open the door. "What on earth is wrong with you? We had a rough night."

"Hey, Major. My fever broke. Vanessa promised to share her breakfast with me."

Major peered over Vanessa's shoulder. Mr. Young was sitting on the sofa with his feet propped up. His face was pale, but he smiled.

"But the note in the window says three," Major said.

"Fine. I'll change it." Vanessa snatched the plate and slammed the door.

Rosalie's mouth was open then Major realized his was too.

"Guess he's better," Major said.

"Guess so." Rosalie giggled. "Aunt Vanessa was mad."

"Sure was." Major smiled. "Will you tell Molly?"

Rosalie raced to the garden, and Major whistled as he headed to the house.

When he opened the door, Stuart jumped away from Aimee Louise.

CHAPTER SEVENTEEN

Major glared at Stuart. *I'll ask about that later.* "I have news. Vanessa's mad at me, and Mr. Young's better. He's sitting up and will have a bite of breakfast."

"That's great news. Not the mad part, but Mr. Young getting well," Stuart said. "Did he have the illness that's supposed to be going around?"

Major narrowed his eyes. *Still pretty close.* "I don't know. Whatever it was, it hit him hard. I suspect Molly and Vanessa will make him slow down."

Stuart stepped farther away from Aimee Louise. "Major, the radio transmissions are fading in and out. Aimee Louise and I would like to spend today troubleshooting and adjusting the antenna."

"There's a toolbox and parts in the shed, if you can't find what you need. I'm going into town to check on Pete."

Shadow rose from his nap and trotted to Major's side.

"Okay, boy. Let's tell Molly."

Major and Shadow strolled to the garden. Molly wore a wide-brimmed straw gardening hat with plastic sunflowers around the band and her pink gardening gloves.

She rose from the row she weeded when she saw Major and waved.

"I'm going into town to check on Pete," he said.

Rosalie dropped her trowel into the wheelbarrow. "I'm coming."

"Stay here and help…"

Molly interrupted Major. "I've got plenty of help. Take Dead Eye Red with you."

When Molly returned to her weeding, Major glanced at Shadow. *Argue for an hour, or take Rosalie and leave now?*

Shadow trotted to the truck, and Rosalie rushed to the house. "Gotta grab my things. Be right there."

Rosalie climbed into the truck with her rifle and go-bag. She wore her ball cap with the brim turned to the back. "Ready."

After they passed the deputies' house and turned onto the paved road, Rosalie pointed. "Trash in the ditch."

"That's not good. I don't think I've ever seen that before." Major frowned.

When they reached Pete's Diner, Major tapped the horn then climbed out. Rosalie jumped out of the truck and eased her door closed then moved to the back of the truck.

She has good instincts.

Major left his door unlatched and opened Shadow's door.

A man called out from the diner. "Who's there?"

"It's Major. I came to check on Pete." Major lifted his rifle out of the truck and eased toward the diner.

"Not here."

"I'll wait." Major moved behind the picnic table that was near the door. His back was to Rosalie, and Shadow assumed his guard stance.

The front door cracked open, and a man peered out. "Anybody with you?"

Major smiled and scratched Shadow's ear. "How's Pete doing?"

"He's fine." The door opened a little farther. "Your dog bite?"

"Yeah. Former police dog. Where did he go?"

The door creaked as it closed to its original position. "With a friend. To see a doctor."

Major turned his head to stare at the road west of Pete's. "Two guys are carrying rifles and coming down the road. You know them?"

"What?"

Major nodded and glanced in the other direction. "Two more."

He put his arm up to shield his eyes from the sun. "It's okay. Old friends of Pete's. He said they were coming to clean the diner for him. They'll be happy to see you opened up the diner for them."

The door slammed then a man ran out the back and into the woods.

"Heel, Killer, heel." Major shouted as he moved closer to the door. He paused then turned the knob and kicked the door open. He stifled his cough from the musky odor of a long-time empty building and old grease.

The burglar had stacked cans of beans and corn and boxes of ammunition on the table nearest to the door. Major searched the building and locked the back door with the deadbolt. After he found Pete's spare key, he left a note on the table then boxed up the food and ammunition and carried it to the truck. Rosalie lowered the tailgate, and he placed the carton in the back. He locked the diner's front door while Rosalie closed up the back of the pickup.

"We interrupted a burglary in progress," Major said. "Pete's not there, and I still don't know how he is, but he's not alone. That's important."

"I kept the guy in my sights as he ran away in case you wanted me to stop him," Rosalie said.

"You did a good job of covering me. Where'd you learn that?"

"I read. I learn things." Rosalie grinned, and Major chuckled.

Major headed to the sheriff's office. On the way, he noticed a rolled-up dirty blanket in an alley. *More evidence of outsiders.*

Sheriff had parked his truck in front of his office. Major pulled around to the side and parked.

"Do I stay in the truck?" Rosalie asked.

"Come with me. Bring your rifle."

Rosalie stayed at the corner while Major knocked on the door.

When Sheriff opened the door, he scanned the area. "Come on in. You come by yourself?"

"Nope." Major waved for Rosalie to join them, and they went inside.

Major leaned back in his chair and closed his eyes while Rosalie caught up Sheriff and Peyton on the news. *Advantage of a brilliant sidekick.*

When Rosalie told them about Vanessa, Sheriff guffawed.

Story sounds good when Rosalie tells it.

"What about you, Sheriff? Can you top that?" Major asked.

"Never. I heard from a sheriff south of us a few minutes ago. Nate and at least one other person stopped early this morning and were sleeping in Nate's car behind the sheriff's office. Roadblocks are causing problems for any travel. We don't have to wait here though. I gave the sheriff directions to the farm but told him to warn

Nate we might be under quarantine." Sheriff rose from his chair. "I've been sitting too long. We don't have to stay."

When he reached the hallway, Sheriff said. "Ready to go, Peyton?"

She carried her things as she came out of the office next to his. "Sure am."

"Remember the olden days when you traveled and stopped at a motel overnight? Slept in a too-soft bed with clean sheets?" Major asked after Sheriff locked the building.

"Pure myth."

Peyton snickered.

When Major and Rosalie reached home, she lowered her window. "Generator. Hear that? We'll have clean sheets tonight."

"And clean bodies. I'll bet Molly has all the generators running," Major said.

Shadow whined to get out of the truck, and Rosalie jumped out with him then they raced to the farmhouse.

Sheriff closed the gate behind his truck then he and Peyton followed Major to the side yard.

"If nobody's made the beds yet," Sheriff said, "I'm taking over that chore. That's my new priority as of today."

"I'll do the laundry, so Molly can focus on supper. I'm still hungry from yesterday," Major said.

When they reached the house, Molly toasted them with her sweet tea as she rocked on the porch. "Aimee Louise finished the laundry, Stuart made the beds, kids are taking showers, and I have our supper in a crockpot. I'm living the life."

Peyton sat on the porch. "I feel like a slug. Is there something I can do this afternoon?"

"Can you drive a utility vehicle?" Molly said. "Annie needs to go to Mr. Young's farm to pick up some plastic and other stuff for her greenhouse. She knows the way."

"I could do that. Annie is building a greenhouse? By herself?"

Molly beamed. "She is a talented architect and carpenter."

While Molly extolled Annie's skills, Major strolled to the trailer. Vanessa sat next to the window and waved when she saw him. He strode to the window and read the sign. *SEVEN*. Vanessa flipped the sign over. *Sorry you make me cranky*. Major laughed and put his palm on the glass, and she placed hers against his. She glanced behind her then waved and disappeared.

Shadow accompanied him back toward the house. "I've been missing Vanessa and didn't realize it until now. I was cranky, wasn't I?"

Shadow yipped, and Major chuckled.

"Lunch!" Molly called, and Shadow raced to the porch.

After lunch, Aimee Louise gave Peyton a driving lesson, and Molly gave Annie strawberry jam to trade for one or two of Jody's survival books. Peyton drove Number 48 from the back to the front of the house then back in a practice run. Annie sat with her back straight in the passenger's seat. After she stopped, Peyton lifted the hood, and she and Aimee Louise leaned over the engine like two old mechanics.

"Did you see that grin on Annie's face?" Sheriff asked. "She's in the big leagues now. Cruising in Number 48. I'll run to the deputies' place to see if they need anything and to let Heather know Mr. Young is improving. I know she's worried."

When Major went into the kitchen, Molly was washing dishes. "We left the generators on for you to take a shower, Major. We can start them up this evening for Sheriff and Peyton. I'll finish these up then join the kids at the garden."

"Don't have to ask me twice." Major hurried to his bathroom and turned on the water in the master bath. When he stepped out of the shower, Number 48 rumbled to life and headed to the driveway.

Aimee Louise must have cleared Peyton to drive. He smiled as he dressed and put away the rest of the folded clothes.

Rosalie had joined Aimee Louise and Stuart in the computer room. Major raised his eyebrows as he listened to Aimee Louise and Stuart argue about how to fine tune the antenna. *I've never heard Aimee Louise argue with anyone before. Or maybe I've never heard anyone challenge Aimee Louise.* He chuckled and slipped outside to turn off the generators. As he reached the porch, he squinted at the road and the car driving toward the farm. He frowned. *Solo driver.*

Rosalie and Stuart appeared at the south side of the house, and Aimee Louise and Shadow trotted to Major's truck on the other side. *They must have gone out the back door.*

He strode away from the house and waited midway to the driveway. The car slowed then parked in front of the driveway.

"Hey there! Is Peyton here?"

"She'll be back soon. Are you Thomas?"

"Sure am. You are?" Thomas opened the gate and sauntered toward the house. His right hand rested on his holstered gun. He flipped the holster snap.

Aimee Louise shouted. "Uncle Dan."

Our code word for danger. Major and Thomas raised their weapons at the same time.

Crack. Crack.

The stranger dropped to the ground. Major approached him and kicked away the gun then knelt to assess him.

"Dead," Major said as Stuart trotted to him, and they examined the man's body.

"This left knee is shattered. That was Rosalie. Head shot was mine. If I missed, Rosalie's shot made sure he'd still go down. That was our plan," Stuart said.

Major searched the man's pockets. "No wallet. No ID."

"I'll check the car. Who's Thomas? Why didn't you ask him if he was Nate?"

"First name that popped into my head. Nothing smelled right."

As the children ran for the front yard, Aimee Louise yelled, "Inside," and they dashed for the back door to go inside the house. Molly and Penny followed them.

Major whistled and waved for Rosalie and Aimee Louise to join him.

* * *

Stuart muttered as he strode to the car, "This family's amazing. Aimee Louise sees clouds. Rosalie's a crack shot. There's a code word for danger and another one for the children to run inside. Major smells things. Where do I fit in?"

Stuart opened the driver's door and called out to Major, "I thought this was a law enforcement antenna on the car, but there's a ham radio installed. Wallet on the seat." Stuart popped the trunk. "Lots of weapons and ammunition back here."

He slipped into the driver's seat and moved the car closer to the man's body where Major waited.

"I can load him into the back seat. There's a tarp in the trunk. I'll wrap him in it then stop at the deputies' house. I'm sure I can get someone to go with me to bury him. He was here for Peyton, wasn't he?" Stuart asked.

"I think so, but I don't know why. The ham radio explains how he found us. But how did he know Peyton would be here? How did he know her name?"

Aimee Louise and Rosalie joined them and stood next to Major. Number 48 rumbled as Peyton and Annie returned.

Peyton parked at the fence line and scanned the area. "Wait inside the fence near Number 48, Annie."

Peyton trotted down the driveway. Her face paled when she saw the body. "What happened?"

Why would the sight of a body affect her? She's an FBI agent. Major glanced at Aimee Louise who stared at Peyton then shifted her gaze to the ground. Stuart cocked his head as he narrowed his eyes at Peyton then glanced at Aimee Louise and raised his eyebrows. Major frowned. *Aimee Louise knows something. Stuart saw it too.*

"You know him?" Major asked.

"He might be a guy from the Miami office. Did he have any ID?"

Stuart handed her the wallet.

She flipped it open. "Carl Kelso. He works in the Miami office on child abduction cases."

Major glowered. "He'd be in the perfect position to cover up a missing child investigation."

She pointed to the car. "Radio antenna. Find anything else besides his wallet?"

"It's a new ham radio," Stuart said. "Just the wallet. Nothing else except what's in the trunk."

She circled the car then peered into the trunk. "This isn't an official car, and none of this is issued equipment." She glanced at Annie. "I returned when we heard the shots. If you don't mind, I'd still like to take Annie to Pastor John's farm."

"We got this," Major said.

"Annie," Peyton said, "our trip's still on. Let's go."

Annie raced around the fence to Number 48 and hopped in then Peyton drove away.

"Somebody needs to catch up Molly and somebody needs to go with Stuart to take care of the body. I can talk to Molly."

"We'll go with Stuart," Rosalie said.

"Nope. That leaves us too short-handed; only one go."

"I'll go," Aimee Louise said.

Stuart smiled until Major narrowed his eyes at him, then Stuart's face reddened.

Major pulled the tarp out of the back and tossed it on the ground. "Let's roll Carl onto the tarp then we can lift him to the back seat."

As Major and Rosalie strolled to the house, she asked, "What do I do?"

Major put his hand on her shoulder. "What you do best: guard the family and make lists. That was an outstanding shot, by the way."

"Thanks, Pops. You're a great teacher."

* * *

"You want to drive?" Stuart asked.

"Yes."

Stuart tossed the keys to her. On the way to the deputies' house, Stuart asked, "Why did you offer to come along with me?"

"Rosalie needs to be at the farmhouse to back up Pops if there's any more trouble."

Stuart's shoulders slumped then he smiled. *I can always count on Aimee Louise for a matter-of-fact answer.*

Aimee Louise honked the horn at the gate then the two of them climbed out and strolled to the house. When Stuart whistled his cardinal call as they got close, Jim ran around the house from the back.

"Can we get everybody together? We've got updates."

"I'd like to talk to Aunt Heather," Aimee Louise said.

"She and Kris are in the garden with the little guys."

Aimee Louise left for the garden, and Stuart whistled a second time as he and Jim sat on the porch.

"What's up?" Wally asked after he and Brad joined them.

"I have a great story for the next time we sit around a campfire, but here's a shorter version," Stuart said. "An FBI agent arrived at the sheriff's office yesterday, and we expected another agent with one or two civilians today. Instead, a crooked agent who must have worked for McNeil showed up with intentions to kill. He tried to shoot Major, but Rosalie and I stopped him. That's his car, and his body is in the back seat."

"Where do we bury the body?" Jim asked.

"I thought of a couple places, but I don't want to go too far."

Brad rubbed his face. "Take him to the old dump site south of town. Nobody goes there anymore."

"I'll go with you." Jim rose and dusted off his jeans. "Will Aimee Louise stay here?"

"We need her to guard us while we dig," Stuart said.

"She's good at that, but does that mean I ride in back with the deceased?" Jim wrinkled his note.

"We can move him to the floorboard so you can sit."

"Then I'll go. I'll grab two shovels."

After Stuart and Jim buried Carl, they tossed the tarp and shovels onto the backseat floor.

"Let me know if you and Major need any help," Jim said when Stuart and Aimee Louise dropped him off at the house. "You can stop and pick me up any time. I'll be ready."

As Aimee Louise drove the two miles back to the farm, Stuart said, "Did Peyton's cloud change?"

"She's had a worried cloud since she's been here, but when she saw the body, her cloud exploded into terrified." Aimee Louise glanced at Stuart. "I don't know if that makes sense. I can't always find the words."

He nodded. "Do you think she recognized him?"

"Yes, but more than just recognized him. What do you think?"

"The same, but I don't know why. We need to talk to Major." Stuart leaned back and gazed at the passing clouds.

"I searched the car while you and Jim were busy."

Aimee Louise never starts a conversation. Stuart sat up and stared at her. "So what did you find?"

"Two spiral notebooks and a passport and ID in another name."

"What? Where did you find them?"

"In the trunk. Under the ammo."

"Have you looked at them? Where are they?" Stuart scanned the backseat, felt under the passenger's seat, and opened the glove box.

"I didn't have time to look at them after I put all the ammo back. They're on my seat. I'm sitting on them."

Aimee Louise pulled up to the gate. After Stuart opened the gate, she drove through and waited.

"Are you going to tell Major, or did you want me to?" Stuart asked.

"I'll tell him, but you talk," Aimee Louise said, and Stuart laughed.

"Rosalie and Sheriff?" he asked.

Aimee Louise climbed out of the car and picked up the notebooks. "Yes."

"I'll gather them and meet you at the barn."

When Stuart threw open the back door, Major and Sara were sitting on the sofa. Sara leaned on Major's shoulder while she read her book about caring for chickens. Major closed the hydroponics book he'd been reading and raised his eyebrows. "Any problems?"

"Aimee Louise and I need a conference in the barn. Do you know where Sheriff and Rosalie are?"

"I do," Sara said. "They're at the greenhouse. They have a surprise for Annie, but they wouldn't tell me what it was. I could go tell them to go to the barn. Except maybe I'll ask them. Mommy says I'm not supposed to tell grownups what to do, but I can ask. Is that okay if I go ask them for you?"

"Yes, thank you," Stuart said as Sara plopped her book on the table and dashed out the door.

"Is Aimee Louise okay?" Major added his book to the table and headed to the door.

"She's fine. We've got a problem we all need to discuss."

As the two men strode into the barn, Major dropped his hand on Stuart's shoulder and growled, "This isn't anything that will make me angry, is it?"

Stuart stuttered, and Aimee Louise waved the notebooks.

Stuart swallowed. "Aimee Louise found two notebooks in the trunk. We haven't had time to look at them."

CHAPTER EIGHTEEN

Aimee Louise handed one notebook to Major and the other to Stuart. The two men sat on hay bales next to each other and opened their notebooks as Sheriff and Rosalie rushed into the barn.

"What's wrong? Sara told us Stuart needed us at the barn right away," Sheriff said.

Major snorted. "Aimee Louise found two notebooks in Kelso's car and don't tell Molly what Sara said." Major rose and held out the notebook as Sheriff strode in.

Rosalie and Aimee Louise sat on either side of Stuart, and he turned back to the first page.

Sheriff scanned the pages and flipped to the end then returned it to Major. "Three pages of handwritten notes. It's a list of boys and their parents, address, phone number, and employment. The circled parent must be the agent or cop. Is that how you interpret it, Major?"

"Exactly. The last column labeled *LOC* could be location, but there are only two entries: SCS or SCW, but I'm not sure what that means."

"Did you see Brandon listed with Peyton and Troy Romero?" Sheriff asked. "It's on the last page."

Stuart jumped up, and Aimee Louise caught the notebook that he dropped in his rush. "Did you see Henry? Is Henry there?" he asked.

Major ran his finger down the page with Brandon and stopped near the bottom. "Here's a Henry. Let me see if there are any others." Stuart crowded Major, and they read each page.

"Two Henrys with the dad circled." Stuart rubbed his forehead. "It's not like I can call Mom to ask her what Henry's last name is. What do we do now?"

Aimee Louise handed the notebook to Rosalie then raced out of the barn, and Stuart smiled.

"Why did Aimee Louise leave?" Sheriff asked.

Major frowned. "She knows something, doesn't she?"

Rosalie snickered, and Stuart said, "You're catching on to interpreting Aimee Louise."

Aimee Louise returned with a folded sheet of yellow construction paper and handed it to Stuart. "Henry drew a picture for me. He said he wanted me to remember he was at your folks' farm."

Stuart examined the picture. "A goat, right? At the bottom it says Henry M."

"This one." Major pointed to the first page. "Henry Morrison. What do you think?"

Rosalie muttered. "Bad guy was a lousy list maker. He should have included ages."

"Right," Stuart chuckled. "Meanwhile, we can get word to Dad. Maybe ask if Mr. Morrison is with them?"

Rosalie pulled her notepad out of her back pocket and jotted an entry then tapped the page. "This evening's call."

"What about your notebook?" Sheriff asked.

"It's four pages of rough map sketches with coordinates listed at the bottom. No indication of what's at the coordinates," Rosalie said. "We'd need an internet connection to determine where the coordinates are."

"Is there another way?" Major leaned against the barn doorjamb and stared at the sky.

"Jody had a stack of state road maps," Stuart said. "We could borrow them."

"That would be a start," Sheriff said. "Who's our best map reader?"

"Mr. Young, but Aimee Louise and I could tackle it," Rosalie said.

"Why don't you and Mr. Young work on it together?" Major asked.

"Because he's sick." Rosalie rolled her eyes. Aimee Louise jumped up and joined Major at the door then peered out.

"Mr. Young and Aunt Vanessa are going into the house." Aimee Louise ran out of the barn, and Rosalie followed her.

"They'll be back in a minute." Major patted the hay before he sat on the bale. "This is my regular seat in the barn conference room."

When the girls returned, Rosalie said, "Mr. Young is still weak, and Aunt Vanessa's making him go back to his trailer for a nap, but he'll eat with us tonight. If we get the maps this afternoon after Peyton and Annie return then he and I can look at the coordinates in the morning."

"Peyton. We need to find out what's really going on. Sheriff, I know you've spent more time with her, but I'm thinking I'm less official and more approachable," Major said.

Stuart coughed. "Sorry. Had a tickle."

"Maybe so," Sheriff said. "We didn't chat much. I thought it was because she was tired, but it must have been more than that."

"What else do we need to do?"

"I'll unload the car trunk if you'll tell me where you want the guns and ammunition, Major," Stuart said.

"We can scrub the inside of the car, but after Peyton and Annie return, I want to pick up maps," Rosalie said.

"I'll go with you," Sheriff said.

Major nodded. "When you go, talk to Jody about Mr. Young's illness and his recovery before you get close to anyone there. Ask her if we need to continue to self-isolate the family here. I need to clear a spot in my bedroom closet for the ammo, and we can put the guns in a gun safe."

"We'll help Annie with her greenhouse," Stuart said, and Aimee Louise nodded.

Major narrowed his eyes. *We?*

"I need to let Sara know I'll read with her later," Major said as the roar of Number 48 sounded at the edge of the field.

On his way to the barn, Rosalie raced past him. "Need my rifle and go-bag."

The entire farm family except for Vanessa and Mr. Young waited for Number 48 in the side yard. Annie's face beamed when Peyton pulled into the yard.

After Peyton turned off the engine, she said, "We think we found everything Annie needs, and Jody loaded us down with books. She made sure we didn't get close to her or their group. She set a box of books on the porch for us, and we picked them up. She said to let her know if we need more."

"I left the strawberry jam on the porch," Annie said.

Stuart loosened the straps that held the sheets of clear roofing onto the back of Number 48. "We'll help unload Number 48, Annie."

Brett ran to the garden for a wagon then he and Josh lifted off the box of books. Josh pulled, and Brett and Sara pushed the wagon to the back door. Molly followed them. "We'll sort the books and find shelf space for them. Excellent afternoon activity for those three."

"Anyone show up?" Peyton asked as she furrowed her brow and scanned the yard before she climbed out of the driver's seat.

Aimee Louise tugged on Stuart's shirt, and Major stepped closer to the two of them.

"Terrified," Aimee Louise said in a quiet voice.

Major answered Peyton. "Nobody."

"Changed to worried," Aimee Louise said in the same low tone.

"Peyton, let's take a stroll and talk about some safe ways we could get you and Brandon together," Major said.

"I could use a walk. I'll take my backpack inside," Peyton said.

Sheriff and Rosalie helped unload the roofing then climbed into Number 48 and left. Rosalie held her rifle across her lap.

* * *

On the way to Pastor John's, Sheriff asked, "You doing okay?"

Rosalie broke away from scanning the surrounding area. "I am overall. I still miss Mom. I always hoped she'd get better, but she…" She resumed scanning the area. "Didn't."

"Your mother was a wonderful person."

"Annie and I have talked about our birth moms and how much we miss them. Annie's worried it might hurt Aunt Molly's feelings if she knew. I miss the dad I had when I was eight. After the drugs were more important to him than Mom or me, we didn't see him much. Mom was sick for a long time, and I was lonely." She snickered. "Not that I can remember what alone feels like, much less lonely. I enjoy being part of the farm family. I grew up thinking I'd always be an only child."

"Farm family took care of that too." Sheriff smiled.

"It's interesting how bad circumstances have good points."

"I heard a coyote last night," Sheriff said. "Hadn't heard one in a long time. Not my favorite animal, but it's a sign that our local wildlife has flourished with fewer people encroaching on their homes."

She pointed to the mockingbird that ran through its repertoire of songs as it perched in a nearby tree. "I loved hearing the birds when I ran in the town park, but I hear birds all the time now. I remind myself to stay in awe of the bird songs."

"How do you feel about Aimee Louise and Stuart?" he asked.

"I'd like for them to get together, and Stuart is smart enough to give Aimee Louise time to think. We'll see." She gazed at Sheriff. "I'm not jealous or anything like that, if that's what you're asking. She'll always be my sister, and even if they don't get together, which will break Stuart's heart, the three of us will always be friends."

When he pulled into Pastor John's driveway, Sheriff said, "I'm supposed to update Jody on Mr. Young's illness and ask about staying isolated. What else are we supposed to do? I'm having trouble with keeping track of all the pieces."

Rosalie laughed. "I'm supposed to ask Doc for maps so we can figure out the coordinates in the notebook."

"That one's yours. That's why I didn't have to remember it, right?" Sheriff chuckled as he tapped the horn and climbed out then shouted, "John. Chuck."

Chuck came out of the house. "This is a surprise, Sheriff. I thought Annie might have forgotten something, but I'm glad to see you. What's up?"

"Jody around?" Sheriff asked.

"She's inside. Need to talk to her?"

Jody stepped past Chuck and sat on the porch steps as Chuck went back inside.

Sheriff leaned against Number 48 and told her about Mr. Young's illness and his recovery.

"I heard more people were recovering than what we originally thought," she said. "Nice to hear about Mr. Young, especially with the news about Pete."

"What happened to Pete?"

"Sorry. Thought you knew Pete died late last night."

Sheriff shook his head. "Losing Pete is a terrible blow. He was a force in pulling our community together." Sheriff furrowed his brow. "It's staggering how many people he saved by providing safe drinking water and even food as long as he could. His swap table was genius; it provided a way for the town to swap for critical items, and almost as important, a spot for retired farmers to socialize. I can't imagine what it would have been like around here this past two years without Pete."

Jody nodded. "Some speculate that his son will continue with the swap table, but you're right that our whole region will miss Pete. The illness skipped our locals so far, except for Pete and Mr. Young. Someone who was passing through town infected Pete."

"Mr. Young spent time in town with Pete. I think it's possible that the same person exposed them."

"How's everybody else at Major's farm?"

"Fine, so far. Vanessa cared for Mr. Young in his trailer. She hasn't shown any signs of the illness. How strict do we need to keep our isolation? Peyton wants to see her son. Should she stay with us for a while?"

Jody rose and paced. "That's a hard call, isn't it? If it was canine parvovirus in a kennel, we'd be sure not to expose any unvaccinated dogs or puppies under the age of four months because it is so contagious and a killer. It's easy to say, keep it in the kennel or, in this case, isolated at a farm. If it were me, I'd maintain isolation a little longer."

"Kind of what we thought, but we hoped Mr. Young might have a different bug."

"I can say with full confidence as an experienced veterinarian that he may or may not." Jody smiled as she rose. "What else? I know you didn't come here for something you already knew."

"My turn." Rosalie returned from the goat pen. "Stuart thought you may have a folder of road maps, and we were wondering if we could borrow your folder? We need to look up coordinates, but we aren't sure where to start."

"I sure do, and I'm happy to give them to you. I'm not going anywhere soon, and I'm cluttering up Vicki's house with all my stuff. It would be nice to clear out a few more things. Can I send you home with another box of books?"

"Only if you insist then I won't get into trouble with Molly," Sheriff said.

"That's great. I've got two boxes of fiction. One of them has middle grade books my sister gave me when her children went to college. Your kids will enjoy them. My sister homeschooled, and I have four boxes of textbooks from third grade through high school. They're six or seven years old. Everything has been online for a while, but she said the books came in handy when their internet went down. I'll send them with the next Number 48 run whenever that might be."

After they left Pastor John's farm, Rosalie said, "Thanks for going with me. I enjoyed the chance to talk to an adult about something besides what we would do about our latest crisis, which is important, but sometimes it all gets exhausting."

"I agree. So, we're bonded now, right? Will you help me with my next prank on your Aunt Molly if I can come up with something good?"

Rosalie laughed. "Sure will."

* * *

Major and Peyton strolled toward the trees. Annie and Aimee Louise had built a bench near the woods for Rosalie to listen to the birds.

"Let's sit here in the shade," Major said.

"Another one of Annie's projects?" Peyton asked as she sat. "It's sturdy. She's amazing, isn't she?"

"Sure is. And speaking of amazing kids, I'm still in awe of Brandon and how he protected a younger boy he didn't even know."

"He's such a goofy kid, and he's so young. It's hard for me to even think of him out in that storm, much less taking responsibility for another child."

"You knew it was Carl Kelso right off, didn't you? What's up?"

Peyton stared at Major then shifted her gaze to the ground. "Troy won't be coming with Nate. I'm positive about that. Both Nate and Kelso work for McNeil. I came across a two-page document with a list of twenty agents, and Nate and Carl were numbers one and two on the list. The second list was almost as long, but when I got the list, someone had already crossed off half the names."

When she glanced at Major, he met her gaze. "Do you think something's happened to Troy?"

"No. When Brandon disappeared, I sent Troy to his brother's place south of Jacksonville. I haven't heard from him, but I'm sure he's okay. He wasn't supposed to contact me because I can find him when it's safe. Can we walk? I'm too on edge to sit still."

They walked across the field to the fence then headed south on the road.

"What about Nate?" Major asked.

"I don't know if Nate realized I learned who he works for. I don't think he has. He replaced my longtime partner who disappeared last month. My old partner's name was crossed off the second list, and my name came right after his. When I told Nate I might leave before he did, he insisted it was safer if we rode together. I agreed but left within the hour with the trucker Troy's other brother arranged for me."

"Where's the document you have?"

"Safe."

Major glared. "We can go back and forth the rest of the day if you want to, but don't make me late for supper."

She laughed. "That's a dirty blow, Major. I don't want to miss Molly's cooking either. I have it with me."

"Can you give us a copy and keep yours? If you're nervous about me, Aimee Louise, Rosalie, or Annie could help you copy it," he said.

Her eyes widened. "Didn't think of that. I'd like to work with Annie."

"Do you think Nate's wife will be with him?" he asked as they turned around to head back.

"Yes. She's number three on McNeil's list, even though she's not an agent."

Major shook his head. "We have conflicting information on who may or may not show up and when, but we need to be ready to throw a surprise party for them."

"I like it. Count me in."

When they reached the gate, Peyton asked, "Did you work with McNeil?"

"Believe it or not, he was a respected agent when I worked with him back in the day."

"Just like Nate," Peyton said in a soft voice. "I was excited when I learned Nate was my new partner."

"Ask Annie to copy your document for you, but she might need Rosalie's guidance, so ask before Rosalie is deep into the maps," Major said.

"I'll do that."

When they reached the gate, the roar of Number 48 caught their attention, and they waited for Sheriff and Rosalie.

After Sheriff pulled through the gate, Peyton ran behind them while Major closed the gate. When Major reached Number 48, he raised his eyebrows and pointed to the two boxes of books. "Jody had that many maps?"

"She sent two boxes of fiction. Everybody will love having something new to read," Sheriff lifted the first box, and Major reached in for the second one.

"Rosalie, I plan to ask Annie to help me copy a document. It's in my backpack," Peyton said.

"Let's find her. I'll hover in case she needs any coaching." Rosalie stuck the maps into a side pocket of her backpack then hurried with Peyton to the house.

"Fast thinking about how excited everyone will be with new books," Major said as they carried their boxes into the house.

"Molly won't buy it. I hope Jody slipped in a cookbook or two. I can't think of anything else that might get me off the hook," Sheriff said.

Josh and Brett waited on the porch. "We saw you and ran to the house so we can open the door," Brett said.

"It was Brett's idea," Josh beamed.

When they set the books down on the table, Molly said, "More books? They better be fiction. This crowd is driving me crazy with the same-old-books complaint."

She turned back to the stove, and Sheriff wiped his brow and flung imaginary sweat then he and Major strolled to the back porch.

"I'll start," Major said. "Peyton said she has a list of agents who work for McNeil and another of agents scheduled for transfer or worse. Carl was on the bad guy list, but the shocker is so are Nate and his wife. Peyton didn't say where the lists came from. Annie will help her copy the list."

"Whoa. Didn't see that coming." Sheriff sat in the nearest rocker. "We received sad news. Pete died late last night. Jody said she would maintain the isolation longer even though Mr. Young is better. I think that's what we should do. Rosalie got the maps. I'm sure she and Aimee Louise will get to them pretty quick. Did Peyton say how she got the list?"

"That's terrible news about Pete." Major sat in his rocker. "Peyton didn't say. I do get the feeling we're being fed information piecemeal, and the inconsistencies bother me."

Rosalie burst through the back door. "Peyton can't find her list. She dumped out her backpack and is going through it again." Rosalie ran back into the house.

"That's convenient," Sheriff said.

Major stared at the sky. *I understand Aimee Louise. Sometimes there is nothing to say.* Major rose. "I'll check on Vanessa and Mr. Young."

"I'll see how Annie is doing." Sheriff's stomach growled as he headed to the steps. "Don't we have a meal coming up?"

Major raised his hand to tap on the trailer door as it opened.

"Hi, Major," Mr. Young said. "Vanessa kicked me out so she can clean."

"Did not," Vanessa called out from the back of the trailer. "Close the door."

Mr. Young winked as he left the door open a crack. "She's fun to tease. Walk me to the house? I thought I'd sit in the kitchen with Molly, so she can boss me around too."

Major chuckled. "Need an arm?"

"Wouldn't mind that at all."

When they reached the porch, Mr. Young said, "I'd rather sit out here. I wasn't sure for a while if I'd ever enjoy fresh air again."

After Mr. Young settled in his rocker, Major said, "Pete has been very ill too, but his condition worsened, and he died last night."

Mr. Young shook his head. "I'm sorry to hear that. I figured if I got better, anybody could. Pete and I have been friends since our sons were in kindergarten together. I bet his son will keep the swap table going, but it won't ever be the same."

"No, it won't. Would you like some water or sweet tea?"

"I'd love some sweet tea. Vanessa wouldn't let me have any. She said I'm not a hummingbird, and I don't need sugar water."

When Major returned with the iced tea, Mr. Young took a long sip. "Did you know Sara's been coming to the trailer window every day and giving us a rundown on what's going on with the family? Absolutely scandalous, at least from Sara's perspective. I must fact-check a few things with you later."

"We have some map coordinates, but we don't know where they are or their significance. Jody sent us some maps. If you're feeling up to it later this afternoon, Rosalie may ask for your help. Thought I'd let you know your afternoon is booking up." Major paused at the steps. "I'll check on the farm animals and garden, unless there's something you need."

"Life's great." Mr. Young saluted Major with his iced tea, and Major sauntered to the goat pen.

Rosalie strolled down the path. "Pops, Peyton lost it because she can't find her list. I left and asked Aunt Molly to calm her down. I came here to hide with you."

CHAPTER NINETEEN

Major leaned on the fence. "What are Aimee Louise and Stuart doing?"

"I don't know. What me to find them?"

Major stretched his back. "Let's look in the front yard. It's the only place I haven't been in a while."

When they rounded the corner to the front, Aimee Louise braced the ladder that leaned against the house. Major gazed up the ladder, and Stuart was on the roof with the antenna.

"I can't watch anyone on a roof," Major said. "I've been meaning to admire Annie's progress, anyway."

"I'll go along."

On their way, Rosalie said, "When Peyton couldn't find her list, she whispered *Oh no. He took it.* But then she went into a frenzy and dumped out her bag. When she started tossing clothes and ranting, I ran for Aunt Molly. Peyton scared me because the only other time I've seen anyone act like that was when dad couldn't find his drugs in the early days when Mom would hide them from him. She wanted him to quit. I'm glad our kids here don't have to deal with anything like that."

Pops put his arm around Rosalie. "I'm glad you're here. You're where you belong, you know. A few years ago, Jody told me about a two-year-old pup that people would adopt from the animal shelter then take him back for owner-surrender. Five families returned him because he ran away. In one way, I don't blame them because they faced a stiff fine for not containing him. Then some folks who lived on a farm adopted him, and he never ran away from them once. Jody said that dog was just trying to find where he belonged. I'm glad you found us because this is where you belong."

"I love that, Pops. Thank you."

When they reached Annie's greenhouse, Annie was on the roof. Sheriff handed her a panel, and she nailed it into place. She stood for the next panel and waved to Major and Rosalie.

"What's this with the roof-climbing?" Major asked. "It's not as high as the house, but this scares me more."

"I can think of something scarier," Rosalie said. "What if Brett was the one handing the sheets to Annie?"

"You win. She'd lean over to reach them, and I would have a heart attack." Major put his hand on his chest and staggered, and Rosalie laughed.

"Inside," Aimee Louise shouted from the front. Rosalie and Annie dashed to the back door, and Major hurried to his truck, picked up his rifle, then crashed into Stuart who was rounding the side of the house.

"Good. You're here. There's a car on the road. Come talk to Aimee Louise."

Aimee Louise waited at the corner of the house, and the ladder was on the ground. Sheriff came up behind Major.

"I was on the roof," Aimee Louise said. "There's a car on the road with three people inside it. One of them has a danger cloud then there are two other worried clouds."

"Find Rosalie, Stuart. Bring her here, and tell Mr. Young to go to his trailer and keep Vanessa with him in the trailer," Major said. Stuart ran into the house then returned with Rosalie. Rosalie had her rifle.

"We've got three people and only one danger cloud?" Sheriff shook his head. "That makes no sense, but it fits in with all the conflicting information we've heard so far. Conflicting." He rubbed his face. "I want Molly and the kids out of the house."

"Go tell the first kid you see that the Starr family meeting in the barn starts now. Your kids and Molly are sharp. They'll get it," Major said.

"True. Be right back."

As a plume of dust appeared on the road, Sheriff returned. "Annie's pulling them together." The back door slammed. "There they go."

"Where's Peyton?"

"As far as I know, still in our bedroom? Want me to check?" Rosalie asked.

Major glanced at the road. "No. car's getting too close. You and Stuart go to the other side of the house. Sheriff, can you position yourself so you can see the girls' windows but not be in anyone's line of fire?"

"Yep. Your truck is the perfect cover."

"Let's go to the front porch, Aimee Louise. After you can tell me who has the danger cloud, I'll need you to run through the house to tell Stuart and Rosalie then back around to Sheriff. It's the best I can think of."

"It's an excellent plan," Aimee Louise said.

Major sauntered near Stuart and Rosalie's side of the house. "Aimee Louise will tell you who has the danger cloud. Remember, only one."

After he strolled across the yard and gave Sheriff the same message, he returned to the porch, and the car slowed and stopped at the gate.

"Back seat passenger is Uncle Dan, the danger man." Aimee Louise disappeared into the house. The front seat passenger, a woman, stepped out of the car and remained at the gate as the car eased forward.

Aimee Louise reappeared. "Done. And I told Peyton to stay down and out of sight or she'd be shot."

"What did she say?"

"*Glad I'm here.*"

The car stopped, and Uncle Dan climbed out of the back seat on the driver's side of the car then waved for the woman to move forward.

After Uncle Dan scanned the house and the yard, he rapped the car roof twice, and the driver stepped out. While the driver had his back to Uncle Dan, he pointed to Major's truck, and the woman brushed back her hair and mimicked his motion.

Well done. Major stepped off the porch. "Shift closer to the edge of the porch, Aimee Louise."

"Peyton here?" Uncle Dan asked.

Déjà vu. "She'll be back soon. Are you Thomas?"

"Who? No, I'm Nate. Her partner."

"He's lying," Aimee Louise said with a soft whisper.

Major nodded. "Good. We've been waiting for you. I have to tell you we were exposed to a deadly, contagious disease and are in isolation."

Major smiled at the confusion that washed over the man's face and hid his smile with his arm as he coughed into his elbow. He prolonged his coughing then said, "Sorry, dry cough is the beginning stages of the infection."

Uncle Dan placed his palm on the butt of this gun and moved his forefinger near the trigger.

"That's rough. Peyton's been exposed too?"

"No. She stays in the guest cottage behind the house." *Shouldn't have said that. If Annie heard me, we'll have a cottage in two weeks.*

"Can we wait there?"

"Sure. Want to check it out first? It was our clinic before Peyton arrived."

I'm getting used to his confused look.

"He's getting ready to shoot." Aimee Louise eased off the porch.

The man swept his gun out of his holster.

Crack. Crack.

When Uncle Dan dropped, the driver grabbed the woman, and they ran toward Major's white truck. Aimee Louise ran to the truck as Sheriff waved for the driver and woman to continue.

Stuart strode toward the fallen man and knelt. "Dead," he called out.

Sheriff came out from behind the truck with the driver and passenger.

"The real Nate and his wife," Sheriff called out.

Rosalie joined Stuart then they sauntered to Major.

"Same shots," Stuart said.

"No reason to mess with perfection," Major said. "Well done."

"I'll grab two shovels and a tarp," Stuart said.

"I'll help," Nate said as he joined the group in front of the house.

Major stared at Nate's wife and her wide brown eyes and ringlets around her face. "You're Dolly's mother," he said.

"You know Dolly? Have you seen her?"

He smiled at the musical tone of her voice. "Dolly and the judge are fine. They're staying on a farm in South Georgia."

As Molly and the children headed to the house, she said, "I'm starving, and the children are starving. We can talk around the table. Come eat."

"Go on inside and get mobbed by children. Rosalie, you can release Peyton. I'll start the generators so we can wash our hands," Major said.

"We'll take care of that," Stuart said as he and Aimee Louise set down the shovels and tarp near the porch then turned to the generators.

Again with we. Maybe I'll get used to it.

"I'll get Mr. Young and Vanessa," Major said.

"Let's go inside, Nate and…sorry, didn't catch your name," Sheriff said.

"Charo," Nate said.

Peyton dashed outside. "I found the list, Major." She froze when she faced Nate.

"Where did you get your list?" Major asked as the generators kicked in.

"Rex Wilson."

"Who's that on the ground in the front yard?"

Peyton frowned and approached the body. "Rex Wilson." She wheeled and said, "What a lying, rotten snake."

"Yes, he was. Let's eat then you can show your list to Nate. The two of you might want to rearrange it," Major said.

While they ate, Stuart told his hilarious version of Dolly and the stinky boy then added how well the children pulled the weeds in his mother's garden. "Mom was touched. It was one more thing off her plate that she hadn't been able to get to."

Major told a story about Dolly coming down the stairs after her bath. "She held her nightgown out to the side in princess style, but when Brandon told her about the snack in the kitchen, she dashed for the table like a linebacker."

"That's my sweet baby girl," Nate said as he wiped away tears of laughter. "Just like her mama."

Charo swatted his arm. "I run like a gazelle, not a linebacker."

"Can I come down the stairs like Dolly in the morning, Mommy?" Sara asked.

"Of course, you can, Sweetie. Then run back up like a gazelle or a linebacker, your choice," Molly said.

At the end of the meal, Charo and the children cleared the table while Molly supervised, and Vanessa filled the sink with soapy water.

"Will you work on the coordinates with us, Mr. Young?" Rosalie asked.

As everyone else headed outside, Molly said, "Don't turn off the generators. Vanessa will strip Mr. Young's bed. We'll be doing laundry for a while."

"What's our next step?" Peyton asked.

"McNeil requested a meeting with Sheriff tomorrow morning then he'll be at Mickleton for another meeting around two," Major said. "We haven't planned our reception party yet, but we know we're having one."

"Are you sniper-trained, Deputy?" Nate asked. "That was a killer head shot: classic, but that knee." He shook his head. "I've never seen a shot like that before at that distance. Was that intentional?"

Major and Sheriff laughed.

Stuart glared. "The head shot was mine. Rosalie's signature shot is the shattered knee. She is awesome. Major was her instructor."

"I knew I'd heard of you before, Major. You're Dave Elliott. Did you know you're a legend? Rosalie must be your star pupil."

"Don't you have to be old to be a legend?" Sheriff asked.

"I am old," Major chuckled.

"You're all old, except Stuart," Peyton said. "What's the party plan? We can include Rosalie, right?"

"That's an excellent point," Sheriff said. "Rosalie and Aimee Louise have unique skills. Can we include them, Major?"

"If we don't include them, they'll track us." Stuart said.

"Right. So we have two opportunities. The meeting with Sheriff, and the large meeting near Mickleton," Major said. "Our first opportunity is in Plainview. If we sketch out two plans, then have to abandon the first, we've learned something we can use to revamp our second plan."

"What if our second plan fails?" Sheriff narrowed his eyes.

"I say we don't consider failure an option. We complete our plan or abandon it before McNeil knows what's happening," Major said.

"I'm positive Rex's orders from McNeil were to kill Peyton and me," Nate said. "It tips our hands if McNeil sees us."

"Major and I attended one of McNeil's sales meetings. He had men dressed in black suits to add an official prestige to his presentation. They weren't typical goons. I suspect they were agents who have shifted to McNeil," Stuart said.

"In that case, Nate and I could focus on them. They wouldn't know who was on McNeil's kill list. We may even know some of them. Black suits? I have one. Nate?"

"I'll check with Charo. If not, I can check Rex's bag. We're about the same size."

"Speaking of Rex, I'd like to bury him," Stuart said.

"Let's break and get back together this evening after supper and radio time. That gives us time to catch any additional updates from McNeil," Sheriff said.

"I'll meet you at the car. My gear is in the trunk," Nate said.

When Stuart arrived at the car, Nate said, "Why don't you drive? You know where we're going."

Stuart dropped his backpack on the driver's seat then spread out the tarp alongside Wilson's body. After they loaded Rex, Nate walked to the gate and opened it then closed it after Stuart drove through.

On the drive to the dump where Stuart had buried Kelso's body, they swapped their personal rookie cop stories and calls they'd been on.

"See that refrigerator?" Stuart pointed. "We rolled it on top of the site to keep any animals from digging. Looks like a monument when you know what's underneath, doesn't it?"

"That's smart. Could we bury Rex close to that freezer?" Nate pointed at an upright near the refrigerator.

Stuart moved the car closer, and they dug. After they buried Rex and rolled the freezer over the grave, Stuart said, "If we're lucky, Molly will still have the generators going, and we can take showers. If she doesn't, Dolly may call you stinky when she sees you."

"That was a funny story about little Henry being a stinky boy. Rosalie's sharp, but there is something deep about Aimee Louise. You know what I mean?"

"Yes."

On their return trip, Stuart talked about Aimee Louise while Nate listened then Nate talked about Charo and how they got together, and Stuart listened.

As they came within sight of the farm, Nate said, "The only thing I can tell you, Stuart, is that you're smart. Aimee Louise isn't typical. When I was a kid, I ran the streets. No social skills needed out there; we lived by the street rules. I've learned the niceties from Charo. I think you're in the same situation except you're learning the social skills for Aimee Louise's world."

After Stuart parked, he said, "Generators are still running. If we hurry, we can get showers before Molly tells Aimee Louise to turn them off."

* * *

After they ate, Aimee Louise, Rosalie, and Annie hurried to the computer room, and Stuart, Nate, and Charo took over the dishes. Peyton and the younger children went outside for a game Peyton promised to teach them.

Mr. Young scooted back in his chair and said, "I need to talk to you about those coordinates before I'm ordered to bed."

Vanessa frowned. "Nobody gives you orders, Mr. Young. I merely…"

Major snorted. "Right."

Vanessa glared. "As I was about to say, I provide gentle suggestions."

Peyton slipped inside while the children played the fast-moving game.

Mr. Young laid out three maps on the kitchen table. "We marked all the coordinates on the maps in pencil so we can erase later."

Stuart leaned over the maps. "These places are where McNeil held meetings or at least had a meeting scheduled."

"Good eye, Stuart," Mr. Young said. "Next step is electricity. You can't tell from these maps, but if you had the right kind of maps..." He glanced at Vanessa who jumped up then dropped a thick book on the table.

"Thank you," Mr. Young said. "This is one of Russell Gaston's books. He was Annie and Josh's birth father and the operations manager for our regional electrical company. He was brilliant. We still have access to all his books because the deputies live in the Gaston house."

Vanessa opened it where a folded sheet of paper marked a page.

"The paper has the references for all our research, but I won't go into that. Back to our maps. All of our coordinates are major regional electrical substations that connect to other regional electrical substations. We don't think McNeil planned another explosion or even another cyberattack. Instead, we think he's moving forward with the plan that Russell Gaston identified before he died. I'm wearing out. I need to move to the sofa."

Vanessa helped Mr. Young to the sofa then positioned the footstool so he could prop up his feet.

"Much better. Everybody with me?"

"Did McNeil kill Russell Gaston?" Peyton asked.

"Yes, and his wife," Sheriff growled.

Mr. Young nodded. "These are also the southeast's regional companies that Russell identified as planned personnel takeovers. The point of ruining farmers, causing animosity with the townsfolk, and crashing the local economy is to drive people away from these areas so McNeil will own the electricity. It's ambitious, but I see how his plans make it doable."

"If we stop McNeil, his entire plan collapses," Nate said.

"That's what we think." Mr. Young shifted his feet to the floor, and Vanessa helped him rise. "You've got our notes and Russell's analysis. The girls can answer questions. Aimee Louise explained how all the pieces fit together then Rosalie checked Russell's documents and corroborated. I'm just the pretty face. See you in the morning."

"What about the disease?" Major asked. "How does McNeil fit into that?"

"Almost forgot. Aimee Louise found evidence of lab environments that introduced previous diseases. One example I knew about after she mentioned it was smallpox. Vaccines eradicated smallpox worldwide until someone took it out of the lab. Makes stealing supplies from the office tame, doesn't it? Russell documented his findings of a lab virus bred for release and guess who would be in tight control of the vaccine? Russell had excellent data, but his findings were preliminary. Good night, all."

Mr. Young and Vanessa made their way to the door and left.

Major leaned back in his chair. "You said that this morning, Molly."

"She did?" Sheriff stared at his wife. "Now we know the urgency. How do we stop him?"

"I liked our revenge motive better," Peyton said. "Why don't I just slit his throat?"

"Works for me," Molly said. "Do you have any knives that need sharpening? I keep my chef knives razor sharp."

"My wife's not kidding," Sheriff said. "Let her sharpen your knife. You can be our back-up plan."

"I have an idea, but I need to talk to Rosalie," Major said.

"I'm here," Rosalie said. "We have interesting news. Aimee Louise will be here as soon as she signs off."

After Rosalie and Aimee Louise sat on the couch; Rosalie elbowed Aimee Louise then raised her eyebrows at Stuart. Stuart glanced at Major as Aimee Louise scooted closer to Rosalie to make room for him. Molly cleared her throat and raised an eyebrow at Major, who sighed then nodded. Stuart sat next to Aimee Louise.

"First, McNeil said he'd be at the county office at ten tomorrow," Rosalie said. "The message didn't mention which county, so the hams discussed and speculated. This morning, the hams said there had been no deaths, which led to a discussion about who was the most skeptical. This evening, no one joked when the hams reported deaths. The hams near Mickelton are excited about the big meeting at noon tomorrow after the announcement of the rescheduled time and the location."

Rosalie handed the notebook to Annie, who cleared her throat and rose to read the note. "The meeting will be at an auction building fifteen miles east of Mickelton." Annie returned the notebook to Rosalie then sat, and Rosalie squeezed her hand. Molly smiled, and Annie's face flushed.

"Remember this is hearsay, not a fact." Rosalie tapped her notebook.

"A ham said his friend in South Carolina saw a bunch of kids at a summer camp that is never open this time of year. Aimee Louise asked for the name and location of the camp, but no one knew. A ham who lives in South Carolina said he'd ask around then check it out. Aimee Louise told him to take friends. He agreed."

CHAPTER TWENTY

Molly dropped her cup and tears flowed as she wiped her face with her apron. "They might have found the children?"

"Could it be possible?" Charo cleaned up the spill, and Stuart filled another cup.

"I'm already packed. We're leaving as soon as we can." Peyton slammed her hand on the table and rose to pace.

"We have friends in South Carolina," Nate said. "We'll pick up our kids at the Newtons' farm then head to South Carolina."

"We don't have confirmation yet, but it sounds promising," Sheriff said.

"I want to leave now, too, but first I want to see the life gone out of McNeil's eyes." Charo glowered.

Major rubbed his forehead. *Dead boys in the truck. I still see them.* "We'll do it."

"One last thing. We may have some storms coming our way. We'll have lots of wind tomorrow while the front blows through then rainstorms around noon." Rosalie closed her notebook.

"Excellent," Major said. "Moderate to heavy winds?"

"Yes."

"McNeil's coming to see Sheriff and to convince him to either be his shill at the Mickelton meeting or at another meeting," Major said. "We can check Mr. Young's map to see where another one might be, but I think it's the Mickelton meeting. We can decide where the best place is for them to meet indoors. That's why the wind is important. We want a neutral spot out of the wind that would be perfect for an ambush. Sheriff can promise coffee."

"We need to take all the children and Molly to the deputies' house tonight," Stuart said. "McNeil might have a contingency in case his charm doesn't work on Sheriff, but we can remove his contingency."

"That's good, Stuart. We know he's been doing that for quite a while," Nate said.

Rosalie stepped to the front door and called, "Inside." The three younger children dashed in.

"Pack up," Molly said. "We're going on a surprise sleepover." The children ran up the stairs, and Molly hurried to her bedroom to pack for the overnight.

Molly, the four younger children, and Penny came into the kitchen. "We're ready. Penny's going with us. I take it Shadow stays."

"We should send Mr. Young, and Aunt Vanessa to the deputies' house when we leave for town in the morning." Aimee Louise said.

"And Ms. Charo," Rosalie added.

"I'll take my family to the deputies," Sheriff said.

"I'll go along." Rosalie grabbed her rifle. "Beauty shop."

The Starr family and Rosalie trooped to Sheriff's truck and left.

"Beauty shop?" Stuart furrowed his brow. "Small shop with limited seating. It's still in good shape because the owner left only a month ago. I'll bet it has a bathroom and a storage room. If McNeil brings his goons, they won't go in. Too girly. Intimidating. Sheriff can take a thermos. So how do we ambush McNeil if he goes into the beauty shop with Sheriff?"

"I'd like to check it out tonight. I need to see how accessible the back door is. What I'm thinking is that Sheriff agrees to open the Mickelton meeting after some hesitancy. When McNeil leaves, Sheriff dashes out the back door, and we nail McNeil on the sidewalk. We'll be in position on rooftops, and we need to take our positions tonight and sleep on the rooftops. We have five shooters if we let Rosalie go."

"Rosalie will shatter his knee, so if we all miss the first time, we have a second shot," Stuart said.

"I can shoot," Charo said.

"But honey, we're all professionals." Nate furrowed his brow.

Charo rolled her eyes. "Did you hear what you just said? I can shoot."

Nate cleared his throat. "My wife's a better shot than I am. She teaches classes for women at our range. If you had to pick between the two of us, I'd have to recommend her. I'm one of the best, but she's at the range every day."

"Six. This is great," Major said.

"What if none of us gets a clear shot at the beauty shop? What's our plan for the meeting?" Nate asked.

"McNeil dashed out the door after his speech at the meeting we attended. Can we slow him down?" Stuart asked.

Major rubbed his chin. "We can let the air out of one tire, but he'll have his professionals around him. How do we split him away?"

"No guarantee, but Rosalie said rain was forecast for tomorrow. He'd either go back into the building or wait in the car," Stuart said.

"Even if it doesn't rain, Sheriff could invite him back inside," Nate said.

"Sounds like we don't need the entire team. When he comes back in, I lock the door behind him and shoot him. I like this idea," Major said.

"What about the goons?" Charo asked.

"That's easy," Peyton said. "Nate and I can join them. If they're FBI, they'll recognize us; if they aren't, we're the special detail and can flash our badges. They can inspect our IDs as much as they like. Nate can order them to leave if they react to the shot inside the building. He's got a magnificent command presence; or I could slit McNeil's throat. That's quieter."

"If they don't leave, we shoot them," Charo said.

Nate chuckled. "Peyton and I can wear civilian clothes. If you still shoot me, I'll know you did it on purpose."

Stuart frowned. "Rosalie and I will need our rifles. We'll be outside, but we can't plan where until we get there."

When Sheriff and Rosalie returned, Major caught them up on the discussion.

"I can't think of anything to add. You, Rosalie?" Sheriff asked.

Rosalie shook her head, and Major rose. "I'll check the beauty shop."

"I'll check roof access and condition of the surrounding buildings," Stuart said.

"I want to see the set up," Sheriff said.

"I'll make a list of what we need for our overnight," Rosalie said.

Shadow trotted behind Major. "Okay," Major said when they reached the truck, and Shadow jumped in.

* * *

Major cruised past the beauty shop then parked at the end of the block. "Might as well start here to check buildings. Shadow and I will be at the beauty shop."

When Stuart opened the back door, Shadow hopped out and trotted along behind Major.

"I'll take this side," Sheriff said, and Stuart crossed the street.

Major tried the doorknob then picked the lock. He scanned the room and opened the bathroom and closet doors then unlocked the back door. He scanned the alley. "This is perfect, Shadow. We have a little table, and the two hairdryer chairs. That's plenty. I'm sure McNeil will open both doors, but if he doesn't, Sheriff can."

Major checked the lock on the back door. "Sheriff can lock the knob then go out if he wants to lock it." He stared at the bathroom door. "Or he could step into the bathroom in case McNeil makes it back into the shop. If he leaves the back door open, it doesn't matter because Sheriff will figure it out. Don't tell anybody that I fell into the details for a second there."

Major stepped outside and noticed that Stuart stepped from one building to the next then disappeared.

When Stuart and Sheriff joined him at the beauty shop, Sheriff said, "These are sturdy old buildings. They all have flat roofs with the false front. They are perfect. I found two buildings with ladders leading to the top."

"I found one, but the access from one building to the next is a short step. We can divide our six into two groups then let the shooters pick their buildings," Stuart said.

"I can stand a few buildings from the beauty shop and flag McNeil down. When I tell him the county locked all the county buildings except for my office, he'll balk at meeting on my turf. He'll recognize the disadvantage he'll have, and I'll suggest a nearby shop."

"I picked the lock. Welcome to my shop."

Sheriff stepped inside. "This is perfect." He stared at the two chairs with the large metal hoods attached. "I've never seen anything like this. What is it?"

"Old style hairdryers." Major chuckled.

"Not sure I'd want to sit there. They don't look safe." Sheriff examined them more closely. "They're even still plugged in. Did you see that? This is great. I'm officially intimidated. I can offer a seat to McNeil and enjoy his reaction."

Sheriff opened the bathroom and closet doors then unlocked the back door and peeked at the alley. "Options. This is good. I may step into the bathroom in case McNeil tries to cut through the beauty shop to get away. If he doesn't check the doors, I'll make a show of it, but I suspect he will."

On their way back to the farmhouse, Stuart said, "What if we get a clear shot at McNeil before he goes into the beauty shop?"

"If it's you and Rosalie, take it," Major said.

Stuart leaned back in his seat. When Major glanced in his rearview mirror, Stuart smiled as he gazed out his window. *He and Rosalie will take McNeil down.*

Major parked his truck at the front door and pointed to the porch. "Gear on the porch. We may leave soon."

Before Sheriff opened his door, he said, "I may take Shadow with me to town. He'll stay with me. Is that okay with you?"

Major cocked his head and furrowed his brow. *If he knew why, he'd tell me.* "Whatever you decide is fine with me."

They loaded their gear and rifles in the pickup bed then piled into the truck. Aimee Louise and Stuart crowded into the passenger's seat, and Nate, Charo, Rosalie, and Peyton squeezed into the backseat. Nate and Peyton had the seats at the windows, and Charo sat next to Nate. As Major climbed into the driver's seat, Nate pointed to the front seat, and Charo elbowed him. Major glanced at the front seat as he climbed in and frowned.

When Major started the engine, Stuart twisted in the seat and stretched then draped his arm behind Aimee Louise. Major growled, and Nate snorted.

"Do you need a tissue?" Charo asked. Major glanced in his rearview window as Charo glowered at Nate.

Major chuckled. "Charo, Dolly asked me that same question."

On the way to town, Stuart told his hilarious version of the story about Dolly and the tissues. *Stuart tells an entertaining story.*

Major stopped the truck in the alley behind the stores across from the beauty shop. Stuart, Aimee Louise, and Rosalie hopped out and removed their gear. Major drove to the alley behind the beauty shop, and Nate, Charo, and Peyton pulled gear out of the back. Major parked the truck two blocks away from the main street and strolled to the alley then diverted. *I want to see what's along the way.*

He stared at the small building across from the county building. The name on the wooden sign had faded. *Donut shop. It's been closed so long that I'd forgotten about it.*

He strode to the beauty shop and stopped in the middle of the road then searched the rooflines until he saw Stuart and Nate. "I'll be at the small shop across from the county building."

After Stuart and Nate waved to acknowledge they'd heard him, he hurried to the alley behind the beauty shop and picked up his bags.

Major carried his gear to the donut shop and spread his sleeping bag near the false front for a windbreak. He lay down and gazed at the sky. *Sleeping under the stars.*

* * *

Sheriff woke before dawn and padded to the kitchen to start a pot of coffee. He peeked out the back door. "Trailer lights are on, Shadow. We'll have company soon."

After the pot finished perking, Sheriff poured a cup and headed to the front door. He relaxed on the front porch with his coffee while Shadow searched the area.

"We'll see them later, boy." Shadow trotted to the porch and flopped down near Sheriff.

"I don't stop to enjoy the sunrise nearly as much as I should."

"I know. I feel the same way." Mr. Young came out to the porch, and Vanessa carried two cups of coffee.

When the sun rose, Sheriff said, "Good morning sun. It's a wonderful day to stop evil."

"That's a fact," Vanessa said. "What about breakfast, Sheriff? I'm scrambling eggs this morning."

"Sounds good. We'll leave right after we eat. Does that work for you?"

"Mr. Young wants to listen to the radio first. Can you wait for us or could you make sure my car starts?"

"I'll check the chickens and goats." Sheriff strode to the chicken coop and refilled their water then checked the goats. "They're fine, Shadow. Ready for breakfast?"

Shadow trotted along with Sheriff to the back porch.

After they ate, Mr. Young left to listen to the radio. Sheriff and Vanessa washed the dishes then loaded the backpacks into the truck.

"We have splendid news this morning," Mr. Young said. "The ham from South Carolina has the name of the camp and is on his way to confirm. He expects to report back this evening, but he said he wasn't surprised."

Sheriff exhaled. "I think I've been holding my breath since last night."

Vanessa sniffled, and her mouth quivered.

After Sheriff turned at the gate, Mr. Young asked, "Is it sad that I'm happy to be going for a two-mile ride?"

"Not at all," Vanessa said as she rubbed Shadow's neck. "I'm enjoying it myself. We've been cooped up long enough."

When they reached the deputies' house, Jim waited in the shade near the road then opened the gate for them. "We're taking turns guarding the road. Anybody going to the farm has to come this way. I have the first shift until lunch."

"That's a brilliant spot," Sheriff said. "I didn't see you until you came away from the trees."

"Good. The folks at the house are waiting for you."

A lanky chocolate lab puppy loped to the truck when Sheriff parked while Heather waited on the porch. The pup danced circles around her as she helped Mr. Young out of the truck.

Heather pointed. "Sit, Teddy."

The dog plopped into a sit and doggy-grinned.

"New dog, I see. Where did you get her?" Mr. Young asked.

"Someone gave Pastor John four six-month-old lab puppies. Kris and I made the mistake of letting Brad and Wally go to Pastor John's for books. They came home with books, a puppy, and a song and dance about security. The toddlers called her *Teddy* as soon as they saw her."

The puppy slipped over to Mr. Young, who held out his hand for a sniff. "I could get used to this special attention."

He waved as he and Heather went into the house while Vanessa grabbed their backpacks and hurried to catch up. Shadow jumped out and investigated Teddy while she danced. Shadow trotted to the backyard, and Teddy trailed him.

"Your choice, Shadow. Don't blame me if the puppy wears you out," Sheriff said.

He pulled away and headed to the highway. After he parked on the side of the county building, he smiled as the light breeze from the south shifted to a brisk northwest wind. *Right on time.*

He found a sheltered spot in the county building portico away from the wind. As he waited, he glanced at the building across the street. *I'll bet somebody's there. Probably Major. He'd have seen it. Dang, we're good.*

He leaned back and relaxed until he heard a car headed his way from the north. He sauntered to the walkway. A black car parked across from the county building, and McNeil stepped out. *Alone. Show time.*

"How you doing, Mr. McNeil? Nice to see you." Sheriff strode to the edge of the sidewalk, and McNeil smiled. A gust lifted his western hat, and he grabbed it before it rolled away.

"Brisk wind you got here. We don't see anything like this on the coast unless it's a hurricane. Now, that's a wind." McNeil sneered.

"The county building is pitch black inside. I'd thought we could just meet outside, but the wind is picking up. Want some coffee?" Sheriff lifted his thermos. "I found an open building where we can talk out of the wind."

"Coffee sounds great, and so does getting out of the wind. I'll get my cup out of the car."

McNeil hurried to his car, threw his hat inside, and grabbed his cup.

"Where's this building?" he asked.

"Just right there." Sheriff pointed.

"Beauty shop?" McNeil chuckled then strode ahead of Sheriff.

You take that lead, Bud.

Crack. Crack.

McNeil dropped. Sheriff strolled to the body and rolled McNeil to his back.

Crack.

Sheriff dashed to the beauty shop for cover then peered up the road at McNeil's car. A body lay on the ground near the back bumper.

Son of a gun, Charlie. You brought backup.

Sheriff drew his gun and approached the car from the sidewalk then jerked open the car door on the passenger side. He stood next to the car with his gun aimed at the trunk. Major joined him. When Major pulled the trunk release, it flew open.

"Empty," Sheriff said. "I knew you were there when I saw the shop across the street."

"Last minute whim."

A gust of wind slammed the trunk shut.

Stuart and Nate peered over their buildings. Major and Sheriff smiled at the cheers.

"Kids," Major said.

"Yep. My truck or your truck?"

"Mine. I'll take Stuart and Nate. I've got a shovel in my truck. We can probably find another at Pete's," Major said.

"I'll give you a second shovel and take Charo and Peyton with me. Aimee Louise can drive McNeil's car. Rosalie will ride with her, I'm sure. I'll pick up my family. It'll be a squeeze, but maybe Annie can ride with Aimee Louise when she picks up Vanessa and Mr. Young. We're getting quite the car collection, aren't we?"

As the rest of the group ran to them, Major asked, "Head and shattered knee shots, right?"

"And right on target."

Charo knelt next to McNeil's body and rolled him over. "Dead eyes. Good."

Peyton offered her hand, and Charo rose. They strolled to Sheriff's truck arm in arm.

Major, Stuart, and Nate were the last to arrive at the farmhouse. Josh and Brett raced to the truck.

"Mom says wash your hands for lunch, and Mr. Young has news," Brett said.

"We already ate," Josh added.

As the three men ate lunch, Peyton and Charo sat at the table with them.

Mr. Young came in the back door.

"You're looking spry," Major said.

"I feel spry." He grinned as he sat on the sofa. "The ham from South Carolina has an idea where the camp is. He gathered a team to check it out."

"I knew it," Charo said. "Peyton and I want to go pick up our families then go to South Carolina."

Major nodded. "Makes sense. You can caravan then Peyton will have a car to get to Troy or caravan to South Carolina. Take Rex's and Carl's cars. McNeil's is a gas hog. I don't know why he didn't have a diesel."

Peyton rose. "Can we leave now?"

"Anytime you want. See Rosalie for directions, and I have a favor to ask. When you come to the roadblock north of Plainview, ask for Phil. Let them know you have a message for Scooter. I'll write a note for you to give them. We want the medical community to know there is an effective vaccine for the illness. Phil's son, Scooter, is a doctor in Atlanta. He'll spread the word and probably find the lab himself."

After the group saw Peyton and the Cabellos off, Vanessa threw her arms around Major's neck and clung to him. He wrapped his arms around her and snuggled her hair with his face.

"You done being a cowboy, old man?"

"Yes, ma'am."

She swatted his behind as he swaggered to the house.

ACKNOWLEDGMENTS

Huge thanks to my husband for his patience, support, talented technical expertise, and guidance, and to my editor for wielding her grammar sword in her battle with my marvelous, convoluted sentences.

Thank you for reading. *You keep reading; I'll keep writing!*

What to read next?

DANGER ON THE ROAD

GRID DOWN SURVIVAL SERIES, Book 3

Stuart, Aimee Louise, and Rosalie travel to rescue the injured, ambushed team, but vicious attacks plague their trip. When the team closes in on the human trafficking ring, the desperate leader is obsessed to kill them.

Subscribe to the newsletter!

Look for the Subscribe button on www.judithabarrett.com

ABOUT THE AUTHOR

Judith A. Barrett, award-winning author, lives on a farm in Georgia with her husband, two dogs, and chickens. She writes series for her readers: thriller, post-apocalyptic science fiction, and cozy mystery novels. Stories with a twist: not your typical characters from not your typical author!

Her motto: *You keep reading; I'll keep writing!*

When she isn't writing, Judith is working on farm chores, hiking or camping with her husband and dogs, or rocking on her front porch while she watches the sunset.

www.judithabarrett.com

Subscribe to her newsletter on her website!

Not into emails, even though Judith's story-focused newsletters are Not Your Typical newsletters? Follow Judith on your favorite bookstore, Bookbub, or her blog for news of her latest release!

Let's keep in touch!

www.ingramcontent.com/pod-product-compliance
Lightning Source LLC
Chambersburg PA
CBHW030359030726
47497CB00002B/404